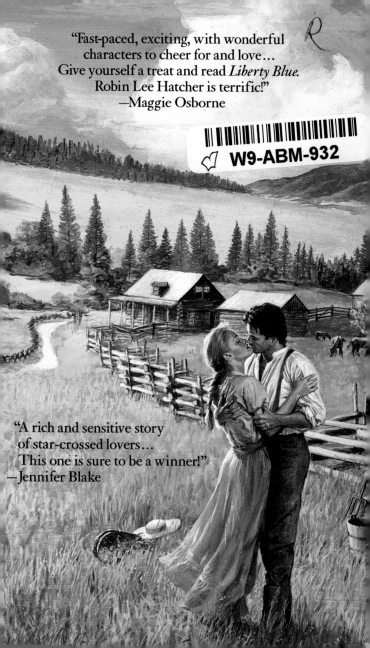

"Fast-paced, exciting, with wonderful characters to cheer for and love... Give yourself a treat and read *Liberty Blue*. Robin Lee Hatcher is terrific!"
—Maggie Osborne

W9-ABM-932

"A rich and sensitive story of star-crossed lovers... This one is sure to be a winner!"
—Jennifer Blake

HER ONLY CHANCE WAS TO HIDE, HIS ONLY CHOICE WAS TO FIND HER

When Libby Blue ran from her ruthless father and her privileged life, she never looked back. In the West, she could run a ranch, be whoever she wanted, and, most important, never have to trust a man again.

Remington Walker would take any risk to find Libby, as long as he was paid for it. Once he had the money he would take his revenge on Libby's father, the man who had destroyed his own father. But soon he found that, while vengeance wasn't nearly enough for life, confession could be fatal to love.

With a wall of lies between them, was the one great truth they shared enough to unite them forever?

"Robin Lee Hatcher is a *tour de force* in the world of romance."

—*Affaire de Coeur*

"A sweet celebration of the West's gentle tamers and the men they loved, *Liberty Blue* sings with all the heart and soul that is Robin Lee Hatcher."

—Kathleen Eagle

Harper Monogram

Liberty Blue

⋊ ROBIN LEE HATCHER ⋉

HarperPaperbacks
A Division of HarperCollins*Publishers*

If you purchased this book without a cover, you should be aware that this book is stolen property. It was reported as "unsold and destroyed" to the publisher and neither the author nor the publisher has received any payment for this "stripped book."

This is a work of fiction. The characters, incidents, and dialogues are products of the author's imagination and are not to be construed as real. Any resemblance to actual events or persons, living or dead, is entirely coincidental.

HarperPaperbacks *A Division of* HarperCollins*Publishers*
10 East 53rd Street, New York, N.Y. 10022

Copyright © 1995 by Robin Lee Hatcher
All rights reserved. No part of this book may be used or reproduced in any manner whatsoever without written permission of the publisher, except in the case of brief quotations embodied in critical articles and reviews. For information address HarperCollins*Publishers,*
10 East 53rd Street, New York, N.Y. 10022.

Cover illustration by Jim Griffin

First printing: October 1995

Printed in the United States of America

HarperPaperbacks, HarperMonogram, and colophon are trademarks of HarperCollins*Publishers*

❖ 10 9 8 7 6 5 4 3 2 1

To Christine Pacheco,
For a friendship that's priceless.
May all your dreams come true.

And to Janis Reams Hudson,
With best wishes for a great term.
May all your memories be good ones.

I'll be watching for your books!

ACKNOWLEDGMENTS

I gratefully acknowledge the faith, support, and advice of my agent, Natasha Kern.

A special thanks to my editor, Carolyn Marino, for her warm welcome to the Harper "family."

My appreciation goes to fellow writers Janet Kuchler, Jo Ann Ferguson, Rainy Kirkland, Anne Amalfitano, Pamela Johnson, Suzanne Brown, Cynthia Holt, Sara Brockunier, Deborah Bedford, Ann Simas, LaRee Bryant, Alice Shields, Gini Wilson, Claudia Yates, Libby Hall, and Margaret Brownley. Thanks for making my term as president of Romance Writers of America so productive and enjoyable. And to Linda Fisher, Marguerite Binkley, and James and Madeline McLain for your invaluable support and good advice.

Finally, with love to my husband, Jerry Neu, who puts up with my flights of fancy.

Stone walls do not a prison make,
Nor iron bars a cage;
Minds innocent and quiet take
That for an hermitage;
If I have freedom in my love,
And in my soul am free,
Angels alone that soar above
Enjoy such liberty.

—Richard Lovelace

Liberty Blue

1

May 1890
Blue Springs Ranch, Idaho Territory

"Not again, Bevins," Libby whispered to herself as she peered through the latticework of sunlight and shadows at the horseman's approach. "Not as long as I've got breath in my body."

While still obscured by the thick grove of cottonwoods and pines, the rider stopped his horse. Already, as dusk settled over the barnyard, she was having difficulty keeping track of him. She didn't know what he was up to this time, but it wasn't something good. It never was with Timothy Bevins.

She stepped back from the window until she was certain she couldn't be seen, then moved to the front door, checking to see if it was tightly latched. It was.

A small sigh of relief escaped her. But her relief was short-lived. Bevins wasn't likely to try to break into her house. No, that method was too direct for such a snake in the grass. He probably thought he could frighten her off just because she was a woman alone.

Well, he's wrong about that, she thought.

Her mouth thinned into a determined line. She wasn't going anywhere, frightened or not. And she wasn't going to wait for Bevins to make the first move, either. She wasn't going to give him a chance to do his dirty work. Not this time.

She grabbed the double-barreled shotgun that rested against the wall. Then, fortifying herself with a deep breath, she turned and walked to Sawyer's bedroom, peeking inside at the boy lying on the bed.

"Sawyer, something's got the horses worked up. Probably another coyote. I'm going out to run it off. If you hear anything, don't be scared. It's just me."

"I don't scare so easy, Libby," he answered with a brave tilt of his scabbed-over chin.

"I know you don't." And neither do I, she thought, trying to shore up her own courage. Neither do I.

She hurried through the kitchen to the back door, opened it slowly and silently, then stepped outside. Dusk had already changed the colors of the earth and sky into varying shades of gray and black. In a matter of minutes, the trees had become threatening silhouettes, looming overhead, their scraggly arms reaching toward her.

Bevins could be anywhere, she thought. Perhaps he was watching her even now.

Low-lying snake in the grass.

She edged along the side of the house, making her way toward the wide clearing at the front, searching every shadow.

You can't scare me, you yellow-bellied bully. You can't run me off my land.

Bevins might not know it, but Libby had quit running over six years ago. This was her home, her land. Aunt

Amanda had entrusted the ranch to Libby, and she meant to protect it and everyone on it. She wasn't going to let Timothy Bevins run her off, no matter what he did, no matter what he threatened to do. And he wasn't going to get another chance to hurt Sawyer, either. Spooking the boy's horse had been the last straw. Absolutely the last straw.

She heard the snap of a twig off to her right. Startled, she turned and, in the waning light, saw him stepping out of the trees. More important, she saw the rifle in his hand.

She reacted instinctively, raising the shotgun and firing before he had a chance to do the same. The kick of the gun slammed her back against the side of the house as she squeezed off the second shot.

She gasped for air, her ears ringing, her shoulder throbbing. For a moment she didn't know if either shot had hit the intruder. Then, as her vision cleared, she looked across the yard and saw Bevins lying in the dirt. He didn't move.

Had she killed him? She hadn't meant to shoot, only to scare him.

Gulping down panic, she dropped the shotgun and cautiously made her way toward him, uncertain what she would do if he wasn't dead, uncertain what she should do if he was.

If he's dead, I won't feel guilty, she promised herself.

It was Bevins's fault Sawyer's father, Dan Deevers, was dead. Her ranch foreman wouldn't have been out in that January ice storm if Bevins hadn't run off more of her sheep. She knew it was Bevins who'd been stealing them, a few at a time, for the past year, even if there wasn't any proof. And yesterday, another of his dirty tricks had hurt Sawyer. The boy could have broken his neck in that fall from his horse—a horse intentionally startled by Bevins, though he'd denied it.

No, she wasn't going to feel guilty if that lying, no-good troublemaker was dead. Not at all.

She steeled herself against what she might find, then looked at the man at her feet.

"Oh, dear God." The words came out on an expelled breath of air.

She dropped to her knees and stared at the man she'd shot. It wasn't Bevins. It wasn't one of Bevins's hired hands. It was someone she'd never seen before.

She'd just killed an innocent stranger.

The stranger wasn't dead, but he would be soon if Libby didn't do something to staunch the bleeding. She hadn't time to wonder who he was or what he'd been doing there, sneaking around her place at this time of evening. Getting shot was his own blasted fault, and she intended to tell him so if he pulled through.

She raced back to the house, wishing for once she hadn't forsaken her long skirts and petticoats for the freedom of denim britches. Cotton petticoats made good bandages and would have come in handy at the moment.

As soon as the door opened, she saw Sawyer, bracing himself against the doorjamb of his bedroom.

"What happened, Libby? What's out there?"

A heartbeat's hesitation, then she hurried forward. She couldn't stop and explain, not if she didn't want to be guilty of murder. "Go back to bed, Sawyer. I'll explain in a little while."

"Libby—"

"*Now!*" she snapped, more harshly than she'd intended.

Just before he turned away, she caught a glimpse of tears in his eyes, but she knew better than to apologize. Sawyer was every bit as proud as his father had been and wouldn't want to know she'd seen him looking that way.

She grabbed a blanket off her bed. It was getting dark and the temperature was dropping. She'd have to get the stranger inside where she could see clearly before she could help him. In another few minutes it would be black as pitch out there, not to mention bone-chilling cold.

Her heart still pounding hard, Libby returned to the wounded man. She laid the blanket on the earth beside him, then paused to assess the situation. The stranger was long and lanky, and he probably had a good sixty pounds on her, if not more. But Libby was strong. She'd wrestled enough obstinate sheep in the years she'd been at the Blue Springs Ranch to make her so. She ought to be able to handle one helpless male.

Bending over, purposefully ignoring the crimson stains on his pant leg and shirt, she rolled him onto the blanket. Then she grabbed hold of one end and began to drag the injured man across the yard. She made slow but steady progress, worry nagging the edges of her conscience.

What would the sheriff do to her if he died? Would anyone believe she'd fired in self-defense? What was the penalty for shooting down someone in cold blood?

She shook off such thoughts. Only a fool or a thief—or both—would ride out alone in this country at night. No honest traveler would hide in the trees rather than ride into the yard and knock on her door. No, this was his own fault, no matter what had brought him to her ranch.

Momentarily she wished Alistair McGregor or Ronald Aberdeen were there to help her, but they were with the sheep, up in the hills north of the ranch.

And just as well, she decided.

As fond as she was of McGregor, she wasn't in the mood for a lecture from the crusty Scottish shepherd. She knew she'd done a foolish thing, shooting a man without cause.

Swearing occasionally beneath her breath, Libby managed to drag the unconscious man into Amanda's old bedroom. Once there, she turned up the lamp and set it on the floor, where it could spill the most light on the stranger's wounds.

She drew a deep breath at the bloody sight, then reminded herself that a woman who made her home in the middle of nowhere had no business getting squeamish at the first sight of blood. She'd seen worse than this. She might see worse yet before the year was out. Life in the Idaho high country was hard. It always had been. It always would be.

With her sewing shears, she cut open his shirt and trousers, swallowing hard as she stared at the torn and bleeding flesh. Again she wondered what would happen to her if he died—which, judging by the sight of him, seemed a likely possibility.

Her gaze moved up, away from his wounds, to his face. He didn't look like a thief. Come to think of it, he didn't look like a fool, either. And he certainly looked nothing like Timothy Bevins.

His features were handsome, aristocratic in appearance, yet there was no hint of softness. His nose was long and straight, his jaw strong and determined. A slight cleft dented his square chin. Black brows capped eyes that bore tiny crow's-feet in the outer corners. Two days' beard growth would have made other men look scraggly and unkempt, but not this man. Instead he appeared—

The stranger groaned.

The sound spurred her into action. She got up from the floor and hurried to the kitchen, where she poured hot water into a large bowl. She dropped a towel into the basin, then picked up the soap and returned to the bedroom.

"Mister," she muttered without looking at his face again, "I sure hope you don't come to, because this is going to hurt."

*   *   *

Pain was Remington's constant companion. He dwelled in utter darkness, haunted by blurry visions and the feel of hot pokers jabbing into his flesh.

He saw his father once, far off in the distance. He wanted to go to him, but he couldn't move. He tried to call to him, but he couldn't speak. Slowly his father faded from view, swallowed in a white mist, leaving Remington alone with the pain once more.

No. Don't go.

But it was too late. Jefferson Walker was gone.

"No . . . don't go. . . ."

Libby leaned over the man in the bed, uncertain whether or not she'd really heard him. "Mister?"

His eyes were closed, his face, drawn with pain, seeming pale beneath his tan. After two days she knew he wasn't going to bleed to death. The wound in his side was superficial, as far as she could tell. She was most concerned about his leg. The buckshot had torn through it, missing the bone but tearing the flesh and muscle. She wondered if he'd ever walk without a limp. And there was still the possibility of infection. So many things could go wrong before he had a chance to recover.

With a shake of her head, Libby straightened, picked up the wash basin, and carried it outside to empty into the underbrush. Overhead, the sky was an expanse of brilliant blue, unmarred by clouds. The air was warm and, if not for the breeze, would have seemed hot.

She sighed as she pushed stray wisps of hair from her face, wondering what she was going to do about the stranger if he didn't show signs of improvement soon. McGregor wouldn't come down from Tyler Creek, where the sheep were grazing, for several weeks. Not until she failed to show up with fresh supplies when expected.

Turning, she noticed Sawyer standing on the corral fence, looking at the horses. She set the empty wash basin near the back door, then crossed the yard to the corral.

"He's a mighty nice horse, ain't he, Libby?" the boy asked when she reached him.

"Isn't. Not ain't," she corrected gently before looking at the stranger's tall, gold-colored gelding. "Yes, he's a fine horse."

Fine was an understatement. The animal was magnificent. This was no ten-dollar saddle horse. This was a steed more commonly found in a stable behind a New York mansion on Fifth Avenue or at a summer cottage in Newport. Not the usual sort of horseflesh to be seen in these parts. But neither was the gelding's owner the usual sort of man to show up at her ranch. Most men who came this way were itinerant workmen, traveling around the country, looking for anything to put a few dollars in their pockets before moving on. No, the man lying in Amanda's bed was no more like them than his horse was like the rangy mustangs found in the mountains of Idaho.

She thought of the beautiful saddle she'd removed from the gelding's back two days ago, the fancy leather saddlebags, the cut of the stranger's clothes, the gold pocket watch, the Colt revolvers and the Winchester rifle. Mentally she recalled every item that belonged to him, including the money she'd found. But there'd been nothing to give away his identity. He remained a mystery—as did the reason for his arrival at the Blue Springs.

"Is he gonna be all right, Libby?" Sawyer asked, breaking into her thoughts.

She glanced at the boy. His coffee-colored hair was shaggy and sorely in need of a trimming. His eyes, like dark brown saucers, watched her with a wariness she understood. Nothing was ever certain out here. Life was precarious. It was a lesson brought home by the death of Sawyer's father only a few months before.

"I'm pretty sure he'll make it," she answered as she brushed his tousled hair back from his forehead.

He frowned, and she knew she shouldn't have done it. Sawyer wanted her to treat him like a man, not a baby. He'd told her so often enough.

Her heart tightened in her chest. She loved Sawyer as much as if she'd given birth to him, and since she would never marry, she knew he was the only child she would ever have. She wanted to do right by him. But what did she know about raising children? She certainly couldn't take anything from her own childhood as an example.

For a moment she recalled dark, paper-covered walls with high ceilings and elaborate moldings, long hallways and whispering servants, a mother with a sad-sweet smile, a father who—

She drove away the memories before she could regret them.

Her gaze focused once more on Sawyer. "I'd better go in. You feed the horses, then get inside and prop that ankle up before the swelling returns."

"It don't hurt no more."

"It *doesn't* hurt *any*more," she corrected automatically.

"Right." He tossed the word over his shoulder as he headed toward the barn.

She smiled as she watched him go. She was being overly cautious, and she knew it. Sawyer could probably run a footrace and still not bother his ankle. She shouldn't try to make an invalid out of him.

Glancing toward the log house, she wished her patient inside could mend as quickly. She had a nagging feeling his presence didn't bode well for her future. She would be glad to see him out of bed and on his way.

*   *   *

Remington drifted slowly into consciousness. At first he thought he'd been dreaming about pain, but quickly enough he realized it was all too real.

What had happened?

He searched his memory for some clues. He remembered arriving in Idaho. He remembered talking to folks in Boise City and Weiser. He remembered learning about, then looking for, the Blue Springs Ranch.

The ranch. That was it. He'd found it at dusk. He'd dismounted and left his horse in the trees, then started to walk toward the house.

And then what?

A noise.

A gunshot.

And then all he remembered was pain. White-hot pain.

With his eyes still closed, he moved his right hand to check his injuries. He felt the strips of bandages binding his chest and winced when he touched a tender place on his left side.

He continued his exploration, moving his hand beneath the blanket toward his left leg and the throbbing in his thigh. Instinctively he knew this injury was more serious. But just how serious?

He drew in a ragged breath, then opened his eyes, squinting against the sunlight that streamed through the open window. The room was unfamiliar to him. He tried to lift his head from the pillow but sank back as agony exploded behind his eyes.

A moment later, he lost consciousness.

2

Sensing another's presence the next time he awakened, Remington lay still, eyes closed, listening and waiting, not ready to let anyone know he was conscious. Even so, he flinched when fingers touched his thigh and slowly began to remove the dressing covering his wound.

"Sorry, mister." The woman's voice was soft and warm toned.

Cautiously he opened his eyes just far enough to catch a glimpse of his nurse. Her rose gold hair was twined in a thick braid that fell over one shoulder. She wore an apple green shirt, a perfect match with the color of her eyes, and her cheeks and the bridge of her pert nose had been freckled by too much time in the sun.

There was little about her that resembled the young lady in the portrait he'd seen hanging above the fireplace in the drawing room at Rosegate, little that matched the detailed description Anna Vanderhoff had given him. Yet he knew without a shred of doubt he was looking at

Anna's daughter, Olivia—and a bonus of two hundred and fifty thousand dollars.

"Libby?"

At the sound of the young voice from the doorway, Remington quickly closed his eyes as Olivia twisted on her chair.

"Libby, I don't think the runt's gettin' enough to eat," the boy continued. "The other pups keep pushin' him out."

Did Olivia have a child? he wondered. No, the boy had called her Libby, not Mother. Was he a stepchild, perhaps? So, there could be a husband after all.

"I think we oughta bring him in the house and feed him ourselves. He oughta be able to suck on one of them bottles, just like an orphaned lamb does."

"You know how Aunt Amanda always felt about dogs in the house."

He liked her voice. It had a whiskey-coated quality and just a hint of a western twang. But he knew Olivia Vanderhoff was not from the West. She'd been born and raised in Manhattan, summering at the Vanderhoff seaside estate in Rhode Island and schooled in the finest women's academy that money and position could buy.

"But Miz Blue's gone," the youngster interjected into Remington's thoughts. "It's up to you now."

He heard her sigh, felt her weariness as she said, "Yes, it is up to me." She was silent a moment. "I'll tell you what, Sawyer. I'll come have a look at that pup as soon as I'm finished here."

"How's he doin'?"

There was a lengthy pause, and Remington sensed Olivia was looking at him again.

"As well as can be expected, I suppose. I just wish he'd wake up. He needs nourishment soon, or . . ." She allowed her voice to drift into silence.

Sawyer moved up to the side of Remington's bed. "He's gonna be okay, Libby."

"I hope so," she whispered. "God knows, I truly hope so."

Remington hoped so, too. He needed to send a telegram to New York City before his year ran out and he lost that two-hundred-and-fifty-thousand-dollar bonus.

Libby worked with deliberate care as she cleansed the stranger's wounds, then replaced the soiled bandages. When she was finished, she picked up the basin of water and bloodstained strips of linen and rose from the chair beside the bed. Only then did she allow her gaze to return to the man's face.

Wake up, she urged him.

It was her fault he was lying there, unconscious and in pain. It was her fault he was wounded, perhaps crippled for life. How would she ever make it up to him—*if* he even survived?

Another thought came to plague her. Did he have a wife waiting for him somewhere, a wife who was worried about him, waiting to hear from him?

Unable to stop herself, she reached forward and brushed his black hair away from his forehead. The moment her fingertips touched him, a strange heat coiled in her stomach, and she quickly turned away.

She just wanted him to get well. She just wanted him to get well and go away.

Libby carried the bowl of water to the kitchen and set it on the counter. She dropped the soiled bandages into a basket, then hurried out to the barn. She found Sawyer in a far corner, kneeling in the straw as he watched the puppies nursing. He was holding the black-and-white runt of the litter in his arms.

Misty lifted her head as Libby approached. The bitch's dark eyes seemed to beg for some relief from the eight rambunctious pups who were latched on to her teats.

Libby knelt beside Sawyer and reached out to stroke the dog's head. "Poor girl," she crooned. "Can't wait until they're weaned, can you?"

Misty licked her hand.

Libby pulled two of the plump pups away from their breakfast, setting them behind her in the thick straw, then took the runt from Sawyer's hands and pressed the pup's nose against Misty's belly, holding him there until he grabbed hold of a teat. "Let's try helping him out this way for a while," she said without looking at Sawyer. "I think he'll make out fine."

"Yeah." His voice revealed his disappointment.

She was tempted to tell him he could bring the puppy into the house, but old habits died hard. She could almost hear Amanda's voice: *These dogs work for their keep. They ain't pets. They're here to tend the flock and send up an alarm if there's trouble and for no other reasons than that. Don't you go makin' pets of 'em, Libby. You hear me?*

She smiled at the memory even as she reached out to stroke Misty's head again. Like it or not, Misty had become Libby's pet, and she'd known Amanda hadn't really minded. She'd understood Libby's loneliness, a loneliness that the collie had somehow helped to fill.

She glanced at Sawyer, her smile fading. The boy was lonely, too. He missed his father. Libby understood. She knew all about missing someone until a body thought they might die from the missing. She'd felt that way about her mother. She still did sometimes.

"You're kind of partial to that runt, aren't you?" she asked, wanting to put her arm around Sawyer to draw him close, wanting to show him she loved him.

He shrugged.

"How about if I make the pup yours?"

The boy's brown eyes widened as he looked up at her.

"It'll be your job to train him, see that he learns to earn his keep. Can you do that?"

Sawyer nodded, and his shaggy dark hair fell into his eyes.

"All right, then. He's yours."

She thought for a moment he might hug her. His smile was bright as he leaned toward her. But he caught himself in time and pulled back.

"Thanks, Libby. I'll make him a good sheepdog. I promise."

"I know you will." Her heart ached for him, wishing she knew how to tell him it was okay for him to be a little boy. It wasn't necessary for him to try to take his father's place.

Resisting the urge to ruffle his hair, she rose from the barn floor. "Don't forget you've got other chores to do."

"I won't," he answered, his gaze still locked on his puppy.

Smiling again, she turned and headed for the barn door. She thought it likely she'd find Sawyer right where she'd left him come lunchtime.

She stepped through the barn opening, squinting her eyes against the bright midmorning sunlight. It was going to be another hot day.

She stopped suddenly, her stomach dropping.

"Mornin', Miss Blue," Timothy Bevins said, his mouth curving in a mockery of a smile. Some women might have found him appealing, but Libby saw only the smallness of his soul behind his hazel eyes. He was mean spirited and a bully. Amanda had always said he was a coward, too, without enough gumption to stand up for himself unless he knew for certain he was stronger than his victim.

"What are you doing here, Mr. Bevins?"

He leaned his forearms on the pommel of his saddle, his body relaxed yet somehow threatening. "Now, that don't sound neighborly. I just come by to see how you're doin'. I'm worried about you bein' here all alone, now that your foreman's dead and old McGregor's gone with the sheep."

She held herself straight. "You needn't be worried about me. I can take care of myself."

"This ain't friendly country. You know that, Miss Blue. Just about anything can happen." He dismounted and took one step toward her.

Timothy Bevins wasn't a tall man, perhaps only three or four inches taller than she, but he exuded strength. He was all muscle, a body sculpted by years of working the range. It wouldn't take much for him to overpower her.

Libby glanced toward the house, longing for the shotgun resting against the wall just inside the door. She was angered by the threat she perceived in his words, in his actions. He had no right to come on her ranch and make her feel helpless. She'd like to give him something to think about. She'd like to give him a taste of buckshot.

Bevins moved into her line of vision. "I just came by to see if you'd given any more thought to sellin' out to me. A gal like you doesn't belong on a place like this, Miss Blue. You should get yourself a man t'care for you. Think how much happier you'd be. It'd be better for that boy, too." He shook his head. "Lord knows what could happen to him out here. Why, he could get hurt real bad just any old time."

Libby forgot her uneasiness. She forgot the shotgun in the house. She stepped forward, her head held high, her hands balled into fists at her sides. "Get off my land. And don't you ever try to hurt Sawyer again."

He smiled, a smile that made her stiffen with fury. "Now, Miss Blue, don't go gettin' yourself in an uproar. I'm just sayin'—"

"I know what you're saying, Mr. Bevins. And I'm saying get off my land."

He grabbed her by the arms and pulled her body up close to his. His smile vanished. "I do believe what you need is a man to show you your place."

"Let go of me." She tried to pull herself free, but his grip only tightened.

"Maybe I'm the man who should show you." His voice had grown husky, and she recognized lust smoldering behind his eyes. "You could be a right pretty woman if you'd fix yourself up some. Yessirree, I think it'd be a pleasure t'show you how t'be a real woman."

She was too angry to have the good sense to be afraid. "Let go of me," she cried again, continuing to struggle, wanting to strike him.

Instead of letting her go, he pulled her even closer, his mouth lowering toward hers. She felt the hardness of his desire pressing against her pelvis. She smelled his hot breath on her face.

Suddenly she realized how vulnerable she was, alone here with no one to help her. Fear replaced rage, turning her mouth dry and her knees to water.

"Let go," she whispered.

Bevins laughed, low and ugly.

"The lady said to let her go."

Libby gasped, and Bevins pulled his mouth away. In unison they turned to look toward the house. There, standing just outside the door, a rifle leveled at Bevins, was the stranger she'd left unconscious not more than fifteen minutes ago. He wore only the bedsheet wrapped around his waist. His chest and feet were bare, his hair tousled, but despite it all, he looked surprisingly strong and threatening.

"Who're you?" Bevins demanded gruffly.

"I don't believe that's any of your business. Now, let the lady go." There was a hard threat in his voice that brooked no argument.

Bevins's hold on her arms loosened, and she pulled quickly away, stepping out of his reach, surprised that her legs continued to hold her upright.

The stranger motioned with his Winchester. "Get on your horse and ride out."

Bevins glared angrily at him, then at Libby.

"Now," the stranger demanded.

Bevins apparently heard the warning in the harsh voice. Without another word, he swung onto his horse's back, then kicked the roan into a canter and rode away, disappearing into the thick grove of trees.

Libby stared after him. It was an effort to breathe, and her legs were still shaking. If not for the stranger, Bevins might have done more than simply kiss her or frighten her. If not for the stranger . . .

She turned to look at her rescuer just as his Winchester clattered to earth. She saw him grab for the doorjamb, miss it, then slump down beside the rifle.

Libby rushed toward him. As she knelt on the ground, she noticed a red stain darkening the sheet where it lay across his thigh. He opened his eyes. Dark blue eyes, the color of the Idaho sky just before a thunderstorm blew through.

"Is he gone?" he asked.

"Yes."

"Good." The word came out on a sigh as his eyes drifted closed.

Six hours later the stranger regained consciousness.

At his bedside, Libby was flooded with relief. "Hello. I'm glad to see you're back."

His eyes focused on her face, but he didn't speak.

"Thank you for what you did. Stopping Bevins, I mean."

"How long have I been unconscious?" he asked, his brows drawing together in a frown of concentration.

"Since this morning. About six hours."

"No. I meant altogether. How long since I was shot?"

"Five days."

He closed his eyes. "How bad is my leg?"

"I'm not sure. I think it will be all right." She sank onto the nearby chair, her guilt returning with a vengeance. "There doesn't seem to be any infection. Of course, it would have been better if you hadn't walked on it . . . "

He opened his eyes again, his gaze locking instantly with hers.

". . . but I'm very glad you did," she finished, feeling just a bit breathless.

"I didn't have any choice," he said dryly. "He was disturbing my sleep."

She shook her head, ignoring his weak attempt at humor. "I'm immeasurably in your debt, especially since I'm the one who . . . especially after I . . ." She let her words drift away, uncertain how to continue.

His blue gaze studied her for an uncomfortably long time before he said, "I take it you had something to do with the reason my ribs and leg hurt like . . . like the blazes."

She remembered the moment she'd shot him. She could so easily have killed him.

"Why?" he asked.

"Why?" she echoed, not really listening, too caught up in the dreadful memory.

"Why did you shoot me?"

She forced herself to concentrate on his question. "I thought you were Bevins."

He released a sigh. "I guess I can understand." He winced. "I'd have shot, too, if I were you."

Unable to help herself, she smiled.

*　　　*　　　*

Remington had thoroughly studied the portrait of Olivia Vanderhoff during his visit to Rosegate, the Vanderhoffs' Seventy-second Street mansion in Manhattan, but it was clear to him now that the artist had failed to capture the real essence of his subject. There had been nothing smiling about the girl of the portrait. There had been no sparkle in her green eyes, no invitation to laughter in her bowed mouth.

At seventeen, she'd posed in a gown of white lace and satin, her hair dressed with pearls, her throat accented with a gold locket. Now she was twenty-five, clad in a man's shirt and, if he wasn't mistaken, trousers. She wore no pearls, no locket, no jewelry of any kind.

What made you choose this stark life? he wondered. *Why this?*

But the why wasn't of any real importance, he reminded himself. The only thing that mattered was he'd found Northrop Vanderhoff's missing daughter. With the money he would collect for locating the beautiful heiress, Remington might be able to keep his promise to his father. He might be able to repay the man responsible for Jefferson Walker's death.

He saw a flush of pink steal into Olivia's cheeks as he continued to stare. All traces of her smile and suppressed laughter vanished. She straightened her back, lifted her chin, then held out her hand toward him.

"I suppose introductions are past due, sir. My name is Libby Blue. I'm the owner of the Blue Springs Ranch."

He took hold of her hand. "It's a pleasure to meet you, Mrs. Blue. My name's Remington Walker."

"It's *Miss* Blue."

He felt an odd sense of relief. So there wasn't a husband after all.

"What brought you to my ranch, Mr. Walker?"

One reason Remington was so successful as a detective

was his ability to read people. Only a very few had ever fooled him. Olivia Vanderhoff wasn't going to be one of them. He could see intelligence in her eyes, as well as a healthy dose of caution and a dash of distrust. She wouldn't believe him if he said he'd been looking for work. He didn't look anything like a sheepherder; he'd bet half the money he had coming from Vanderhoff on that.

He allowed himself a self-deprecating chuckle. "I thought it was sheer luck until you shot me."

The blush in her cheeks heightened, but her gaze didn't waver.

"The truth, Miss Blue, is I was lost. I was in the territorial capital on business and decided I'd have a look at the country before returning to my home. I had a map, but unfortunately, I thought I could head off into the wilderness, explore a bit of the territory, then find my way back, none the worse for wear. As you've no doubt guessed, I lost my way. But, as fortune would have it, I came across your place before I met with a worse fate."

"Why didn't you ride up in the open where you could be seen?" Her eyes narrowed. "Why were you carrying your rifle?"

"Bad judgment on my part. I truly didn't mean you any harm."

He could tell she was weighing his words. For a moment he feared she wasn't going to believe him. Then he saw the suspicion leave her gaze. A hint of her pretty smile touched the corners of her mouth.

"You're not from around here, Mr. Walker. I can tell by your accent. Just where are you from?"

"I was born and raised in Virginia, ma'am."

"Well, I suggest you return there as soon as you're able to travel." She rose from the chair, her expression stern but her tone teasing. "We do things a bit differently here in Idaho."

Remington nodded. "Shoot first?" He rested the palm of his right hand on his left side. "I noticed." Then he grinned to take the sting out of his words.

Libby's pulse quickened. Instinct warned her that the stranger she'd shot was potentially more dangerous than she'd at first assumed, perhaps even more dangerous than Bevins ever thought to be.

She stepped back from his bedside. "You must be hungry. There's a kettle of stew on the stove. I'll bring you some broth. You need food in your stomach." She turned and hurried out of the bedroom.

Trust no strangers, she reminded herself moments later as she pulled a bowl from the kitchen cupboard.

It was a rule she had followed faithfully for over six years. Even after all this time, it was a rule she couldn't afford to forget—not even for this particular stranger's devastating smile.

Unbidden, unwanted, she envisioned her father. A regal man with steel gray hair and eyes to match. A man who bought and sold people the same way he bought and sold property or ships or anything else. A man for whom everything and everyone had a price. Even his daughter. She was to have brought him the southern railroad he'd coveted for so many years—and the devil take her feelings.

She closed her eyes as she leaned against the sideboard. She didn't want to think about her father. To do so only made her unhappy. She couldn't change who he was or how he'd felt about her.

Her mother's image drifted into her thoughts, and Libby felt the sting of tears. "Oh, Mama," she whispered, her heart aching.

She wondered if her mother knew she was all right, knew she was well and happy. Dan Deevers had mailed Libby's letter from Cheyenne when he'd been there last year, but of course she would never know for certain whether or not Anna Vanderhoff had received it. It had been a foolish thing to do, writing to her mother after so many years of silence. But she'd been lonely after Amanda's death, and she'd missed her mother with a keen freshness.

Even now, she wished . . .

Libby sniffed and opened her eyes. She was being emotional and melodramatic. She'd found the life she wanted right here at the Blue Springs. She owned her land and her sheep and her home. She had Sawyer to love, and she had McGregor and young Ronald for trusted friends. Most important of all, she had her freedom. Nobody owned her. Nobody could tell her what to do or what to say or what to wear or what to feel. She was free, and she meant to stay that way.

Drawing a deep breath, she filled the bowl with broth, placed it on a tray, and carried it back to the bedroom. She was going to get Mr. Walker well and on his way—and the sooner the better.

3

When Libby entered the bedroom the following morning, carrying salve, fresh bandages, and a bowl of warm water, she discovered her patient sitting upright, his back against the headboard.

"Good morning," he greeted her.

For five days she had tended his wounds without hesitation or embarrassment, but that had been when he was lying unconscious and helpless. Suddenly he didn't seem so helpless. He was alert and watching her, and she knew he understood how intimately she'd cared for him while he'd been ill.

As the heat rose in her cheeks, she reminded herself she was no stranger to the male anatomy. Amanda Blue hadn't had any patience with unnecessary modesty. There wasn't time for such nonsense, Amanda had told Libby the day Robert McLain was carried in and placed on the kitchen table, the broken leg in his thigh poking through the tear in his pant leg. In her years at the Blue Springs, Libby had tended men with just about every kind of injury and ailment she could imagine. This was no different.

Remington peered at the bowl in her arm. "I hope that's not breakfast," he teased.

"No, Mr. Walker. I'm here to change your dressings." She set everything on the bedside table, then drew in a quick breath of air before bending over her patient and drawing the sheet down to his waist.

His chest was well muscled and broad. A swath of dark hair—which she found disturbing to look at—narrowed as it grew closer to his navel, then disappeared beneath the bedsheet. She hoped he didn't notice the slight tremor in her hands as she carefully removed the bandage from his side wound. She knew he was watching her. She could feel his gaze upon her like a physical touch.

"Just a flesh wound," Remington commented as Libby dropped the soiled bandages on the floor. "I was lucky. Five inches to the right, and I'd have been a dead man."

She glanced up and met his gaze. "Yes." She thought again how terrible it would have been if she'd killed him. What if she'd never seen the blue of his eyes or the curve of his smile or . . .

She returned quickly to her task, washing the wound, smoothing on the salve Amanda had taught her how to make from roots and herbs, then covering it all with clean linen. She'd almost convinced herself she wasn't the least bit bothered by his bare chest or the way she knew he was watching her. She almost believed this was no different from caring for Sawyer when he was sick. Almost.

Libby drew in another long, deep breath as she moved the sheet aside to reveal his thigh and began to repeat the process.

Remington was amused by her embarrassment and impressed by her resolve. If he didn't know better, he'd think the young woman who called herself Libby Blue had spent her entire life doctoring wounded men in the back-country instead of hobnobbing with the sons and daughters of New York's Knickerbocker families. He wondered what she'd been like as a pampered debutante.

"There's still no sign of infection," she said as she reached for the wet cloth.

Remington turned his attention to his leg and got his first good look at what the buckshot had done to his thigh. It didn't take more than a glance to tell him this was no flesh wound. It would take time to heal, time he didn't have. But he didn't exactly relish losing his leg, either, and he suspected that might happen if he tried to leave too soon.

He clenched his teeth as Libby cleansed the wound. Stabs of pain shot up and down his leg as she worked. To distract himself, Remington studied Libby's profile as she leaned over him. He memorized the tiny wisps that curled at her temples, the unusual color of her pale, rose gold hair. He noticed her tiny, shell-shaped ears and the small point of her chin. He admired the sweep of her thick eyelashes, the delicate arch of her golden brows, and the smoothness of her skin. He decided he even liked the splash of freckles over her nose.

What made you run? he asked her silently. *Why did you leave that life of ease for this?*

He thought of Northrop Vanderhoff, standing behind his large cherrywood desk, a glass of brandy in his hand, his thick gray eyebrows drawn together as he'd glared at Remington.

"I hear you're the best, Walker."

"If she can be found, I'll find her," Remington had answered confidently, his gaze never wavering, his expression hiding the seething bitterness that burned in his chest.

"I want my daughter returned to me. I'll make it well worth your time, Walker. You find her and bring her back to me."

Remington had initially suspected Northrop's daughter had run off with a man her father didn't approve of. Although rare, it wasn't an unheard-of occurrence in a society that too often selected mates with the same cool deliberation accorded potential business investments. But his investigation hadn't turned up a mystery lover, and now he knew she had no husband.

So what *had* caused her to go into hiding?

"Has this ranch always been your home, Miss Blue?" he asked, knowing the truth but wanting to hear her version.

A strange expression flickered in her eyes as she lifted her gaze to meet his. "I came to live with my aunt over six years ago."

Remington knew she had no aunt, living here or anywhere else, but he didn't let on. "And before that where did you live?"

"I came here from San Francisco."

That much was true. San Francisco was where he'd managed to pick up her trail. Of course, she was leaving out that she'd lived all but a few months of her life in New York City, right up until she'd disappeared.

Libby straightened. "I'll bring you something to eat. I thought some porridge might sit well on your stomach."

He couldn't keep from making a face. He'd never cared for oatmeal.

She laughed, a light, airy sound that filled the room and made him feel like grinning.

"Mr. Walker, you and Sawyer have something in common. He doesn't think much of my porridge, either. But Aunt Amanda always said it was a good food for the sickbed, and she was seldom wrong. So I'll fix it, and you'll eat it."

"Yes, ma'am," he drawled obediently.

Smiling and shaking her head, Libby picked up her doctoring supplies and left the room.

Well, he thought, if he was going to be laid up for a while, at least he wouldn't be bored. Discovering how Olivia Vanderhoff had transformed herself into Libby Blue should prove to be an interesting diversion until he could finish the job he'd come here to do.

Sawyer waited until Libby was hanging clothes on the line before he ventured over to the bedroom door and peered inside.

"Hello," the stranger said. "You must be Sawyer."

He nodded.

"Come on in."

Sawyer glanced toward the back door. Libby had told him to stay away from the stranger, but she came in here all the time. Besides, this man had run off Mr. Bevins when he'd tried to hurt Libby. In Sawyer's mind, that made him someone to trust.

"Come on. I'll tell your mother I invited you in."

He stepped into the room, then stopped. Eyes squinted in concentration, he stared hard at the man in the bed. He looked like any other scraggly ranch hand who had ever worked the Blue Springs. Hair needing trimming. Dark stubble on his chin. But Sawyer doubted he'd ever been a ranch hand. His horse and saddle were too fine, and his hands weren't rough and callused.

"My name's Walker. Remington Walker. What's yours?"

"Sawyer Deevers. And Libby ain't my ma. My ma's dead. Long time ago, 'fore I could remember."

"I'm sorry to hear that." He held out his hand. "It's a pleasure to meet you. Excuse me if I don't get up, but I've had a bit of an accident." His smile was friendly.

Knowing he probably shouldn't, Sawyer moved forward to shake Mr. Walker's hand. "'T'weren't no accident.

Libby meant to shoot you. She just thought you were somebody else."

Mr. Walker laughed aloud. "So she told me. I guess I'm lucky she's a good shot."

"You're lucky all right. Libby can't hit nothin' she aims at. She prob'ly meant to kill you, which is why you're still alive."

The man's smile faded to a frown. "I see," he muttered. Then, changing the subject, he asked, "Why are the two of you all alone out here? I thought ranches always had lots of men around the place."

"McGregor, he's with the sheep. Ronald Aberdeen, too. The others were all let go. Libby can't afford to pay more help right now. Things have been kinda hard 'round here since my dad died."

"Your dad worked here?"

"He was the foreman for Miz Blue and Libby. He got caught in a storm and froze to death up on Bear Mountain last winter. He was lookin' for the sheep Mr. Bevins run off." He squeezed his hands into tight fists. "It's Mr. Bevins's fault my dad's dead, and someday I'm gonna get him for it."

Remington watched the boy struggle with his anger. He knew firsthand what it meant to lose a father. He knew what it was like to have someone else be responsible but get off scot-free because there wasn't any proof.

Hoping to divert Sawyer's thoughts, Remington asked, "Have you been taking care of my horse for me?"

Sawyer's brown eyes grew as wide as saucers, all trace of anger disappearing. "I sure have. He's just about the best horse I've ever seen. What's his name?"

"Sundown. I've had him a long time. Raised him from a colt. He means a great deal to me, and I wouldn't want anything to happen to him. I'll tell you what, Sawyer. You take good care of him for me while I'm laid up here, and I'll pay you fifty cents a day."

"Fifty cents! A *day*?"

"That's right."

"Thank you, Mr. Walker," Libby interrupted from the doorway, "but Sawyer can't accept."

Both Remington and Sawyer turned to look at her as she entered the bedroom. She frowned at the boy.

With his chin nearly touching his chest, Sawyer turned toward the bed once more. "I'll take good care of your horse, Mr. Walker, but you don't need to pay me for it. Thanks anyhow." That said, he hurriedly left the room.

Remington lifted his gaze to meet Libby's.

"I'm sure you meant well," she told him, "but Sawyer should help because it's the right thing to do, not because he can make money doing it."

"I only wanted—"

"I'll see that he doesn't disturb you again." She stepped out of the room and closed the door.

Remington sighed as he leaned against the pillows at his back. He'd only been trying to help. Sawyer had said money was short, and Remington was fairly certain the boy would take good care of Sundown. Was it such a terrible thing to pay him for his work?

"Sawyer should help because it's the right thing to do, not because he can make money doing it. . . ."

Libby might not be Sawyer's mother, Remington decided, remembering her stern expression, but she sure did act like one.

Then he thought of Libby's father. He doubted Northrop Vanderhoff had ever done anything without considering the bottom line. He couldn't help wondering how that unscrupulous old man had managed to raise a daughter with real principles.

Perhaps he should also wonder why an honest, kindhearted man like Jefferson Walker had befriended Northrop. How could his father have been fooled for so many years? How could Jefferson have allowed Northrop to drive him to such desperate measures? How could any of it have happened?

But those were questions without answers. Jefferson Walker could not respond to them. Jefferson Walker was dead. Dead because of Northrop's greed.

Weariness swept over Remington suddenly, and he closed his eyes, swearing even as he drifted into sleep that he would have his revenge. . . .

One way or another.

4

The sun was barely a promise on the horizon as Libby made her way toward the barn. The morning air was crisp, a lingering chill mocking the coming of summer, and dew lay heavy on the ground. The moisture sparkled like tiny diamonds scattered over the earth.

Libby loved mornings, especially this time of year when everything smelled fresh and new. She never minded awakening early. She never minded the chores that awaited her as she began her day. This was her time.

Pulling open the door, she heard the sound of whimpering puppies, obscured a moment later by a loud moo.

"I'll be with you in a minute, Melly," she told the Jersey milk cow as she set the bucket near the stall. Then she walked to the back of the barn and knelt beside Misty. "How're you doing, girl?"

She stroked the small collie's head before picking up one of the black-and-white puppies.

"Look at you. If you're not a charmer, I don't know

who is." She pressed the pup into the curve of her neck and jaw, enjoying the feel of his soft coat against her skin.

Melly let out another noisy complaint and kicked the side of her stall for good measure.

"All right. All right. I hear you."

Libby returned the pup to its mother, then stood and crossed the barn once again, this time entering the milk cow's stall.

"Getting a bit cranky, aren't we?" she said as she patted Melly's fawn-colored neck.

She tethered the cow near the manger, then pulled a three-legged stool up close and set the pail beneath Melly's swollen udder. As soon as she was settled onto the stool, she leaned close, grasped the Jersey's teats, and began to milk.

She'd enjoyed this chore ever since Amanda first showed her how it was done. She'd always found the warmth of the barn and the rhythmic sound of the milk sloshing into a pail to be a soothing combination. She could allow her thoughts to wander at random.

This morning they wandered to Remington Walker.

Last night her patient had requested a crutch so he could get out of bed. Libby had found the one Robert McLain used back in 1884 and had taken it into Remington's bedroom. He hadn't tried to use it yet—at least, not in front of her—but she suspected he would soon. She only hoped he wasn't rushing things, since a setback would delay his departure. And the sooner he left, the better.

At least, that was what she'd been telling herself.

She thought of Remington's slightly crooked smile, the way the corners of his eyes crinkled when he laughed. She remembered how his stormy blue gaze followed her whenever she was in the bedroom, the intenseness with which he studied her, listened to her. She recalled the way his voice affected her, making her insides soften. Something about him made her feel both safe and at risk. Even as she wished for his quick recovery so he could leave the Blue Springs, she felt a secret sorrow knowing he would go.

She thought of the way he had driven off Timothy Bevins. The man had barely had strength enough to stand, yet he'd forced Bevins to release Libby and ride out. Once Remington was gone, what would keep Bevins from coming back to bully her again?

Nothing.

Her hands stilled as she leaned her forehead against the cow's side. She knew Bevins wasn't going to give up. He was determined to get control of the Blue Springs. If things kept up as they were, he just might get it, too.

She wished Amanda were there. Amanda Blue hadn't had an ounce of fear in her tiny body. Amanda Blue had known how to handle Bevins.

Libby closed her eyes, remembering the night she'd met the feisty little sheep rancher from Idaho. . . .

Olivia felt icy tentacles of fear wrap themselves around her heart and squeeze. It was difficult to breathe, and her pulse was racing. Impatiently she watched the other passengers filing down the aisle, taking their seats, and she silently begged them to hurry.

Go, she thought. Let's go.

She glanced out the train window, staring at the darkness, wondering if he was out there, the man her father had hired to bring her back, wondering if she'd managed to slip away unnoticed. Nervously she felt to see if her hair was peeking from beneath the poke bonnet she'd tied on before leaving the hotel. She wished there had been time to dye it even as she cursed herself for not doing so sooner.

"Mind if I join you?"

Olivia turned her head and looked at the wizened face of the short-statured woman in the aisle. She opened her mouth to say she'd rather be alone, but it was too late.

"I'll be glad to put San Francisco behind me," the woman said as she sat across from Olivia. *"Too many people for my taste."* She set a carpetbag on the seat beside her, then held out her hand toward Olivia. *"My name's Amanda Blue. What's yours?"*

"Oli—" She stopped herself before she could finish, remembering the mistake she'd made in using her given name before. In a flash of inspiration, she substituted the nickname her nurse had used when she was a little girl, the name her father had forbidden anyone to use again after he'd fired the nurse and sent her packing from Rosegate. *"Libby. My name is Libby."* She took pleasure in her small defiance.

"Nice to meet you, Libby. I'm on my way home to Idaho. You ever been there? Pretty place. I got me a sheep ranch up in the high country. Best dang sheep ranch in the whole durn territory." She shook her head and tried to look contrite. *"Pardon my language. It comes from livin' with too many foul-mouthed men. A body gets where she's not careful about what she's sayin' when she lives out in the middle of nowhere like I do."*

Olivia didn't know how to respond. But then it didn't seem to matter. Amanda Blue was content to carry the burden of the conversation. As the train chugged its way out of the station and sped away from San Francisco, she regaled Olivia with story after story about the mountain country of Idaho Territory, about the men who worked for her, about the sheep and the lambs, about shearing seasons and lambing seasons. She talked on as the miles fell away beneath the churning wheels of the train. She talked into the wee hours of the night.

Then, suddenly, Amanda leaned forward and covered Olivia's hand with one of her own. Her gray eyes were solemn, her expression understanding. "You're in trouble, aren't you, dearie? I can tell by the look on your face."

Olivia tried to deny it, but the words wouldn't come.

"Don't you worry." Amanda patted her carpetbag. "I got my Colt forty-five in here, just in case I need to do any persuadin', but my guess is, whoever you're runnin' from isn't on this train or he'd've made himself known by now. You're safe with me."

Strangely enough, the little woman made her feel safe, too.

"Why don't you come to Idaho with me, Libby? I got lotsa room on that spread of mine. Won't nobody come lookin' for you there."

"But you don't even know me, Miss Blue," she whispered, her throat tight.

"Don't have to know you t'see you need help, young lady. You come and stay just as long as you want."

Olivia glanced out at the dark night beyond the train window. She had little money and no idea where she was going. She'd simply purchased a ticket on the first train out of San Francisco and had hoped it would take her beyond her father's reach. But where was that place? In all the months she'd been running and hiding, she had yet to find a place beyond her father's reach.

Could that place be in Idaho?

She turned and met the older woman's friendly gaze once again. "All right, Mrs. Blue, I'll come with you."

Amanda's smile was gentle. "Don't you worry, Libby. It'll work itself out, whatever your problem is." She patted her hand again. "And there ain't no missus in front of my name. Never been married. You just call me Aunt Amanda. It'll make us both feel like we got family."

For the first time in nearly a year, Libby smiled in earnest. "I'd like that . . . Aunt Amanda."

* * *

Melly moved restlessly, nearly upsetting the pail of milk. Brought abruptly back to the present, Libby shook off her memories. Like it or not, she would have to handle her current problems herself. Amanda wasn't around to solve them this time.

Rising from the stool, she grasped the heavy milk pail, then left the barn.

When she opened the back door to the house, she was surprised to discover Remington standing at the stove. He leaned heavily on his crutch as he scooped ground coffee into the blue-speckled coffeepot. He'd apparently found the clothes she'd taken from his saddlebags and placed in the dresser. He wore a pair of his trousers, although his chest and feet were still bare.

Hearing her enter, he glanced over his shoulder. "Good morning."

"What do you think you're doing, Mr. Walker?" she asked as she lifted the milk pail onto the counter near the sink.

He raised one eyebrow, as if the answer should be obvious. "Making coffee." He flashed one of his crooked grins.

For some reason, his response irritated her. "I can *see* that." She took the spoon from his hand. "Go sit down. You shouldn't be putting so much weight on that leg. Do you want to start your wound bleeding again? That's just what I need, to have you laid up longer than necessary."

He didn't argue with her, and she suspected he was in pain. She watched as he limped over to the table and sat on one of the chairs.

It was on the tip of her tongue to scold him some more for trying to do too much, to warn him of the permanent damage he might do to his leg. Then he met her gaze, and the words died in her throat. She turned away from him, unsettled by the way she felt whenever he was near.

"I wanted to apologize for yesterday, Miss Blue."

She didn't look at him. "Apologize? Whatever for?"

"For offering to pay Sawyer. You see, he told me things had been difficult for you since his dad died and—"

"Sawyer shouldn't be bothering you with our troubles, Mr. Walker."

"The boy wasn't bothering me." He paused, then said, "And it sounds to me like you've got more troubles than you can handle."

Libby turned around. She would have denied the truth, but she found a challenge in his dark blue eyes that she couldn't resist. "Life isn't ever easy in this country. Struggle goes part and parcel with living here. We'll handle what comes, just as we always have."

"Why do you stay?"

"This is my home, Mr. Walker. Where else would you have me go?"

Remington watched as Libby held herself a little straighter, saw the stubborn lift of her chin, caught the determined glint in her apple green eyes, and he felt a spark of admiration for her courage. He knew she had somewhere else to go, a place where her every whim could be satisfied, a place where want was unheard of.

And soon enough she would return to that life. Just as soon as Remington could send his telegram.

He frowned, feeling an odd sense of disquiet.

"Mr. Walker?"

He looked up as she drew closer to the table.

She placed her hands on a slat-backed chair. "I would be remiss if I didn't tell you about Timothy Bevins. He won't take lightly to what you did yesterday, making a fool of him in front of me. He's got a mean temper, and he fancies himself a cattle baron who's going to own this valley someday. He'll be after your hide next."

Remington felt a powerful urge to stand, take her in his

arms, and hold her close while whispering words of comfort. If he'd had the strength, he might have given in to it. He was thankful he didn't have the strength. He wasn't about to be the second Walker to fall victim to a Vanderhoff. And no matter what Libby called herself, she was still a Vanderhoff. He would do well to remember it.

Northrop stood at the window of his study and stared out at the Rosegate gardens. Beneath a gray sky, raindrops glistened on dark green leaves and lush lawns. In a few more weeks the flowers would bloom, creating an explosion of color.

Rosegate's gardens were the envy of every society matron in Manhattan. Northrop took immense pleasure in anything he owned that others coveted, and the gardens were no exception. That he had his wife, Anna, to thank for those magnificent rose gardens didn't even cross his mind. Northrop wasn't the sort of man who thanked others for doing what he expected of them. And even if he had been, he certainly wouldn't have thanked Anna for anything today.

Anger roiled through him. That she should defy him in this manner was unforgivable.

The door opened behind him. He didn't have to look to know it was Anna. No one else would dare enter without knocking first. Neither would she if he hadn't sent for her.

"Bridget said you wanted to see me, Northrop."

"Sit down, Anna."

He listened to her footsteps as she crossed the spacious room and settled onto a chair opposite his desk. He waited, allowing the moments to stretch one into another, knowing she would grow more anxious with each passing heartbeat.

At last he turned.

Anna's face was pale, her gaze uncertain, as she watched him return to his desk. At forty-five she was still a handsome woman. Her hair had retained its golden hue without a trace of gray. Her skin was smooth, with only a hint of lines around her eyes. She had even maintained her youthful figure.

"Have I done something to displease you, Northrop?" she asked hesitantly.

"Now, what would make you think that, my dear?"

Her face grew even more pale as she considered the possibilities.

Northrop took perverse pleasure in watching his adoring wife squirm. In twenty-eight years of marriage, they had played out similar scenes many times, and he'd never ceased to enjoy himself. He'd married Anna for the generous settlement her father had bestowed upon the newlyweds and because her family's social standing was equal to his own. Anna had married him for love. Her one wish through all their years of marriage had been to please him.

She seldom did.

Northrop picked up the folded paper on his desk. He knew the moment she recognized it. Her gaze fell to the floor.

"Why didn't you tell me about this, Anna?" He spoke softly, without a trace of the anger he was feeling.

"I . . . I was going to, Northrop, but—"

"But what? What possible reason could you have to keep this a secret from me? It was written almost a year ago."

Anna spoke in a near whisper. "It was addressed to me, Northrop, and there was nothing in it that revealed Olivia's whereabouts. I didn't think—"

"You never think!" he bellowed as he leaned his knuckles on the desk. "Never once in twenty-eight years!"

"Northrop . . ." Tears pooled in pale blue eyes as she reached for the letter.

He snatched it away, crumpling it into a ball. "Get out!"

"But—"

"I said get out."

She rose from her chair and held out her hand toward him. "May I have my letter, please?" she asked softly.

His answer was to throw the wadded paper into the fireplace.

Anna stared at the flames, her eyes glistening, her chin quivering. She watched until only ashes remained of her precious letter, then she turned without another word and left her husband's study.

The moment the door closed behind her, Northrop regained his seat.

Blast all females to perdition!

He swiveled his chair around to stare at the fireplace. He thought of Olivia, the daughter whose beauty had promised to strengthen the kingdom of wealth and power he'd worked all his life to build, the daughter who had defied and betrayed him.

Damn her! Damn her for her defiance!

But he would find her. For seven years he'd continued his search, hiring the best detectives money could buy. He would continue until he brought her home. He didn't care how long it took or how much it cost him. He would teach her yet what disobedience meant. She would bend to her father's will or be broken.

Northrop Vanderhoff never quit. He never gave up. He never admitted defeat. And Olivia knew it. Wherever she was, she knew her father was still looking for her. She knew he was searching, and she was afraid.

He grinned and lit his cigar.

5

Leaning on his crutch, Remington made his way outside. He paused just beyond the doorway to catch his breath.

It irritated him that he tired so quickly. He was impatient with his slow recovery. He wasn't acquainted with inactivity. The hours and days dragged by with agonizing monotony.

To make matters worse, Libby had avoided him completely for the past two days. She'd let him doctor his own wounds, sending Sawyer in with the water, salve, and bandages. Without her brief visits, there was nothing to occupy his thoughts except thinking about what he could be doing if he weren't stuck in that room. He couldn't even satisfy his curiosity by trying to find out more about Libby.

The sounds of hammering jolted him from his thoughts. For the better part of an hour he'd listened to that racket coming from the far side of the barn, and he couldn't help wondering what Libby was building. He considered working his way back there to see for himself, but then he caught sight of Sundown in the corral off to one side of the barn.

The gelding whickered a greeting as Remington limped toward him. Sundown thrust his head over the top rail and stomped a front hoof in the dust, as if he too were impatient with his master's slow progress. Remington noted the horse's well-groomed appearance and knew Sawyer had been caring for him, just as he'd promised.

When he reached the corral, Remington stroked the gelding's muzzle. "Bored, fella?"

Sundown bobbed his head.

"Yeah. Me too." He glanced around him.

The burnt red barn was large and in good condition. The corral posts and rails were sturdy. The paddock, where a small flock of ewes and lambs grazed, was surrounded by a whitewashed fence. The yard was swept clean. In all, Blue Springs Ranch appeared to be a well-run enterprise.

He looked at the house. Although crude by eastern standards, it was roomy and solidly built. It would keep its inhabitants warm in the winter and cool in the summer, something he suspected was of prime importance in this country. The interior of the house had been furnished to satisfy an assortment of tastes. Hanging in the parlor was a landscape by one of Europe's most renowned artists, a painting that would have commanded a high price in Manhattan. But many other items in the house had undoubtedly been ordered by catalog from Sears & Roebuck or Montgomery Ward, with attention paid only to cost.

This seemed an odd place for the daughter of Northrop Vanderhoff to have settled. It seemed even odder to him that she should have chosen to remain. Despite Remington's ill will for her father, he couldn't deny Northrop's eagerness to find his daughter. His love for his only child was obviously beyond measure. Why else would he offer such an exorbitant fee and agree to the outrageously high bonus Remington had demanded?

Yet Libby obviously did not want to go home. Why? he wondered. Why did she remain in hiding when she could so easily leave her troubles behind? Was it pride alone? Had she left because of a love gone awry or because of some silly spat with her parents?

Remington gave his head a shake, reminding himself that he didn't need answers to silent musings. He'd found Olivia Vanderhoff: that was the only thing that mattered. As soon as he could travel, he'd send his telegram, and once his fee and bonus were collected, he would be on his way back to New York. He had a promise to his own father to keep, and he couldn't be concerned with Libby's relationship with Northrop or Anna or her reasons for going into hiding.

"Mr. Walker . . . "

He turned at the sound of her voice.

Libby stood near the corner of the barn, watching him with a gentle frown. Her hair was swept back and cap-tured in the now familiar thick braid that fell over her shoulder. She was wearing an oversize man's work shirt, denim britches, and boots. A battered hat hung against her back from a leather tie around her throat.

"You shouldn't overdo," she reminded him.

"I won't."

Her frown disappeared as she started forward. She moved with a natural grace, and it wasn't difficult for Remington to imagine what she would have looked like in satin and lace, her hair dressed with jewels.

"I'm surprised you made it this far. You're certain you're not putting too much weight on that leg?" Her gaze moved down and then back again.

He found he rather liked her concern. "I'm certain."

He motioned with his head toward the barn. "What are you building out there?"

"A new chicken coop. We had a coyote get into the old one a few weeks ago. He made off with one of our best layers."

Again Remington was struck by the incongruity of the situation. The daughter of one of the wealthiest men in America, wearing trousers, swinging a hammer, fighting coyotes, and shooting trespassers.

"I made lemonade this morning," she told him. "Would you like some?"

"Lemonade?"

Libby nodded. "I bought some lemons last time I picked up supplies. You'd think they were pure gold for what they cost, but sometimes . . ." She shrugged off the remainder of her sentence.

"To tell you the truth, I'd love some lemonade."

Libby smiled. "Go sit in the shade under the willow. I'll bring you a glass."

He watched her walk toward the house, enjoying the way her hips and legs looked in her trousers. Folks back east would be scandalized by the inappropriate apparel, but he thought he could grow to like the fashion, should it ever take hold.

Once Libby disappeared through the doorway, he gave his head another shake. He'd do well to remember what had brought him here.

With slow steps, he made his way toward the tall willow growing near the west corner of the house. A bench made of thick planks rested against the trunk of the tree, and Remington settled himself there just as Libby came out of the house, carrying a tray with three glasses and a pitcher.

As she handed him one of the glasses, she asked, "What sort of business is it you do, Mr. Walker? I failed to ask you before."

"My father raised the finest Arabians in Virginia. I hope to carry on the tradition."

It was a cover that had served him well in the past. It was true, after all. Before the war, the stables at Sunnyvale had been filled with blooded Arabian horses. And Remington still owned several mares and stallions whose bloodlines could be traced back to Sunnyvale. But horse breeding wasn't how Jefferson Walker had made his living, and it wasn't how Jefferson's son made his. The words, although technically true, felt like a lie as he spoke them.

But all that mattered to Remington was for Libby to believe they were true. And apparently she did.

"I should have guessed," she said, glancing toward Sundown. "He's not your usual saddle horse. Not in these parts." Once again she brought her gaze back to meet his. "Has your trip been a successful one?"

Had it been successful? he wondered as he looked at her pretty face, as he stared into her eyes and thought how very little she resembled the woman he'd expected to find.

Successful? Yes, but not in the way she meant. And real success wouldn't be his until he was well enough to travel. Real success would come just as soon as he sent a telegram to her father. Just as soon as she was returned to the bosom of her family and whatever she'd run away from.

Just as soon as he'd betrayed her.

Libby's mouth went dry and her breathing became shallow even as her pulse quickened. She wanted to look away from Remington, but she couldn't seem to do it. His blue eyes seemed darker, stormier than usual. He looked angry. Angry at himself. Angry at her.

Yet she wasn't afraid. Instead she felt strangely drawn to him, driven to touch him.

She took a sudden step back, as if to break an invisible hold he had upon her. Lemonade sloshed over the rim of the glasses and onto the tray.

"I . . . I'd better take Sawyer his drink. He's got to be wondering if I've forgotten him." She turned away.

"Maybe I could be of help, Miss Blue."

Unable to help herself, she glanced over her shoulder. Remington had risen from the bench. His dark eyebrows were drawn close in a frown. He didn't look eager to help.

"I built a chicken coop myself when I was a boy," he offered.

Trust no strangers.

She had lived by those words for nearly seven years. She shouldn't forget them. Not with this man.

"Please," he said with a slight shrug. "Allow me to help." His smile appeared slowly, erasing the effects of his frown, bringing a humorous sparkle to his eyes. There was something charming about the look he gave her, something difficult to resist. "To tell you the truth, Miss Blue, I'm bored. I need something to do."

What was it that made her want to trust this man despite herself? She didn't know a thing about him. Not really. It was dangerous to forget the rules she'd played by all these years. It was dangerous to let someone else into her life, no matter how briefly. It was dangerous. . . .

"There's nothing wrong with my arm. I can still swing a hammer."

She had a sudden vision of him holding her in his arms, of his head lowering toward hers until their mouths could touch. She saw it, felt it, as clearly as if it were really happening, and she suspected then that there would be no rules where Remington was concerned.

She turned away a second time. "All right, Mr. Walker. You may help if you wish. But it's your own fault if you hurt yourself again."

*   *   *

There might not have been anything wrong with his arm, but Remington's energy gave out before he'd driven two dozen nails into the new chicken coop. This time he didn't argue when Libby told him to sit down and rest. He was glad to obey.

He squinted against the bright sunlight as he watched her climb to the top of the ladder and lean over to drive more nails into the roof. Her Levi's pulled tight against her shapely backside.

Yes, he could get used to this particular fashion. Especially on Libby.

But she wasn't really Libby Blue, he reminded himself. She was Olivia Vanderhoff, and as soon as he was able, he would be helping to send her back to Manhattan, to Rosegate, and to her father—the man Remington was determined to destroy.

He closed his eyes, remembering what he had against Northrop Vanderhoff, remembering the importance of the two-hundred-and-fifty-thousand-dollar bonus he would collect as soon as he betrayed Libby.

The manor house of Sunnyvale Plantation was large and airy and as bright as its name suggested. It was a happy home, too, despite the lack of a mistress. Remington's mother had died of childbirth fever within days of his birth, and Jefferson was never inclined to marry again.

Remington was just a small boy when the War Between the States began, and to him those years were a great adventure. His mammy made a game of hiding Sunnyvale's heirlooms and silver and paintings. She was responsible for saving the best of Sunnyvale's breeding stock from both the Yankees and the Confederacy. The

Walkers suffered during the war, just as every Virginian suffered, but Remington didn't notice it at the time.

At the end of the war, Jefferson Walker returned, looking weary and years older than his true age. But he returned with an iron determination to rebuild his plantation and the JW Railroad.

He would have succeeded had it not been for Northrop Vanderhoff.

Jefferson and Northrop had been friends before the war. JW Railroad and Vanderhoff Shipping had supplied goods from around the world to much of the South. Jefferson hoped to do so once again. But he'd given his rail cars to the cause of the Confederacy, and most of them had been destroyed. In addition, railroad tracks had been ripped up throughout the South. Jefferson knew it would take time, time he didn't have as creditors pressed him for payments.

Then Northrop offered to buy into the company, promising much needed cash for JW Railroad and the Walkers. But Jefferson declined the offer. He knew that once he allowed Northrop to own even just a small part of the railroad, he would lose all of it. Northrop always sought complete control of everything he touched. Not even his friends were safe from his desire to acquire more and more.

The day Jefferson refused Northrop's offer was the day their friendship ended. Northrop deliberately and methodically set out to destroy both Jefferson and the JW Railroad. It took him nearly a decade, but at last he achieved his goal.

Remington was away at college in that fall of 1875, blissfully, thoughtlessly unaware of the trouble his father was in. Seventeen and on his own for the first time in his life, Remington was concerned only for himself and the good time he was having with his new friends and with the young ladies.

But while Remington was enjoying his new status as an adult, the JW Railroad fell into bankruptcy. Anything of value at Sunnyvale was sold until the house was stripped bare. Finally, the plantation itself was lost.

And one morning, Jefferson Walker, despondent, financially ruined, closed himself in his study, placed a gun in his mouth, and pulled the trigger.

Remington opened his eyes and looked once more upon Northrop Vanderhoff's daughter. She was pretty and kind, and it was clear even to him that she was nothing at all like her father.

But Remington couldn't allow that to interfere with his mission. He was going to bring Northrop to his knees. He was going to do his best to destroy him, just as Northrop had destroyed Jefferson. Remington had waited years for revenge. He might never have another opportunity like this one. He couldn't let it slip away.

Not even for the woman who called herself Libby Blue.

6

Libby tossed restlessly in her bed. She couldn't rid herself of thoughts of Remington. Every time she closed her eyes, she envisioned him, and those visions were about to drive her mad.

From the day she'd escaped her father's clutches, Libby had promised herself she would never again allow a man to have that kind of power over her. Never would she fall in love, she'd vowed, and she would rather die than marry. Anna Vanderhoff had suffered for love; her heart had been broken time and time again. Affection could become a tool for manipulation, Libby knew, and she would never allow it to happen to her.

Nothing would ever seduce her into giving up the freedom she'd found. Certainly not a stranger from Virginia.

She buried her face in her pillow and cursed the image of Remington that refused to leave her in peace. She saw his raven black hair, so desperately in need of cutting. She saw the stormy blue of his eyes, the way his gaze seemed to look through all her barriers and see inside her soul.

She saw the crooked curve of his smile, the dark stubble on his jaw at the end of the day. She saw the breadth of his shoulders, the chest hair that narrowed as it trailed down to his navel, the taut muscles of his stomach, the . . .

Groaning, she rolled onto her back and stared up at the ceiling.

What's wrong with me? she chastised herself.

In a short time, he would be well. He would return to his home in Virginia. She would never see him again. And that was best for everyone. She didn't *want* to see him again. She didn't *want* him confusing her. She had no need for a man unless he liked to work sheep and keep to himself. She was happy with her life just the way it was.

She was about to close her eyes when she realized her room wasn't as dark as it should be. Light flickered across the ceiling. Light that shouldn't be there.

She sat up and turned toward the window. Beyond the barn, she could see flames.

"The shed! Oh, dear God—not the wool!"

She flew out of bed. "Sawyer, help me! The shed's on fire! . . . Sawyer!"

She didn't wait to see if the boy heard her. Barefoot, nightgown flaring behind her, she raced outside, grabbing a bucket from the ground as she went.

She rounded the corner of the barn and came to an abrupt halt. The full length of the shed was ablaze, and she knew it was already too late. No amount of water could save the shed or its contents. She could only hope the fire wouldn't spread to the other outbuildings or to the house.

The bucket dropped to the ground, and her eyes filled with tears.

Half of this spring's wool crop was in that shed. Sacks filled with fleeces, each of them weighing close to four hundred pounds. Now it was all going up in flames.

She felt Sawyer's hand slip into hers, but she didn't look down. She didn't want him to see her despair.

The wool had been scheduled for shipment at the end of this week. The wagons were coming for it in just a few days. The heavy sacks would have been hauled into Weiser, put on the train, and shipped back east. The money from the sale of those fleeces would have put the Blue Springs back on sound financial footing. She could have replaced the sheep they'd lost this year. She could have hired more herders. She could have—

"What started it?"

She turned to look at Remington through the haze of unshed tears. Firelight flickered over him, bronzing his bare chest. He wore only his drawers, and she knew he had wasted little time in coming to help her. But there was nothing he could do to help her now.

"I don't know," she whispered after a lengthy silence.

But she *did* know. It was Bevins again.

Remington seemed to read her mind. "You suspect that Bevins fellow?"

The best she could do was nod. She couldn't speak around the lump in her throat.

She wasn't certain how it happened, but suddenly her face was pressed against Remington's bare shoulder. His right arm circled her back, and his hand patted the spot at the base of her neck.

"Don't worry," he whispered. "It'll be all right. I'll see to it."

Surprisingly enough, she almost believed him.

Remington knew his words were insane even as he spoke them. Yet it had felt right to say them. As right as the way she felt nestled against him.

Shards of pain shot through his left leg. Even leaning heavily on the crutch didn't provide much relief. Still, he was reluctant to let go of Libby. He wanted to go on holding her, go on reassuring her that he would make things right, that he could make a difference.

After several minutes Libby raised her head and their gazes met. The light from the burning shed made the tears on her cheeks glitter. He wanted to pull her back against him, but he sensed her resistance.

"I . . . I'm sorry, Mr. Walker," she said in a broken voice. "I . . . I don't know what came over me."

"It's all right. It's perfectly understandable."

She was the most beautiful thing he'd ever seen, standing there in her white cotton nightgown, her hair flowing loose around her shoulders. In the glare of the fire, he could see the dark tips of her breasts pushing against the fabric of her nightgown, and he remembered the way she'd felt, pressed against him, as he'd comforted her only moments before. He remembered how fragile she'd felt, how small and vulnerable.

"It's all right," he repeated, his voice thick. "You've had quite a shock."

Libby took another step back, then turned to face the blaze once again. He could barely hear her when she said, "We needed the money so badly."

She reached out for Sawyer and took hold of the boy's hand, drawing him up to her side. They remained there, the three of them, until the shed and all its contents were destroyed and the fire had burned itself out, leaving only smoldering remains. Then, with dawn a promise on the horizon, they turned in unison and made their way back to the house.

Even as exhausted as she was, Libby knew she wouldn't be able to sleep. After she helped Remington to his room and saw Sawyer to bed, she went into the kitchen and made a large pot of coffee. Then she sat down at the table and tried to sort through what she should—or could—do now.

What would Aunt Amanda have done? she asked herself.

A sad smile touched her mouth. She could almost hear the spunky little woman. *"What do you do now? You pick yourself up and go on with what you got, that's what. You don't let nothin' keep you down, dearie. You just spit in life's eye and show it what you're made of."*

But what *was* Libby made of? In the sixteen months since Aunt Amanda had died, everything had gone wrong. Maybe she wasn't capable of running the ranch on her own. She'd had to let most of the herders go last fall. Dan Deevers was dead. Instead of buying new ewes and rams last year, she'd had to sell off more of her herd. Some of the sheep had gotten ill this past winter, a few dying, some of the ewes aborting their lambs. And then there was Bevins, always making more trouble for her in one way or another.

What made her think she could make a go of the Blue Springs without Amanda's help?

"Can't sleep?" Remington asked from the doorway.

For some reason she wasn't surprised he hadn't stayed in his room. Looking up, she observed the dark circles under his eyes, and she knew he was in pain. She also saw he'd slipped into his trousers and donned a shirt. His feet were still bare. He had narrow feet with long, crooked toes. It seemed she noticed even the smallest details when it came to Remington Walker.

Subduing a sound of frustration, she said, "You'd better sit down, Mr. Walker. You've already used that leg too much for one night."

He came forward slowly, his stiff movements confirming the truth of her words.

"The coffee should be ready. Do you want some?"

He nodded as he settled onto a chair.

Libby remembered how safe and secure she'd felt

within the circle of his arm. She'd never thought it could feel so good to have a man hold her that way. She'd never imagined she might wish to be held that way.

With a shake of her head to chase away the memory, she rose and fetched two mugs from the cupboard. After filling them with hot coffee, she returned to the table, setting one of them in front of Remington.

"I know it's none of my business, Libby," he said as she regained her seat, "but what does the loss of that shed mean to you? To this ranch?"

His eyes were filled with concern, and she couldn't resist the pull his words had on her. Especially the sound of her name as he spoke it. Libby. He'd called her Libby instead of Miss Blue. That simple act touched her as nothing else had, forcing her to give an honest reply.

"Just about everything," she admitted. "It means just about everything."

"I don't know anything about the sheep-raising business. Tell me about the Blue Springs."

Libby took a sip of the hot, black coffee, then stared into the cup. "We raise mostly Rambouillet sheep on the Blue Springs. Aunt Amanda always said they're one of the finest breeds. They're hardy and do well in the hot summers and cold winters of Idaho. The lambs are a good size, so we can sell them for meat in the fall, and the breed yields a high quantity of wool at shearing time." She looked up at him. "But not so much that we can afford to lose half of it."

"Half? Where's the rest?"

"I didn't have the men or the wagons to haul the sacks to Weiser after the shearers were done a few weeks ago. I barely had enough to pay them their wages. So I sent what I could and planned to use some of the money from its sale to ship the rest to market. Now . . ." Her voice drifted into silence.

"Why don't you tell me what Bevins has to do with all of this?"

Her fingers tightened around the coffee mug in her hands. "Plenty."

Remington waited in silence for her to continue.

"He's wanted this ranch ever since he first came to the territory. He wants to control the water from the springs. If he could do that, he could drive anybody else off for miles around. Aunt Amanda was always generous. She didn't try to dam the water up. But Bevins . . . he would. He wants control of all the grazing land hereabouts."

"Mmm."

Libby sat a little straighter in her chair. "Bevins has made plenty of offers to buy the ranch, but Aunt Amanda wouldn't sell. And neither will I. He's going to have to drive us out. That's the only way he'll get control of the Blue Springs. He may do it. We're nearly broke, and we haven't got much left other than the flock up on the summer range and the ranch house here. But we'll fight him to the last."

Remington knew he must be crazy. Clean out of his mind insane. That was the only explanation for what he said next.

"I'd like to help."

"Mr. Walker, you're scarcely able to walk. What could you—"

He leaned forward, placing his arms on the table. "I heal fast."

"But you'll be leaving—"

"I'll stay until I'm sure you and Sawyer aren't in any danger, until you're back on your feet again."

Remington figured he might still get the bonus money. He had a few weeks left before his year was up. But he couldn't go until he knew Libby was going to be safe— which didn't make a whole heck of a lot of sense, given that her father would plan to take her back to New York City as soon as he received Remington's telegram.

Libby rose and walked over to the back door. She pulled it open and stood framed in the opening, staring at the sunrise. Light filtered through her cotton nightgown, revealing the womanly curves beneath it.

"I can't pay you, Mr. Walker."

Her hair was set ablaze by the sun, shimmering red and gold. And soft as silk. He remembered the feel of it as he'd held her against him, his arm around her back. He also remembered the feel of her warm tears on his bare skin.

Clean out of my mind insane . . .

Using the crutch for leverage, he got up from his chair. "I don't expect pay, Libby. This is something I want to do."

She glanced over her shoulder. Her green eyes revealed quiet despair. "Your family will be wondering what's happened to you."

"I don't have a family." A trace of bitterness worked its way into his reply.

Her gaze fell away from his. "Neither do I."

There was a sea of lies and half-truths between them.

He wasn't who he'd said he was. He wasn't a southern gentleman who raised Arabians on his ancestral plantation. The war and Northrop Vanderhoff had seen to that.

And she wasn't who she'd said she was. She had another name and another home and a family to return to.

Yet the lies didn't seem to matter to him at the moment. All he saw now was a young woman whom he wanted to help.

Help her and then what?

But he didn't have an answer to his question, and he wasn't willing to look for one just yet.

7

Northrop settled back into the leather-upholstered chair. "Well, O'Reilly, do you want the job?"

He couldn't imagine the man would turn him down. True, he'd offered a mere fraction of what he'd agreed to pay Remington Walker, but it was far more than he figured any Irishman was worth. Northrop wouldn't even have considered the fellow if Gil O'Reilly hadn't come highly recommended by several trusted sources.

"So, 'tis not your daughter you want me t'find, but the detective you've already hired t'find her. Am I understandin' your meanin', sir?"

Idiot. "Yes, that's right."

"And does this detective have a name?"

Northrop felt like grinding his teeth. "Of course he has a name," he snapped. "Remington Walker."

O'Reilly let out a long, low whistle. "'Tis Mr. Walker himself you've got workin' for you." He rose from his chair. "I'd not be honest in takin' your money, Mr. Vanderhoff. Remington Walker was the best agent

Pinkerton ever had. Though I've not had the pleasure of meeting him, I know his reputation right enough. He's got a nose for findin' people, he has. He'll find your daughter if anyone can, and when he knows somethin', he'll contact you. I'd swear to it on my dear departed mother's grave."

"Are you saying you don't want the job?" Northrop raised an eyebrow. "Not even if I give you a bonus in addition to your fee? Say, a thousand dollars if you find Mr. Walker by the first of September?"

"Didja not understand me, Mr. Vanderhoff? You'd be throwin' your money away t'hire me, what with Mr. Walker already on the job."

"It's my money, O'Reilly."

The red-haired Irishman shook his head. "That it is, sir. That it is." He seemed to think the matter over a moment or two, then said, "I guess if you're determined t'throw it away, you may as well throw it my way. I'll take the job—and your money, too."

"Good." Northrop leaned forward and slapped the palms of his hands on the top of his desk. "Sit down, O'Reilly, and I'll show you the last correspondence I received from Walker."

By the end of the week, Remington's side scarcely bothered him at all. His thigh still hurt like the blazes and he couldn't walk without the crutch, but he could move a lot faster and his stamina had improved as well. Perhaps Libby's cooking had something to do with his returning strength. The meals she prepared were delicious, the portions generous.

"Where did you learn to cook like this?" Remington asked as he dished another helping of potatoes.

"Aunt Amanda taught me."

He'd known, of course, that she hadn't learned to cook

at Rosegate. "Your aunt sounds like an interesting woman. Tell me about her."

Libby smiled. "She was interesting all right. I've never known anyone else like her. There wasn't anything she couldn't do. She could rope a cow as well as any man. She sheared the sheep and helped with the lambing and patched the roof when it leaked. She could rustle up grub for twenty shearers in the blink of an eye. And she could have shot the ear off a cougar at two hundred yards with her Winchester, if she'd wanted to." She shook her head. "Aunt Amanda tried to teach me how to do everything like her, but I'm afraid it was hopeless. I'm merely adequate in comparison."

"From personal experience, I'd say you learned at least a few of your lessons well enough." He grinned wryly as he spoke, rubbing his ribs with one hand. Then, as he spooned some of the canned beets onto his plate, he asked, "Was she your mother's sister or your father's?"

Libby hesitated briefly before answering, "Aunt Amanda was unlike either of my parents."

Not quite the truth. Not really a lie.

He lifted his gaze to look at her across the table. She was pushing her food around her plate with her fork, obviously troubled by either his question or her reply. Perhaps both.

She doesn't want to lie to me, he realized. The thought pleased him. "I wish I could have met your aunt," he said, meaning it.

She glanced up. "I wish you could have met her, too. Aunt Amanda was special."

She had the most unusual eyes. The shade of green was like none other Remington had seen. Once again, he thought that Northrop hadn't received his money's worth for the portrait of his daughter that hung at Rosegate. The painter had completely failed to capture his subject. While

Remington had expected to find a lovely woman, he hadn't expected a startling beauty.

But it was more than just her looks. The portrait hadn't captured her . . .

Her what?

In some way he couldn't quite define, this woman was very different from the one who had stood for that portrait. It had nothing to do with the unique color of her eyes or the pale rose gold of her hair or the more womanly curves the years had wrought in her. This difference had more to do with an essence, an aura, a strength and vitality. Had it all been there before and simply beyond the artist's ability to capture it? Or was it something new? Had she taken on this difference with her new name and identity?

Remington longed to know the answers.

Libby felt a blush rising in her cheeks as Remington continued to stare, his gaze intense and thoughtful. Sometimes she felt as if he could see right into her mind, as if he knew what she was thinking, what she was feeling. As if he could read all her secrets. She, on the other hand, could never guess his thoughts. Even when he smiled, a part of him was closed off, held in reserve, mysterious. She wished she could break through that barrier. She wished . . .

She looked away from him, suddenly afraid, not wanting him to see inside her head. She didn't want him to know how often her thoughts were of him.

She tried to calm the irregular beat of her heart. She tried to school her face into a nonchalant expression. As she cut the meat on her plate, she said, "I'm going to ride up to Tyler Creek tomorrow."

"How long'll we be gone?" Sawyer asked, a note of excitement in his voice.

"I'm going alone," she replied with a shake of her head.

"You need to stay here. Melly will need milking, and someone has to keep an eye on Misty and her pups."

"But—"

"Don't argue with me, Sawyer."

"All right," the boy grumbled, his acquiescence less than enthusiastic.

"What's at Tyler Creek?" Remington asked.

"The flock. Tyler Creek's part of our summer range. I think McGregor and Ronald should know what's happened here." She sighed. "Losing the wool could mean I won't be able to pay them their wages. Not for quite a spell. They should have the choice to stay or go elsewhere."

Remington frowned. "I'm not sure you should be riding up there by yourself."

"What alternative do I have, Mr. Walker?"

"I could go with you."

She felt a strange tightening in her chest and knew she wanted him with her, but she shook her head. "I'm not in any danger from Bevins. He's a thief and a troublemaker, but he's not really dangerous." She remembered the way Bevins had grabbed her, the lust she'd seen in his eyes, but she pushed the memory away. "Besides, you aren't ready to ride a horse. It's a long way up to Tyler Creek."

He leaned forward, his expression austere, implacable. "Then I think you should wait until I *can* ride. You must think Bevins poses some danger to you or you'd never have shot me."

He was right. She had been afraid. She was still afraid sometimes, and it was tempting to agree with him. It was more tempting than anything she'd felt in a long, long while. She would like to wait until he was well and strong. She would like to let him take care of her, if only for a short time. She would like to depend on someone else for a change.

But she couldn't. Remington had said he wanted to help, to stay until she and Sawyer were back on their feet. He hadn't said anything more than that.

And if he had implied more?

Once again Libby shook her head. "I can't wait. I've got to go now."

She'd made her choice long ago. She couldn't put her destiny in the hands of another. She was responsible for her own life. She couldn't get into the habit of leaving it up to someone else.

"Libby—" he began.

"I'm sorry. McGregor and Ronald need to know what's happened. If Bevins manages to run off any more of our sheep . . . "

Remington's scowl reminded her of her father. "I still say you ought to have someone along to protect you."

She closed her eyes, trying to escape the image of Northrop Vanderhoff, the determined glare of his eyes, the intractable set of his shoulders. She could almost hear his condescending tone as he explained to her that he knew what was best for her. That she was merely a girl and unable to take care of herself, unable to *think* for herself.

But she *was* able to take care of herself. She *was* able to think for herself. She wasn't helpless. She wasn't mindless. And she wasn't going to forget it. She wasn't going to let a handsome stranger make her forget everything she'd learned in the past seven years.

She opened her eyes and stared straight at Remington. "I can't wait for you. This is my ranch, and I'm responsible for what happens here." She rose and picked up her supper dishes. "My mind's made up, so there's no point in continuing this discussion. Sawyer, help me clear the table. Then you've got some reading to see to, young man. I haven't seen you open your primer in nearly a month."

* * *

That night, when the house had fallen into silence, Libby sat in her room, a book of poetry open in her lap, lamplight flowing over the pages. But she stared down at the words without seeing them as she remembered that wonderfully terrible moment when she'd been willing to let Remington take control of the situation. When she'd wanted him to take care of her. When she'd trusted him, not just with everything she owned, but with all that she was.

But that was everything she'd sought to escape when she'd left New York. She'd wanted to make her own decisions, to be mistress of her own life. She knew too well what it meant never to enjoy that simple freedom.

She focused her gaze on the book.

> *I feel like one,*
> *Who treads alone*
> *Some banquet hall deserted,*
> *Whose lights are fled,*
> *Whose garlands dead,*
> *And all but he departed.*

She closed the book, trying to blot out the loneliness the author's words stirred in her heart, but the phrase continued to play through her mind, taunting, painful, cruel.

Libby set the book on the table and extinguished the lamp. She wouldn't think about being lonely. She wouldn't let herself give up all she had gained. The price was too high.

Unwelcome, her father's image—strong, domineering, impervious—flared to life in her mind, and her thoughts were dragged backward in time.

* * *

"You've kept us waiting," Northrop announced as Olivia entered his study.

Her mother was already in the room, seated in her usual chair off to the left of Northrop's massive desk. Olivia took the chair on the right, as she always did for these meetings with her father.

"I'm sorry," she said, not bothering with an explanation. Her father wouldn't care what her reasons were for her delay in answering his summons.

"I have some important news, Olivia. You are to be married this summer."

"Married?" she echoed softly.

She glanced quickly toward her mother. Anna's eyes met hers only briefly, just long enough for Olivia to see the compassion written there.

She looked back at her father. "To whom?"

"Gregory James."

"Mr. James? But he's—" She'd been about to say that Gregory James was an old man, but she knew it would make no difference to her father. It wouldn't matter to him that Mr. James was thirty-five years his daughter's senior. Not if he'd decided this was whom she was to marry.

"Northrop"—Anna spoke up hesitantly—"Olivia is only seventeen. Isn't there someone—"

"She'll be eighteen next month, and it's time she was married. James has agreed to turn over full control of his railroad to me upon his marriage to Olivia. It will give Vanderhoff Shipping the access it needs to most of the South. We've needed to own such a railroad for years. It's an opportunity I cannot ignore."

Olivia would never know where she got the courage to speak up. Perhaps it was because she'd recently learned from a gossiping servant that her father kept a mistress and had sired two illegitimate sons. Perhaps it was because she'd tricked her father's man of business, using *a few carefully worded questions, into revealing that those same illegitimate sons were being groomed to inherit Vanderhoff Shipping. Or perhaps it was because she'd been silent all her life and suddenly saw herself as she would be in another twenty years, a copy of her mother, obediently doing, without question, whatever her husband bade her to do.*

"I cannot marry him, Father."

Northrop turned wide, surprised eyes in her direction. "What?"

"I said I cannot marry him," she whispered, her insides twisting as they always did when her father looked at her as he was now. "I . . . I don't love him. He . . . he's too old and I . . . I . . . I don't want to marry him."

Her father rose from his chair. "But I have said you will marry him."

"When I marry, Father, I intend to choose my own husband."

He stared at her, temporarily dumbfounded by her defiance.

Olivia lifted her chin and quoted, "'Marriage, to women as to men, must be a luxury, not a necessity; an incident of life, not all of it. And the only possible way to accomplish this great change is to accord to women equal power in the making, shaping and controlling of the circumstances of life.'"

"Great Scot!" Northrop bellowed. "Where have you learned such drivel?"

She shivered. "It's from a speech Susan B. Anthony gave in—"

Her father turned suddenly toward his wife. "Where were you when our daughter was filling her head with that nonsense? By Gawd, Anna, I have a mind to—"

"It's not Mama's fault!" Olivia jumped up from her chair, frightened by the rage she saw in her father's face.

Northrop rounded the desk with surprising speed. He grasped her by the upper arms, his fingers biting into her flesh. "I'll not have this impudence from you, girl. Do you hear me? You'll marry Mr. James. It's your duty to do as I command." He gave her a shake. "Do you hear what I'm saying, Olivia? I won't be disobeyed."

She wanted to ask him why he couldn't love her, why he couldn't love her mother. She wanted to ask him why he was so willing to barter and sell her as he would any other commodity that belonged to Vanderhoff Shipping.

In the end, all she said was, "Yes, Father, I hear you."

But she could not marry Mr. James. She knew then that she would have to escape. She didn't know how or when, but she would have to get away before it was too late.

She remembered something else of Miss Anthony's that she'd read: "Woman must not depend upon the protection of man, but must be taught to protect herself."

Olivia prayed it wasn't too late for her to learn that lesson.

Libby stood up, repeating aloud Miss Anthony's words as if to remind herself of their importance. "'Woman must not depend upon the protection of man, but must be taught to protect herself.'"

She couldn't forget all she'd fought so hard to learn. She couldn't allow herself to forget what she'd given up, what she'd endured, in order to have her freedom. She'd proven she was capable of taking care of herself. She had no need for a man in her life, not even a man like Remington Walker.

I feel like one,
Who treads alone . . .

Unbidden, she remembered the feel of Remington's arm around her back, the gentleness of his hand as it stroked and patted and soothed. She remembered how safe and secure she'd felt, and she knew she was in more danger from her feelings for Remington than she was from either Bevins or her father. Remington had the power to destroy far more than mere property, the power to take away far more than mere freedom.

Remington had the power to break her heart if she let him get too close. So she simply wouldn't let it happen.

8

Remington watched as Libby slipped her shotgun into the saddle scabbard, then mounted the ugly, Roman-nosed horse. The white, swaybacked gelding didn't look strong enough to get her over the first foothill, let alone carry her up to the high pastures where the sheep were grazing.

As if Sawyer had read Remington's thoughts, he said, "He don't look like much, but ol' Lightning's the most surefooted critter you ever seen, and he can outlast just about anythin' on four legs."

Remington raised a doubtful eyebrow but said nothing.

Libby turned the gelding so she could look at Sawyer. "I'll be back tomorrow evening. The day after at the latest." She frowned slightly. "You do your lessons and make sure Melly is milked on time. I'm counting on you."

"I'll do it," the boy replied, "but I still think I oughta be goin' with you. Mr. Walker's right, ya know."

For the first time that morning, Libby met Remington's

gaze. "I'm perfectly able to take care of myself. I've been doing it for years."

She was telling him she didn't need him. She couldn't have made it any clearer. But Remington believed she *did* need him. She just didn't know it yet. And as crazy as it sounded, he wanted her to need him.

"Just be careful out there."

Something in her expression softened. "I will." Then she nudged Lightning with her heels and rode off.

Remington watched Libby disappear into the grove of aspens and pines, knowing he wouldn't rest easy until she was safely back at the Blue Springs. He told himself he was worried only because of the healthy bonus he meant to collect from her father, but the words no longer rang true.

"I guess I'd better milk Melly," Sawyer said with an exaggerated sigh.

"Yeah," Remington murmured in response. Then he turned and stepped inside, frowning thoughtfully.

Just why was he worried about Libby, he wondered, if not for the money?

He hadn't come to Idaho to make certain she was safe or happy or for any other altruistic reason. His job was to let her father know where she was, collect his bonus, and then get back to the business of destroying Vanderhoff Shipping the same way Northrop Vanderhoff had destroyed Remington's father and the JW Railroad. He had to forget everything else.

Besides, Libby didn't want his help. She didn't want his concern. That was what she'd been telling him out there. He should take her words to heart. He had no business becoming entangled in her problems. And she wouldn't have any problems once Remington told Northrop where she was. Her father would take her back to Rosegate, where she would be waited on hand and foot. She'd have nothing more pressing to worry about than what color gown to wear each morning.

He would do well to remember that Libby wasn't the niece of an Idaho sheep rancher. She was a Vanderhoff and, therefore, his adversary.

When Libby cleared a bend and recognized McGregor's camp in the distance, a ribbon of smoke rising from the central cookfire, she was never happier to see anything in her life. The sun already rode the crest of the western mountains as she guided Lightning down the trail toward the camp.

The dogs saw her first. As soon as one sent up a warning bark, McGregor was on his feet and on the lookout. He raised an arm and waved when he saw her. She waved back, then nudged Lightning into a trot.

"What're ye doin' here, lass?" he asked as she drew near. "Is there anythin' amiss? The lad all right?"

"Sawyer's fine." She eased back on the reins, stopping the gelding. "But we've had trouble." She dismounted, then turned toward the grim-faced Scot. "The wool was destroyed in a fire. The shed burned to the ground early last week."

"How'd it start?"

She shook her head. "We don't know."

"The bloody bastard."

Libby didn't have to ask who McGregor meant, nor did she dispute it. "I thought I should warn you. I don't know what he'll do next. He came to the house a couple of weeks ago and made some trouble, but Mr. Walker ran him off."

"Wait a minute, lass," McGregor said with a note of alarm and a deepening frown. "Who's Mr. Walker?"

"It's a long story."

He took the reins from her hands. "Then ye'd best go sit by the fire and get ready t'tell it t'me. Ye'll be hungry. There's supper in the pot. I'll see t'yer horse."

"Thanks. I am hungry."

A short while later, with Libby fed and her horse tethered alongside the team of mules that pulled the camp wagon, Libby told McGregor everything, starting with how Bevins had intentionally spooked Sawyer's horse. She didn't have to tell him what the loss of the wool crop meant to them all; the old sheepherder knew.

But McGregor didn't seem overly concerned. "Ye can pay us when ye're able, lass. And don't ye be worryin' yerself about the sheep. We've got the dogs t'warn us of trouble comin', and we'll be ready for him if he comes." He poured himself some coffee from the battered pot, kept warm at the edge of the fire. "But are ye sure ye can trust this . . . Walker, did ye say his name was?"

"Remington Walker." His name felt warm on her lips.

Could she trust him? She hoped so, for more reasons than McGregor wanted to know.

"Yes, I think we can trust him," she finally answered.

"Maybe we should bring the sheep down off the mountain, at least until we thinka what t'do next."

"We can't do that, McGregor. We haven't the feed in the valley to see them through summer."

"I'd rest easier if I could keep an eye on ye and the lad."

"We're not in any danger. We'll be fine." She didn't tell him Remington had said he wanted to stay until he was certain she and Sawyer were safe. She suspected the old sheepherder wouldn't be pleased to hear it. "It's the sheep I'm worried about. If we lose any more of them . . ." She let her words drift into silence; she knew McGregor understood.

"Ye leave them t'Ronald an' me, lass. We'll see that naught happens t'them."

Libby smiled weakly. McGregor would do his best. She just wasn't certain his best would be good enough.

And if she failed, if she lost the ranch, where would she go? The Blue Springs had been a place of safety for her for six years. It had been her home, and she had actually learned to be happy. Would she be able to find another place like it if she were forced from the ranch?

She thought of Remington then. Her pulse quickened, her stomach tumbled, and she wondered again if she weren't in more danger from her feelings for Remington Walker than from anything Bevins might do to her.

She didn't share her thoughts with McGregor. She thought it best to keep them a secret for now, perhaps forever.

Sawyer was playing with Misty and her puppies out in the yard as dusk settled over the earth. The boy's laughter, the dog's barking, and the whine and yip of the pups floated on the evening air through the open window of Libby's bedroom. The sounds were strangely pleasant, but Remington hadn't time to be lulled by them.

He glanced around the bedroom, knowing this might be his best opportunity to investigate the life Libby had been living. He felt only a small twinge of guilt as he moved toward the sturdy oak dresser in the corner.

The top drawer held several flannel shirts, just like the ones Libby had worn every day since Remington's arrival. The second drawer contained two pairs of men's denim trousers. The third drawer contained feminine undergarments, accented with ribbons and lace. He grinned, both surprised and glad that Libby hadn't taken to wearing men's underdrawers along with the shirts and trousers.

The bottom drawer of the dresser contained more surprises—two dresses, one black, one the same apple green as Libby's eyes. The dresses were well worn and out of fashion, and Remington suspected she'd had them ever since she'd left Manhattan.

In this drawer he also found a gold locket, wrapped in tissue paper. He picked it up, letting the chain slip through his fingers. He recognized it as the locket Libby had worn for her portrait. Had she kept the pearls as well?

He opened the locket and found tiny portraits of Anna and Northrop Vanderhoff inside. He wondered how often Libby opened the locket and remembered what she'd left behind. He wondered if she was ever sorry she'd left Manhattan. Would he be doing her a favor when he notified her father of her whereabouts? Would he be doing what she secretly wanted to do herself?

He frowned as he wrapped the locket back in its paper and returned it to the drawer.

No, he thought, she didn't secretly want to return to her father's home. He knew it as surely as he'd ever known anything. And she would hate Remington when she learned what he'd done. He knew that with certainty as well.

But it couldn't be helped. He would be doing what he'd been hired to do. He would be doing what he *had* to do. He owed it to his father to see this through to the end. This was his one and only chance to have the revenge he'd wanted for fifteen years. Such a chance would never come again.

Remington closed the drawer and straightened, his frown deepening as he tried to picture Sunnyvale and the life he'd known there, as he tried to picture his father. But it was Libby he kept seeing, her face filled with sadness.

He cursed as he reached for his crutch and limped out of the bedroom, as if running from the accusation he could already see in her eyes.

*   *   *

Anna Vanderhoff could hear her husband's snoring, even through the heavy oak door that joined their bedrooms. Northrop always slept soundly after he'd visited her bed and partaken of his conjugal rights. The same could not be said for Anna.

Shoving aside the bedcovers, she rose and then crossed the room to the large window. She held aside the draperies and stared down at the moonswept gardens. She smiled sadly. The rose gardens were the one place she could feel a measure of real happiness. She'd often wished they were larger, so large she could lose herself in them forever. Perhaps then . . .

She leaned her forehead against the cool glass and tried to forget the feel of Northrop astride her, his body invading hers as he grunted coarsely. At one time, when she was young and foolish and still hoping to make him love her, she had looked forward to the act of marriage. She had been eager to have his children, eager to be a good wife, eager to do anything and everything that would please him.

Anna closed her eyes, remembering the joy she'd experienced during her pregnancy. Even after all these years, she remembered exactly how she'd felt. Northrop had demanded that his child be a son, a son to inherit the vast empire he had built. When Olivia was born, he had blamed Anna for her failure. She had been certain the next child would be a boy. But there hadn't been another child, only a near dozen miscarriages.

She wasn't certain exactly when Northrop had taken his mistress, but she knew the woman—Ellen Prine was her name—had given him two sons, and illegitimate though they were, Northrop intended they should inherit Vanderhoff Shipping. The boys must be about ten and twelve years old by this time.

Anna wondered if Miss Prine looked forward to Northrop's visits to the house he provided for her and their sons. She wondered if Miss Prine welcomed his kisses, his embraces, his fornication. Did she love Northrop? And did Northrop love her?

Anna opened her eyes again and turned her back to the window. Moonlight spilled across the floor, illuminating the room in a soft white glow.

Did Northrop love Ellen Prine? she asked herself again. No, she was quite certain he did not. Northrop was incapable of that emotion. For many years she had hoped to teach him how to love. She had prayed to be able to teach him, and she had agonized over her inability to do so.

He hadn't even been able to love their daughter. Not even their lovely Olivia.

Olivia.

Tears pooled in Anna's eyes as the familiar ache pinched her heart. If only she could see her daughter . . . If only she could know Olivia was well and happy and safe . . .

Anna remembered the scene in Northrop's study just over a week ago. She remembered watching the precious letter burning, her one and only link to her daughter destroyed before her eyes. She'd hated Northrop then. For the first time in twenty-eight years of marriage, she'd truly hated him.

Anna supposed love had died long before that day, but she'd refused to acknowledge its death. A wife was supposed to love her husband. To love and honor and obey. She had always honored his wishes, obeyed his orders. She had promised to love him when they'd wed, and she had been faithful to doing so, despite his cruelty and his betrayals. But she couldn't love him any longer.

One more time she turned to face the window. She stared across the rooftops of the stately homes that lined

Seventy-second Street. She stared toward the west and prayed her daughter was safe. Most of all, she prayed the men Northrop had hired to find Olivia would fail. As much as she longed to see her only child, she wanted even more for her daughter to be happy, and she knew Olivia could never be happy if Northrop brought her back to New York.

"I love you," she whispered, hoping the words would somehow touch her daughter's heart and Olivia would know who'd sent them.

9

"Come on, Lightning."

Libby nudged the gelding with her heels, hoping to get a little more speed out of him. The ranch house was less than an hour away, and she was anxious to reach it. She told herself it was because she didn't want Sawyer to worry about her or because there might have been trouble of one kind or another while she was gone. She told herself everything except the truth.

She wanted to see Remington.

Throughout the previous night, she'd dreamed of stormy blue eyes and raven black hair and a smile that could stop her heart. She'd dreamed of warm embraces and fiery kisses. She'd dreamed of Remington Walker.

He'd said he wanted to stay and help. But how long would he stay?

A few weeks. A few months.

Forever?

Her heart skipped a beat.

Forever.

Did she *want* him to stay forever? she wondered.

The answer came with a sharp thud in her chest. *Yes!*

Libby pulled on the reins, stopping Lightning in his tracks. Breathing was difficult. Her pulse danced a rapid beat, and she felt light-headed.

"Oh, no," she whispered.

She'd warned herself. She'd warned herself not to let this happen. Not ever. And she hadn't thought it would. How could it, feeling the way she did? But it *was* happening. Against all good sense, against all reason, it was happening to her.

She was falling in love.

Libby closed her eyes and remembered the feel of Remington's embrace. It shouldn't have felt so wonderful. The memory should not have stayed with her.

"There'll come a day when you'll want a man's kisses. . . ." Unbidden, Amanda's words invaded her thoughts. *"Mark my words, Libby. The day will come when you'll want a man's kisses and more besides. . . ."*

Libby had told Amanda she was wrong. She didn't want or need a man in her life. She had seen what love did to a woman, what marriage really meant. She had watched her mother suffer a broken heart and shattered illusions, and she'd wanted no part of it for herself. She'd told Amanda that she wanted the same liberty Amanda enjoyed, the same freedom to make her own decisions and choose her own destiny. Amanda had never married, and she'd been content, even happy. Libby wanted the same for herself. Nothing a man could offer was worth losing her freedom of choice.

She drew in a long, ragged breath, then opened her eyes and started Lightning forward again. She was worrying needlessly, she told herself. He wouldn't be staying. Remington had a home in Virginia to return to. He would ride out of her life as abruptly as he'd ridden into it. And when he was gone, she would look back and laugh at her foolishness.

Libby repeated those words to herself often in the next hour. She repeated them so often, she almost believed them. Then she rode into the yard at the Blue Springs and saw Remington step through the back doorway, and she knew she wouldn't laugh when he left her.

She knew she would want to die.

Remington was surprised by the surge of relief he felt when Libby rode into sight. Strands of hair had pulled free from her braid. Her shirt and trousers were covered with a fine layer of dust. There was a smudge of dirt on her right cheek and another on the tip of her nose. She looked tired and sweaty.

She looked adorable.

Leaning on his crutch, he walked to the corral. She glanced at him as she dismounted, then looked away. She looped the reins around the top rail of the fence and began to loosen the cinch on Lightning's saddle.

"You found McGregor all right?" he asked.

"Yes."

"Everything okay? They hadn't had any trouble?"

"No. No trouble." She glanced toward the house. "Where's Sawyer?"

"He took Misty and the pups down to the creek."

She nodded, then turned her back to him as she continued to unsaddle Lightning.

Remington leaned against the fence, taking some of the weight off his bad leg. He thought of the dresses in the bottom drawer of Libby's dresser and wondered if she ever wore them. Especially the green one. Not that her trousers weren't affording him a rather nice view of her slender legs and shapely derriere.

He grinned, enjoying himself more than he should have.

Libby lifted the saddle off Lightning's back and set it on the corral fence. In a swift, easy motion, she yanked off the sweaty blanket and laid it, bottom side up, over the saddle. Then she removed the horse's bridle, replacing it with a halter and rope.

During his years in New York, working first for Pinkerton and then opening his own agency, Remington had made use of his business connections and family background to gain acceptance among Manhattan's privileged set. Although he'd purposefully avoided the Vanderhoffs—easy enough to do with his moderate income—he'd known his share of debutantes and society matrons. He'd sat at their supper tables and been entertained at their Newport estates and danced at their charity balls. He'd even known his share of unusual women, those who rebelled against society's strictures. But he couldn't imagine any of them doing what Libby was doing now. Nor looking like she looked now. In fact, the images flashing through his head nearly made him laugh aloud.

As if she could feel his amusement, she turned. Their gazes met, and his humor left him. He didn't want to laugh. He wanted to kiss her.

And she *wanted* him to kiss her.

He could feel it in the air, like the crackle of electricity during a thunderstorm. He could read it in her eyes as easily as he could read the stars on a clear summer night.

Libby moved suddenly to the opposite side of the horse, hiding herself from his view, breaking the spell that had bound them, however briefly. He knew she'd done it on purpose, and he was glad. He'd be wise not to complicate things more than he already had.

He placed his crutch beneath his arm and stepped away from the corral. "I've got a stew on the stove for supper. I thought you'd be hungry when you got back. I'll go check on it." He started away.

"Remington."

He stopped and glanced over his shoulder.

There was an uncertainty in her expression that served only to make her look more desirable. "Thank you," she whispered.

"For what?"

"For watching after the place while I was gone. For keeping an eye on Sawyer." She shrugged. "For staying to help."

Damn! The desire to kiss her returned with a vengeance, along with a desire to do much more. With those trousers outlining her shapely figure, it was too blasted easy to imagine her without clothes. It was too blasted easy to imagine what it might be like to remove those clothes and make love to her.

She offered a tentative smile. "It's nice to have someone here I can trust."

Her words doused his ardor like a splash of cold water in the face. Trust him? She didn't know how wrong she was.

He started walking toward the house again. "I'll check on our supper," he replied gruffly. He was angry at himself—but even more angry at Libby.

For being born a Vanderhoff.

Falling in love with Remington would be the most foolish thing she had ever done, Libby told herself again as they sat at the supper table that evening. She simply couldn't allow it to happen. She must remember he would leave her one day. One day soon. Perhaps in only a week or two.

Drawing a deep breath, she looked across the table at him. "I've never been to Virginia, but I've heard it's lovely there. Would you tell me about your home?"

"My home," he repeated softly. There was a subtle change in his expression, a change she couldn't quite read. "You mean Sunnyvale."

"Sunnyvale. It sounds lovely."

"It was beautiful . . . before the war."

Bitterness? Sadness? Was that what she saw in his eyes, in the firm set of his mouth?

"But the war was a long time ago, and I doubt you want to hear about that." He was silent a moment, and Libby sensed that he was looking back across time and remembering. "When I was a boy, we raised tobacco at Sunnyvale, but we were best known for our stables. Sundown is a good example of the famous Sunnyvale Arabians."

"He's a beautiful animal," she said. Then, unable to stop herself, she added, "You must be in a hurry to return to Virginia."

He met her gaze, and something in his eyes made her feel cold and frightened. "Yes, I'd love to be able to return to Sunnyvale."

"Well," she replied, her voice quavering slightly, "then we must get you well and on your way soon." She glanced at Sawyer, eager to change the subject. "Have you decided on a name for your pup yet?"

"Yeah. I been callin' him Ringer 'cause of the white ring around his neck. He's mighty smart, Libby. He's gonna be the best dang sheepdog we've got on the place."

"Don't swear, Sawyer." She picked up her fork. "And I'm sure he'll be a wonderful sheepdog if you train him right." She tried to smile for the boy's sake.

But inside she was hurting. Hurting in a way she'd never hurt before. Longing for something she couldn't have and shouldn't want.

Remington was eager to return to his place in Virginia. He was rightfully angry with her for shooting him, for keeping him here. He was probably angry at himself for offering to stay and help. And could she honestly blame him? She was nothing to him.

Her appetite was gone. Looking at the food on her plate nauseated her. She rose suddenly from her chair, saying, "I'm afraid I'm too weary to eat. I'm going to bed. Just leave the supper dishes. I'll do them in the morning." She made a hasty retreat before either Remington or Sawyer could respond.

Once in her room, the door closed behind her, Libby drew a deep breath. It was for the best, she told herself. It was for the best he was leaving. She didn't want a man to love, didn't want a husband or children. She didn't want any of that. She wanted only her freedom.

But the familiar phrases no longer rang true.

10

Timothy Bevins tipped his chair back on its hind legs, leaning it against the wall of the house as he stared at the cattle grazing in the distance. A warm breeze stirred the tall grass. The valley was green now, but if this heat persisted and the late spring rains didn't come, the land would be parched before the end of June.

He cursed as he dropped his chair back into place with a thud and rose to his feet. He needed *all* the range hereabouts if he was going to increase his herd. He needed those damn sheep to quit eating the feed his cattle could use, and he needed to control the springs that provided water to the valley. Once he controlled it, he'd be able to keep out ranchers like Libby Blue and farmers like the Fishers, who had settled alongside Blue Creek.

Spurs jingling, he crossed the porch and went down the steps, swift strides carrying him to the hitching post where his horse waited. He freed the reins, then stepped up into the saddle. Jerking the animal's head around, he spurred the red roan into a gallop and headed west, toward Pine Station. He needed a drink.

Blast Libby Blue! Why was she hanging on? He'd given her plenty of chances to sell, lots of opportunities to leave without trouble, just like he'd done for the old woman before she died. But Libby hadn't listened, and he was running out of patience.

He didn't know how, exactly, but he was going to make the Blue Springs his. Maybe he was just going to have to get tougher with her. Maybe stealing sheep and burning a shed weren't enough.

Libby spent the morning in the garden, weeding and hoeing and watering. The growing season was short in Idaho, and the vegetable gardens were too important to ignore. Without the food grown there, she and Sawyer and the sheepherders wouldn't have enough provisions to see them through next winter, let alone to feed the shearers when they arrived in the spring.

Besides, she'd hoped the work would clear her thoughts after another restless night.

For a while, she was successful in keeping her mind on other things, but eventually Remington drifted back into her thoughts. Instead of the smell of freshly turned soil, she caught a whiff of his uniquely male scent, something very subtle, something very Remington. It was so real, she sat back on her heels and looked about, half expecting to find him beside her.

But, of course, he wasn't there.

Once he left Blue Springs, she knew she would still be able to close her eyes and remember everything about him. The way he'd looked. The way he'd smelled. The feel of his arms around her, her face pressed against his chest. Everything.

"Oh, Mama," she whispered, understanding as she never had before how easy it could be for a woman to forget what she believed in just because she loved a man. She realized how harshly, how wrongly, she had judged her mother. She'd never understood before, but now she did.

She wished she didn't.

Libby sucked in a deep breath, then released the air slowly. She wasn't like her mother. She couldn't—*wouldn't*—forget who and what she was, not for any reason. Not even for Remington Walker.

As if conjured up by her thoughts, he came out of the house, pausing just beyond the doorway. She felt her heart quicken as it always did at the sight of him. In only a moment, his glance found her.

He would go and leave her behind. He would go back to his place in Virginia, to his plantation and his horses, and she would remain here with the life she had made for herself, with Sawyer and McGregor and Ronald and the sheep and the dogs. She didn't belong in his world, and he wouldn't stay in hers.

She knew all this, but suddenly it didn't matter. Suddenly she wanted to know what it was like to love, completely and without question or reserve. She wanted to know what it was like to lie in a man's arms and know his body even more intimately than she knew her own. She was tired of being afraid to risk her emotions. She'd been afraid for so long, and she was tired of it.

She dropped the short-handled spade and rose to her feet.

She would let herself love him. She would live every moment he was here to the fullest. She would know and understand everything about loving him, and when he went away, she wouldn't regret it. She would have her memories, and perhaps that would be enough.

*   *   *

During the night, Remington had decided he could live with the guilt of his deception. This was his job. This was what he'd been hired to do. He'd been paid to find Olivia Vanderhoff. Withholding pieces of information, twisting the truth, and telling lies went hand in hand with being a good detective. There was nothing wrong with what he'd done. Libby would be better off because of what he was doing. Even if he succeeded later in crumbling a part of the Vanderhoff empire, as he'd sworn he would do, Libby would still be better off than she was here. After that . . .

Well, it wasn't his responsibility what happened after that.

So he'd told himself during the night, and he'd been convinced it was the way it had to be. But he wasn't so sure when he saw the trust in her eyes as she walked toward him, looking ridiculously pretty in her men's clothing, her rose gold hair gleaming in the midday sunlight.

"Morning," she said as she stopped before him.

Lord, but she was a beautiful sight.

"How's your leg?"

"Better."

She brushed her hair away from her face with the back of one hand. "I was weeding the garden. I've been neglecting it."

She was tending to me instead, he thought.

Libby glanced over her shoulder at the tidy rows, then returned her gaze to him. "Pine Station doesn't carry much more than basic staples, so we try to grow as much of our own food as we can."

"Pine Station?"

"It used to be a trading post. Later it was a way station for the stagecoaches on their way north. Folks thought it might grow into a real town, but the stage route changed because of the railroad, and Pine Station never grew much beyond a saloon and the general store."

He frowned thoughtfully. "I didn't see it on the map I bought in Boise City."

"I doubt it's ever been on a map," she replied with a soft laugh.

"Do they have a telegraph in Pine Station?"

She shook her head. "No. Weiser's the closest town of any size. That's where Aunt Amanda always picked up what supplies she couldn't at the Pine Station general store. Of course, I don't know for certain Weiser has a telegraph. I always stayed at Blue Springs whenever Aunt Amanda went over that way. But I imagine they'd have one, now that the railroad comes through there."

Remington knew the reason she'd never gone to town with Amanda Blue. She'd wanted to avoid being seen. She must have known her father would be relentless in his search for her. She'd known there would be detectives on her trail. For reasons he didn't understand, she had placed herself in self-imposed exile, here in the mountain country of Idaho, about as far from the wealth and opulence of New York society as a person could get. She'd made a new life, a new identity, for herself, and she'd hoped her father would never find her.

But she'd forgotten she still needed to be wary, that her father—and his hired men—would still be searching for her. Remington was one of those men, and he was here. She'd been found. She just didn't know it yet. She hadn't escaped her father after all.

"Do you need to send a telegram?" she asked, drawing his attention back to her.

Remington shook his head. "No hurry. It can wait."

"I suppose I could send a message with Pete Fisher. He and his wife have a small farm south of here. He might be going to Weiser, and—"

"It's not important, Libby," he interrupted. "It can wait until I leave."

Her gaze fell away. "Yes . . . you can do it when you leave," she said softly. When she looked up again, her eyes seemed brighter than before, and she was wearing a smile that looked strangely sad. "Do you feel up to a walk? If you do, I'll show you some of our sheep."

Remington wished he could drive off whatever had caused her sadness, but he suspected he was the reason. And if he wasn't now, he would be soon enough.

"I'd like that," he answered, hoping she would one day forgive him for what he planned to do.

Libby led the way to the pasture where a few ewes and lambs were kept during the summer months. Some were there because of injuries that needed attention. Others remained to be slaughtered for food over the summer. Libby tried never to think of that part. If she and Sawyer and the herders didn't need to eat, she could have happily made pets of all of them.

Misty, followed by her growing offspring, came out of the barn and preceded Libby and Remington to the pasture. The black-and-white collie slipped beneath the bottom rail of the fence and immediately began working the ewes and lambs into a tight bunch. Misty's puppies seemed to think it was all a game for their enjoyment. They gamboled into the midst of the sheep, scattering them in all directions. The air was filled with a cacophony of bleating and barking.

Libby whistled, then signaled Misty to leave the pasture. The collie obeyed after first rounding up her rambunctious brood.

She heard Remington chuckling and glanced his way. Her spirit brightened at the sight of his smile. "As you can see, we'll need to do some training before those puppies are able to join the herders and the flock."

His smile broadened. "Yes, I can see that."

She knelt as Misty trotted toward her, then reached out

to stroke the collie's sleek head and scratch her behind the ears. "Hello, girl," she whispered. "How's my Misty?"

The dog wagged her tail and whimpered.

Glancing up at Remington, Libby said, "Misty's grandparents came from Scotland with McGregor." She feigned a Scottish accent. "Me good friend McGregor claims these dogs are smart enough t'cook yer breakfast an' serve it t'ye, if that's what ye want of 'em, an' he willna let ye say otherwise. He gave this bonny lass t'me not so many years ago. She's nearly proved him right a time or two."

Remington leaned against the fence, still smiling as the puppies crowded around her, whining and wiggling, begging for attention. The look in his eyes made her go all soft and warm inside. She'd never seen anything more beautiful than the blue of his eyes or the cut of his jaw or the curve of his brow or . . .

Her heartbeat quickened and her breathing slowed. She found herself staring at his mouth, wondering what it would be like to be kissed by him. Libby had never been kissed before. At least, not a real kiss on the mouth. She'd had a young gentleman or two kiss her cheek, but there'd never been time for more than that. Her father had guarded her social activities as closely as he'd guarded everything else in her life.

Gently pushing away the puppies, Libby rose. Something irresistible pulled her toward Remington, like an invisible cord tied about her waist, drawing her helplessly into dangerous waters.

What are you doing? her mind screamed. *Stop!*

But she couldn't stop. She kept moving closer to him. Slowly. Ever so slowly.

His eyes darkened and his smile faded. She didn't see so much as feel him move away from the fence rail, straighten to his full height.

It's going to hurt when you go away, she thought as she

stood before him, only a whisper of air separating their two bodies, staring up to meet his stormy gaze.

She heard the crutch drop to the ground, felt the puppies scampering around their feet, investigating the strange object in the grass, but it was the feel of Remington's arms as they encircled her that dominated her awareness.

He lowered his head. She tipped hers back and to one side, then closed her eyes. It seemed the most natural thing in the world when his mouth covered hers. She felt herself grow hot, grow cold. Blood pounded in her ears, yet she felt as if her heart had stopped. Her skin tingled. Her knees felt weak.

He might stay. . . . He might stay. . . . He might stay. . . .

He raised his head. She opened her eyes.

He might stay. . . . He might stay. . . .

He brushed her cheek with the side of his thumb. "Libby . . ."

Her stomach tumbled.

He might stay. . . .

"I . . ."

She shook her head. "Don't say it," she whispered. "Please don't say it." She wrapped her arms around him and pressed her cheek against his chest. "Don't explain it or apologize for it. Just let it be for now."

"Ah, Libby." He rested his cheek against the top of her head. "You don't understand."

"You're wrong, Remington. I understand."

His arms tightened around her. "No, Libby, you don't. But I do."

And then he lifted her chin with the tip his finger and kissed her again.

11

Black clouds blew across the sky as evening approached, driven by gusts of wind that bent the tall pines into arcs and rattled the leaves of the quaking aspens and cottonwoods. A shadow blanketed the earth, making the whistling winds sound ominous. Minutes later the lightning began, a thunderous display that brightened the heavens above and shook the ground below.

Libby and Sawyer ran to the pasture and, with the help of Misty, drove the sheep into the shelter of the barn. Then they led the skittish horses, prancing and whinnying in alarm, into their stalls and closed them in. Only Melly seemed oblivious of nature's uproar. The milk cow stood quietly in her stall, chewing her cud and flicking her tail, her brown eyes dolefully observing all the frantic activity.

Libby felt a flash of envy for Melly's calm. She wished she felt the same. Instead she was as skittish as the horses and felt as storm tossed as the black clouds tumbling and crashing overhead. She'd felt that way ever since Remington had kissed her earlier in the day.

"We better hurry, Libby," Sawyer shouted at her from the doorway of the barn. "The rain's comin'."

Libby followed the boy outside, racing to beat the deluge that was about to fall from the sky. She didn't reach the house in time. In a matter of seconds she was drenched clear through to the skin.

"Wow, ain't it somethin'?" Sawyer said with a laugh as they entered through the back door.

She shook her hands and wiped the rain from her face. "Yes, it's something." She would have corrected his grammar, but then she saw Remington, watching her from the doorway, and the words vanished right out of her head.

"Sawyer's right. That's some storm." He limped over to the window and looked outside.

From the moment he'd kissed her, everything had changed between them; yet nothing had changed. She was falling in love with him, but he remained a stranger to her. They hadn't talked after the kisses or the embrace they'd shared. They'd simply gone about their normal routines, which led Libby to wonder what Remington might feel for her—if he felt anything at all.

"Yes," she replied at last, "it's some storm."

He turned his head and met her gaze. "You're soaked." The hint of a smile curved his mouth.

"I know." Her pulse began to race.

"You'd better get out of your wet things."

"Yes," she whispered.

Remington glanced at Sawyer. "You too."

The boy nodded and headed off to his room.

"I made a fire in the fireplace." Remington's gaze returned to Libby. "I think it's going to be a cold night."

She couldn't seem to reply, so she, too, simply nodded and left the kitchen, hurrying to her own room and closing the door behind her.

As she leaned against the door, her heart pounded a

rapid and unsteady beat, and she felt tears burning the back of her throat. She wanted him to love her. She wanted him to stay.

But she didn't know how to make him want to stay, how to make him love her.

Once, long ago, in a totally different life, she had learned the fine art of courtship. She had been taught the things a well-bred young woman should say and do when in the company of men. Her lessons had been detailed, right down to the proper way to hold and wave a fan and how to light a man's cigar. She had learned how to waltz and how to walk and how to sit. She had learned how to flirt and how to sing and how to play the piano.

But she'd forgotten all those lessons. She'd put that world—and the girl she'd been—completely behind her. When she'd donned her flannel shirts and denim trousers and become a sheep rancher, she'd forgotten how to be a woman. She'd been so certain she would never need to know.

Her eyes flicked toward the dresser in the corner of her room.

Would a woman be able to make Remington want to stay?

Remington returned to the parlor and added another log to the already blazing fire. The room was toasty warm, and now that the lightning storm had passed, the sound of the rain upon the roof was comforting and peaceful.

But Remington didn't feel peaceful. He kept berating himself for complicating things with a kiss.

He didn't deny Libby was a beautiful woman, but he had never been a man who gave in easily to the temptations of beauty. He had learned long ago how to curb his desires. He needed to remember that, now more than ever.

Wearily he sank onto the sofa, staring at the orange-and-yellow flames in the fireplace while his thoughts drifted back in time.

Remington had enjoyed a reckless, carefree youth, unaware of his father's burgeoning debt. At seventeen he'd gone off to college, more intent on having fun than on learning. He'd known, of course, that hardships had been endured in the decade following the war, but there had always been enough money for him to do as he pleased. JW Railroad, from all he'd been told, had been returning to its prewar strength. Sunnyvale Plantation, although hard hit by the war and lacking in servants, had remained in the Walker family, as it had for six generations. What could possibly disturb the carefree life he'd been living?

How ignorant he'd been. How selfish and thoughtless. Maybe if he'd paid some attention to his father's worries . . .

He closed his eyes and leaned his head against the back of the sofa.

He remembered the shock he'd felt when he'd heard of his father's suicide, when he'd learned that Sunnyvale and the railroad and all he'd ever known was gone. He remembered the fury that had raged through him when he'd learned the part Northrop had played in Jefferson's destruction. He'd sworn then not to rest until he'd had his revenge. He'd sworn on the memory of his father that he would repay Vanderhoff in kind.

It had taken him over fourteen years to find a way to have that revenge. In truth, he'd nearly given up. He'd begun to think it would never happen, that he would have to resign himself to letting go of the promise that had been made beside his father's grave.

But the opportunity for revenge had presented itself last summer, and that was why he was here in this parlor tonight. He couldn't forget that. He couldn't allow his heart to soften toward—

"Remington?"

He opened his eyes and turned his head and saw her standing just inside the room, wearing the green dress he'd seen in the bottom drawer of her bureau. Her hair, still damp, had been twisted into a bun at the nape of her neck, caught in a net made of emerald satin ribbons. Her hands were clenched at her waist, and she watched him with an uncertain gaze.

He rose from the sofa, placing his crutch under his arm.

She glanced down at her dress, smoothing the wrinkles with the palms of her hands. "I don't ever wear this anymore, but I thought . . ." She let the words die away, then gave a helpless shrug.

"You look lovely." Hellfire and damnation! Why did she have to be Vanderhoff's daughter?

She took a hesitant step forward. "I haven't had much occasion to wear a dress since I came to the Blue Springs."

"To live with your aunt," he added.

"To live with my aunt," she echoed.

How many lies would form the wall that separated them? he wondered. How many lies before they were through, before she despised him completely?

He smiled, trying to disguise the sadness he felt over what was to come, over what he knew he would do. "It's a pity. You should be seen like this often."

It wasn't her fault she was a Vanderhoff, but that's who she was. He would hurt her because of it, and she would hate him when it was over. But he couldn't help wishing there was some way he could lessen the hurt, lessen the hate she would feel.

She answered his smile with a tentative one of her own. "Aunt Amanda said they used to have dances in Pine Station on occasion, but when the stage route changed and the railroad didn't come through, folks moved away, and . . ." Again she finished her sentence with a small shrug.

"Do you miss dancing, Libby?"

She shook her head, then nodded.

"Would you like to dance?"

Her eyes widened.

Remington glanced down at his leg, then set his crutch aside. "You'll have to come to me."

Her eyes rounded even more. "You shouldn't, Remington. You—"

"Come here."

Even as she obeyed him, she said, "There's no music."

"Of course there is."

She arrived before him. He could smell the clean scent of her rain-dampened hair. He could see the fresh glow of her skin.

He took hold of her right hand with his left and placed his other hand in the small of her back. He drew her closer to him and whispered, "Close your eyes, Libby."

She did, her long lashes fanning above her cheeks. Her mouth was parted slightly, and he could hear the quick breaths she took.

"Listen. . . . Can you hear the rain upon the roof?"

She nodded.

"Can you hear the crackle of the fire?"

Again she nodded.

"It's music, Libby."

He drew her closer yet, then began to sway slowly from side to side. He ignored the needles of pain in his leg. The pain was worth it, just to hold her. He hoped, when it was over and she was back in New York, this would make up for some of his deception. He hoped, when he'd destroyed the Vanderhoff fortunes as he planned, she would remember tonight and not think too harshly of him.

He rested his cheek on the crown of her head and breathed in the fragrance that was uniquely Libby Blue.

I'm sorry. I'm sorry I must use you this way. If it weren't for your father . . .

As if she'd heard his thoughts, she lifted her head, opened her eyes, and gazed up at him, and the look she gave him sent a stab of guilt straight through his heart.

As he stared into eyes filled with love, Remington knew he was a greater bastard than Northrop Vanderhoff could ever hope to be.

Libby found it nearly impossible to breathe as she watched Remington's blue eyes grow darker, stormier. She could feel the anger emanating from him as clearly as she could feel the warmth from the fire. Yet she wasn't afraid. She believed in her heart he wouldn't hurt her, although she had no reason to think so.

He slipped his right hand from her back, pulled his left hand from her grasp. Then he took hold of her upper arms and gently set her one step back from him.

"I think maybe you were right. I'm not up to dancing." He turned and reached for his crutch, then made his way with a *thump-step, thump-step,* toward his bedroom. At the parlor entry, he paused and glanced behind him. "You do look pretty in that dress, Libby. You ought to wear it more often. The men hereabouts would be buzzing around you like flies."

Something fearful tweaked her heart, but she shoved it away. She forced herself to smile. "A dress just gets in the way when I'm working."

"Yeah, I suppose it would at that." He stepped into the hall. "Good night, Libby."

When he was gone, Libby sank onto the sofa and stared at the dancing flames in the fireplace. She listened to the crackle of burning wood and the patter of rain on the rooftop and knew she would never hear them again without remembering the moment he'd held her in his arms and swayed with her to the imaginary music.

She wondered if the anticipation of his leaving was worse than the leaving itself would be.

The loneliness of her future closed in around her while outside the rain continued to fall, as if nature understood the pain in her heart and wept for her.

She knew she would never want to wear this dress again.

12

For the next week, while Remington's wounds continued to mend and his strength improved, Libby did her best to deny her feelings for him. She tried to prepare herself for the day he would leave. She avoided being alone with him, which wasn't difficult since he seemed to be avoiding her, too.

Perhaps that was the reason she was so surprised, early one morning, when he came into the barn while she was milking Melly. Her hands stilled on the cow's udder as she watched him walking toward her. His limp wasn't nearly so exaggerated, she noticed, and he was leaning less upon the crutch. His movements didn't seem as stiff or painful as they had just a few days before.

How soon before he's able to ride? she wondered, and felt the now familiar sadness she always felt when she thought about Remington leaving the Blue Springs.

For his part, Remington also wondered what he was doing there. He'd seen Libby walk out to the barn, milk pail in hand. For a week he'd been purposely distancing himself from her. It was for her own good. He didn't want her thinking he was something he was not. He had to protect her from her own innocence, from the trust she'd placed in him so erroneously.

He hadn't had a single good reason to follow her out to the barn this morning—except simply wanting to be with her.

"You're up early," he said as he stopped at the stall opening.

"I always am." She turned her gaze downward and began milking again.

Remington watched the frothy white liquid squirt into the bucket and wondered how a woman could look so fetching while seated on a stool and leaning up close to the belly of a cow. He'd always been one to appreciate a woman in feminine trappings, yet he thought Libby looked more enticing at this moment than any society beauty he'd ever seen, no matter how elaborate her dress or how sparkling her jewels.

"Aunt Amanda always said milking was the best way to start a day. It gives a body a moment of peace so she can think before all heck breaks loose, as it's sure to every now and again." A pinch of color spread over her cheeks. "That's what she always said."

"I'm sure she was right." He stepped farther into the stall. "I never milked a cow before. Care to show me how it's done?"

Her hands stilled. "You want to learn how to *milk?*"

To tell the truth, he was as surprised as Libby by his request. He knew it had more to do with needing a reason to remain in the barn than with any real desire to learn how to milk a cow.

Why can't I have the good sense to just leave her alone? he wondered.

"Are you sure?" she asked softly.

"I'm sure."

"All right." She released her grip on the cow's udder and slid the stool backward, then rose. "Come over here and sit down."

He leaned his crutch against the wall of the stall and limped the few steps to where Libby was waiting for him. She took hold of his arm as he sank onto the short-legged stool. When he was settled, she knelt beside him, the straw crunching beneath her knees.

"The first thing you must know," she said, taking hold of one of his hands and guiding it beneath the cow, "is that you don't yank. You'll only succeed in making Melly mad." Her hand covered his as it closed around the engorged teat. "Squeeze firmly, starting with your thumb and forefinger and rolling downward with a gentle pull."

He could feel the warmth of her body, so close to his own, right through his shirt.

"Use your other hand, too," she instructed.

She always smelled so clean and fresh, even here in the barn.

"Now alternate. It's easier when you get a rhythm going. That's right."

A spray of milk shot into the bucket.

Libby laughed. "You're a quicker study than I was. I thought I'd never learn how to do it."

The pleasure he felt had nothing to do with the splash of milk in the pail and everything to do with Libby's laughter. The last remnants of his restraint slipped away, and he did what he'd been wanting to do for a solid week, the very thing good sense told him not to. He turned his head and kissed her cheek. Afterward he kept his forehead close to her temple, knowing she could feel his breath upon her face, wishing he knew what she was thinking, cursing himself again for not being stronger, for not staying away from her.

The barn grew hushed and still. For an endless heart-beat, neither of them moved.

"You'll go away soon, won't you?" she asked breath-lessly.

He thought of his father and the promises he'd made. "I can't stay here."

She turned to look at him. "I know."

"Libby . . ." He cupped her cheek with the palm of his hand.

She pressed her face against his touch and closed her eyes. "It doesn't matter."

"You don't understand. There are so many things you don't know about me. You—"

"I don't care."

"You will care," he warned, yet he couldn't keep him-self from drawing her against him and kissing her again, this time on the mouth.

When the truth comes out, you'll care, he told her silently.

But Libby didn't care. Not that day or the next. Not that week or the next. Not as long as Remington held her in his arms. Not as long as he kissed her whenever they were alone together and allowed her to pretend they had forever.

It was a desperate kind of happiness she felt, always conscious, somewhere deep below the surface, that she was pretending, that her joy was temporary. Remington hadn't denied he would leave her one day, and she knew she couldn't hold him there. When it was time, when he was well, he would go. He'd told her it would be so.

There was nothing for her to do but enjoy to the fullest each and every day they were together. Then at least she would have her memories to turn to when she was alone again. She would be able to say that for a brief time she had discovered the wonders of love.

Libby set out to collect remembrances with the same determination of a miner seeking the mother lode. She was always watchful, always observant.

She memorized the crooked slant of Remington's smile. She memorized the way one eyebrow lifted when he was amused. She memorized the gentle cadence of his Virginian accent. She memorized the way his black hair brushed the collar of his shirt, the dark shadow that formed beneath his skin on his jaw as the day waned. She memorized the way the shading of his blue eyes altered, depending upon his mood.

Nothing Remington did, nothing he said, went unnoticed by Libby. And so the days of his recovery passed.

13

Standing on a chair, Libby reached for the earthenware jar atop the cupboard. Her fingers closed around the narrow neck of the vessel, and she pulled the jar toward her, carefully drawing it up close to her body before stepping off the chair. She pulled off the lid and tipped the container sideways, emptying its contents onto the table.

The smattering of coins seemed to mock her. There were so few of them, and now that the wool crop was lost, there weren't going to be more of them soon.

It crossed her mind that Remington had money, but she pushed the idea away. She couldn't seek help from him—for more reasons than she could understand. She simply knew she couldn't ask.

With a sigh, Libby scooped the coins into her hand and dropped them into the pocket of her trousers, then she walked to the back door and opened it. Her eyes quickly found Remington and Sawyer, standing inside the corral. Sawyer was brushing Sundown's neck and chest while Remington leaned against the golden horse's back.

She paused for a moment, simply to enjoy looking at the two of them—Remington so tall and strong, Sawyer small and wiry but growing fast. Remington was always patient with the boy, always willing to talk to him, spend time with him, and Sawyer's affection for the man was obvious.

He'd make a wonderful father.

Her heart skipped a beat.

Remington's child . . .

She could almost see herself, holding an infant in her arms, Remington standing beside mother and baby.

She gave her head a quick shake and tried to still the tumble of emotions in her chest. She had no time for such thoughts. Remington wasn't going to stay at the Blue Springs, and she couldn't leave. They had no future together. There was no point in wanting the impossible.

With quick strides, she crossed the yard to the corral. Remington and Sawyer turned as she approached.

Libby deliberately set her gaze on the boy. "I'm going into Pine Station for supplies. McGregor will be expecting us soon."

"I'd like to ride into Pine Station with you."

She looked at Remington, and again her traitorous heart skipped a beat. *When are you going away?* she wanted to ask. *How long do I have before you go?* Instead she said, "You should probably stay here and rest. Sawyer can go along to help me with the supplies."

"I'm rested, Libby," Remington protested gently. "I'm not an invalid. The outing would be good for me."

Her brief flash of self-preservation had vanished. She wanted him with her every moment of the day, and she was too greedy to let this opportunity slip away. "All right, if you want to come." She glanced at Sawyer. "Help me hitch up the team to the wagon."

As the three of them set out toward Pine Station—

Remington with his rifle across his knees, Libby driving the team, Sawyer in the back of the wagon with his pup— Remington told himself again how much better off Libby would be when she was out of there, when she was away from all the work and worries of this ranch, when she was safe and secure in New York.

He glanced at her without turning his head. She was leaning forward, her forearms resting on her thighs, the leather reins looped through her gloved fingers. She was wearing a floppy-brimmed felt hat, pulled low on her forehead. Her eyes were hidden in the shade of the brim, but he could see the splash of freckles across her nose and the firm set of her mouth.

She had more worries than a woman should have to bear. She shouldn't have to work so hard. She shouldn't have to live this hardscrabble life. Her father was one of the wealthiest men in America. She should be living in ease and luxury. Why would she choose to live like this? What had driven her here?

He had to know why she'd run away. The reason hadn't mattered to him before. His questions up to now had been part of a game he'd played to satisfy his curiosity.

But now her reasons mattered. They mattered because Libby mattered. She mattered too much.

"Libby."

"Hmm?"

"Tell me about your family." *Tell me what you were running from. Tell me why you're hiding.*

Her glance was quick and sparing. "I haven't any family. It's just Sawyer and me."

Another lie between them.

"Everyone starts out with a family. You told me you came from San Francisco to live with your aunt. What was your life like before you came here? Tell me about your parents."

She was silent for a long time, and he thought she wasn't going to answer him. But then he heard her sigh.

"My mother's name was Anna." Her voice was soft, wistful. "Mama was a pretty, gentle woman, always kind to others, no matter what their status. Our servants loved her. Everyone loved her. Everyone except—" Abruptly she broke off what she'd been about to say.

Remington waited for her to continue.

"I never liked our house. It was always too large and dark. I don't think Mama liked it, either. That's why she spent so much time in her rose gardens." She stared off into space, remembering.

But Remington didn't have all his answers yet, so he pushed for more. "What about the rest of your family?"

"There wasn't anyone else. I suppose I was lonely when I was little. I wanted a brother"—a pained expression flashed across her face—"or a sister, but Mama never had any more children. But I wasn't unhappy. My mother was there. Sometimes she would come to my room late at night, after I was supposed to be asleep, and she would read to me from storybooks about magical places and people. Sometimes she read poetry, beautiful sonnets about . . . about love."

"And your father?" Remington persisted, noticing the way her fingers tightened around the reins.

Her voice became brittle. "My father didn't believe in fairy tales or storybooks. And he hated poetry."

Remington should have let it go. He should have let her be, but he couldn't. "What made you leave home, Libby? What made you come to Idaho?"

She turned, and he could feel the hardness of her gaze upon his face. "Because I had no choice."

"What happened?" *Tell me the truth.*

"I lost my parents," she said, her voice cracking. She looked away. "I lost everything. I have no home but Blue Springs, no family except for Sawyer."

There was a long, pregnant pause. Libby had told him little, yet Remington understood so much more. He knew now, beyond a shadow of doubt, that Libby had run away from her father, that Northrop had hurt her, wounded her deeply. She hadn't run off with a lover. She hadn't simply set out on some escapade, a spoiled rich girl looking for adventure. Even after all these years, she was afraid she would be found. The worst thing that could happen to her would be for someone to return her to New York and her father's house.

And that was exactly what Remington intended to do.

He cursed silently, hating himself for what he'd done already, hating himself for what he had yet to do. He never should have kissed Libby, never should have allowed her infatuation to grow.

And for his part, he shouldn't let himself care whether or not she was safe, whether or not she was happy. He couldn't change who he was or who she was. He couldn't change the past.

Straightening suddenly, as if she wanted to escape the questions he'd asked, Libby slapped the reins against the backs of the horses. "Get up there!"

The team quickened their strides, and the wagon continued on toward Pine Station, the occupants cloaked in silence.

Bevins watched the wagon moving along the road below, and his anger mounted. That gal didn't have two licks' worth of sense or she'd've been out of this country by now. She'd've sold him the Blue Springs and hightailed it off to town where she belonged.

He ground his teeth, remembering how his most recent attempts to get at the sheep had been thwarted by that damned Scot and his dogs; then his eyes narrowed as he watched the wagon disappearing over a rise. He'd like to know who that fellow sitting next to Libby was and what he was doing at her ranch.

He cursed, then spit out a stream of tobacco. Hell, he knew what the fellow was doing. He'd been wearin' nothin' but a bedsheet last time he'd seen him. Having a grand old time in Libby's bed, just like any other red-blooded man would do if he had the chance. Just like he'd do himself if he ever had the chance.

He wondered what Amanda Blue would think if she knew she'd left her ranch to a gal who'd take in a man like that. He wondered what others would think.

With a sudden grin, Bevins turned his mount in the direction of Pine Station. He wanted to be there when Libby arrived.

The sign above the Pine Station general store was faded but still legible from a fair distance away. The store was housed in a long log building, single story and low roofed. The proprietors, Marian and Walter Jonas, were an elderly couple who'd come to the territory nearly thirty years before. They'd opened the way station when the gold rush was at its peak and miners were moving back and forth between camps in the north and those in the south. They'd stayed on after the boom, selling supplies to the farmers and ranchers who'd settled in the lush mountain valleys of Idaho Territory.

Next to the general store was Lucky's Saloon, run by a crusty old gold miner who'd broken his leg after his can-tankerous mule threw him down the side of a mountain. Somehow—no one knew exactly how—Lucky had managed to drag himself to Pine Station. He'd lost his leg to gangrene, but he'd always figured he was lucky to be alive at all and told folks so every chance he got. The nickname stuck, and everyone, including Lucky, seemed to have forgotten his real name.

All of this Libby had learned from Amanda during that first year at the Blue Springs, but Libby didn't share any of the information with Remington as the wagon crested the top of the hill and the two buildings came into view.

"Pine Station?" Remington asked.

They were the first words either of them had spoken for over an hour.

She nodded, her throat still tight with warring emotions. She wished Remington had never asked about her parents. The questions had brought up too many memories, too many things she had tried so hard to forget. They had reminded her why she had left New York and why she could never leave Idaho or her ranch. She'd remembered, too late, why she'd never wanted to fall in love.

With a sinking sensation, she knew she'd been behaving the fool.

She glanced sideways at Remington and tried to tell herself she was mistaken about her feelings for him. It wasn't love she felt; it was simply loneliness.

But in her heart she knew the truth.

"Libby, ain't that Mr. Bevins's horse?" Sawyer asked from behind her.

She spied the piebald tied to the hitching rail in front of the saloon. "Yes. It's his horse." She drew back on the reins, almost glad to have Timothy Bevins to think about rather than the thoughts that had troubled her the past hour. "At least we know he's not at our ranch causing trouble."

When the wagon stopped, Libby set the brake, then looped the reins around the brake handle and hopped to the ground.

"Leave Ringer in the wagon," she told Sawyer as she headed for the door of the general store, not waiting for Remington or the boy.

There wasn't a square inch of the interior of the store that hadn't been put to good use. Only narrow walkways had been allowed between the display tables. The Jonases carried a little of everything. Folks hereabouts could make the trek into Weiser or even down to Boise City, if they chose. Or they could purchase their supplies from one of the mail-order catalogs. Walter Jonas was a shrewd enough businessman to try to keep his limited number of customers happy.

"Mornin', Miss Blue," Marian called from behind the back counter.

"Good morning, Mrs. Jonas." She wound her way through the display tables, silently rehearsing what she planned to say. Amanda had said that Marian Jonas could be a pain in the backside, but she was a decent woman at heart, even if she did fancy herself the moral watchdog of the area. Surely she would be willing to help Libby now.

"I figured it was 'bout time you were in for supplies." The plump, short woman offered a smile. "I could just about set my clock by Amanda's visits."

Libby nodded. "I know."

"I got plenty o' cornmeal and flour and salt." Marian turned toward the large sacks stored in the back corner. "Imagine you'll want a bit of sugar for the boy."

"Mrs. Jonas . . ." Libby paused, took a deep breath, then began again. "Mrs. Jonas, I need to talk to you about payment for the supplies. I was hoping we could put them on account. You see, we . . . we had a bit of trouble out at the ranch." She held herself a little straighter. "As soon as we can market some more of our sheep—"

"Sellin' off your sheep's gonna make it hard to keep the ranch goin', ain't it, Miss Blue?"

She twisted, surprised to find Bevins standing near the wall of canned goods, hidden in the shadows.

"Your herd's already been thinned down, from what I

hear. How're you gonna pay Miz Jonas if you're broke?"
His tone mocked her as he stepped forward, into the light
from the window.

Libby had thought Bevins was over at the saloon. She
wouldn't have been so frank with Marian if she'd known
he was there.

His smile was merely a sneer in disguise. "But then,
maybe you plan on marryin' that fella you got livin' in
your house with you."

Libby felt heat rise in her cheeks. "No, Mr. Bevins, I do
not plan to marry Mr. Walker." She lifted her chin. "Nor
do I intend to sell my ranch to you." She turned to find
Marian watching her with a disapproving expression.
Before she could explain the situation, the door opened
and Sawyer and Remington entered the store.

Everyone turned to look at Remington, and the air
became charged.

"And you with that boy staying with you," Marian
scolded in a low voice. "Have you no shame, Miss Blue?
What would Amanda think if she were alive?"

Libby knew exactly what Amanda would have
thought—and what she would have said to Marian at that
moment. However, she kept hold of her temper, saying
instead, "It's not like Mr. Bevins made it sound."

But Libby knew her protest wasn't believed, just by
looking at the prim set of the woman's mouth. She could
have explained why Remington was there. She could
have, but she didn't. She didn't want to explain anything
in front of Bevins, especially when the explanation would
be wasted.

Libby squared her shoulders. "I was asking about being
able to put some supplies on account. I'd be happy to
trade mutton, if you'd prefer."

"Mutton upsets my stomach, so I don't suppose we'd
have any interest in a trade."

Libby knew that was a lie. The Jonases had bought plenty of mutton over the years from Amanda Blue.

Marian glanced at Remington as he approached. "Besides, Mr. Jonas has decided we can't give credit right now. Money's short for everyone. I'm afraid we can't help you."

Libby heard Bevins's soft laughter but refrained from looking his way. "Thank you anyway, Mrs. Jonas," she said, managing to keep her anger and frustration from her voice as her thoughts raced. How was she to outfit her herders without those supplies? How was she to properly care for Sawyer?

But pride made her stand tall and not let Bevins or Marian see her despair. She wouldn't give either of them that victory, no matter how small.

She turned, found Sawyer, and said, "We'd best be on our way."

"But, Libby—"

"Please don't argue with me, Sawyer." Her resolve was disappearing, and she felt close to tears. "We've a long drive back to the ranch." She glanced toward Remington, uncertain what to say to him.

"I need to pick up a few things for myself," he told her. "Why don't you wait for me in the wagon? I won't be long."

She couldn't do anything but nod and hurry out of the store before Bevins succeeded in seeing her cry. She would rather choke on her own tears than have that happen.

Remington stared at Timothy Bevins as the door swung closed behind Libby and Sawyer. Bevins returned the look with a glare of his own, obviously hoping to intimidate. But Remington wasn't easily intimidated, especially not by the likes of Bevins.

It didn't take long to assess the man. Bevins was muscular and probably had plenty of brute strength. Remington guessed he also suffered from a short fuse and a blinding temper, serious handicaps in a game of wits.

As the seconds ticked by, counted off by the large clock sitting atop a high shelf, the corner of Bevins's right eye began to twitch. A light sheen of perspiration appeared on his forehead and upper lip. His weight shifted from one foot to the other, then back again.

"I suggest you keep away from Miss Blue and her ranch." Remington's words were deceptively mild.

Bevins's face turned red. "Who do you think you are, tryin' t'tell me what to do?"

"Who do *you* think *I* am?" Remington returned calmly.

Again, silence stretched between them. Remington waited it out without even a blink of his eyes. He'd known other men like Bevins, cowards who struck from behind, who picked only on those smaller or weaker than themselves. Bevins wouldn't take up Remington's unspoken challenge. He would turn tail, at least for now.

A few minutes later, just as Remington had expected, Bevins swore beneath his breath, then strode down one aisle and left the store, the door slamming at his back.

Remington felt only a small twinge of satisfaction as he turned to face the proprietress of the general store. "Good afternoon. I'm Remington Walker."

"Hmm." Even though she was short and had to look up to meet his gaze, she still managed to look down her nose at him. "I'm Mrs. Jonas. What can I do for you?"

"I need some supplies." His smile was congenial, carefully hiding his true feelings. "I'll be paying cash, of course."

He guessed, correctly, that Mrs. Jonas wasn't so offended by him that she wouldn't take his money. Fifteen minutes later he helped load the back of Libby's wagon with everything he'd thought might be of use to her.

14

"I shouldn't have let you do that," Libby said softly once Pine Station was behind them. "You shouldn't pay for our supplies."

"Why not?"

Her throat hurt. "Because I don't know when I'll be able to pay you back."

"I'm not asking you to pay me back." He reached out and covered her hand with his. "I'm sorry. About what Mrs. Jonas said, I mean."

"It doesn't matter," she whispered.

And it didn't matter, not the way Remington thought. She didn't give a plug nickel for what Marian Jonas thought of her. What mattered was how miserably she'd failed. What mattered was letting down the people who had counted on her. What mattered was not living up to Amanda Blue's expectations.

Amanda had given Libby a new life when she'd brought her to the Blue Springs. She'd given her a new identity. She'd taught her how to be free and independent.

And she'd trusted Libby enough to leave the ranch to her when she died.

And now Libby was losing it, little by little by little. Remington had saved her this time, but what would she do when he was gone?

Remington's fingers tightened around hers. "Libby . . . "

She blinked again, then turned her head to meet his gaze. But whatever she might have seen, whatever he might have said next, was interrupted by the crack of rifle fire. Dirt flew up in the road mere feet in front of the horses. In the next instant, the reins were torn from her hands as the team bolted into an uncontrolled gallop.

Libby screamed as the wagon hit a rut and bounced into the air, tossing her over the seat into the bed. She landed on her back amid the supplies, barely missing Sawyer's head with her boot. The air *whoosh*ed from her lungs, and pain shot up her spine. She thought she heard another gunshot, but she couldn't be sure over the thunder of horses' hooves and the rattle and bang of the wagon.

Grabbing hold of whatever she could, she pulled herself to her feet and looked for Remington. He was leaning forward on the wagon seat, reaching for the errant reins.

Libby envisioned him falling forward beneath the runaway wagon. "Remington, don't!"

He didn't seem to hear her. He rose, and her heart stopped as she realized what he intended to do.

"Remington!"

He vaulted forward onto the rump of one of the horses, his hands grasping the harness as his lower torso and legs bounced dangerously close to the flying rear hooves of the animal.

The wagon hit another rut, and Libby was tossed backward a second time. Her head smacked against a barrel. For a moment everything dipped and whirled, but she fought the dizziness as she righted herself again.

She couldn't see Remington. The wagon seat blocked her view of the horses. Had he fallen off? He wasn't strong enough yet. How could he possibly hold on? What if—

She scrambled to her feet, whispering his name as she tried to reach the front of the wagon.

The horses slowed their breakneck gallop, tossing Libby forward. She grasped the back of the wagon seat just in time to keep from falling yet again.

She saw him then, sitting astride the lead horse, pulling back, sawing with the reins, slowing the team. A rush of relief filled her heart, a feeling so profound it frightened her.

She glanced down at Sawyer. "Are you all right?"

"I'm okay," he answered.

"And Ringer?"

"He's okay, too."

She let out a sigh. "Good."

The moment the wagon stopped, she was over the side and hurrying toward Remington as he slid off the horse. She saw the way his leg buckled under his weight, saw him grab hold of the harness to steady himself.

"Remington," she whispered.

He looked over, then reached for her, pulling her close against him, pressing his face against her hair. "Are you all right?"

She nodded.

He kissed her cheek, then held her away from him as he searched her face with his eyes. "You're sure?"

"Yes."

His gaze moved to the surrounding trees and hillsides. "This is my fault. I shouldn't have intentionally provoked Bevins."

"We don't know it was him."

"*I* know." He looked at her once more, and he raised

his hand to cup the side of her face. His voice softened. "I'd never forgive myself if anything happened to you."

Her heart fluttered like the wings of a hummingbird, and she felt joy spreading a warmth through her body, a warmth like nothing she'd ever known before.

He cares. . . .

Remington read the swirl of emotions in her green eyes and knew his soul was damned for eternity. If there was a shred of goodness left in him, he would have let her be, but he couldn't.

Desire, torrid and unrelenting, flared through him. He wanted Libby as he'd never wanted a woman before. This went beyond mere physical hunger. It went deeper and burned hotter. She'd slipped inside his defenses undetected.

Damn you, Libby.

He cradled her face with both hands and leaned down to kiss her, unable to resist the temptation, too hungry for the taste of her. He played with her lower lip with his tongue until her mouth parted. He heard her small gasp of surprise as his tongue touched hers, felt a new jolt of desire as she turned her head slightly to receive him better.

She tasted sweet and warm. He could smell the fresh scent of the soap she used. She filled his senses, like water from the springs spilling into a bucket.

When at last they parted, both were breathing hard. Her eyes appeared sultry. Her cheeks were flushed. He watched as she lifted her fingers to touch her lips, as if she couldn't quite believe what had happened.

"You . . . you've never kissed me that way before," she said softly.

His body ached with wanting her. "With good reason," he replied darkly.

He saw understanding dawn in her eyes, saw her mouth form an O, saw her flush deepen.

Damn you, Libby, he thought again. But it was really her father he was damning. His own father, too. Damning the past that stood between them.

Remington took hold of her arm and turned her toward the wagon. "Come on. It isn't safe for us out here."

But would it be any safer for them back at the Blue Springs? he wondered, knowing that something irrevocable had happened there on the road from Pine Station, something that couldn't be forgotten.

"But you never married," Libby said as she curled her legs beneath her on the floor and leaned back against the wall.

"No, I never married," Amanda conceded, *"but it's not because I never fell in love."*

Libby was surprised by the confession, and she turned to look at the woman who had befriended her.

Amanda Blue's expression was soft and dreamy, and in the flickering light of the fire, she appeared younger than her fifty-five years.

"Tell me," Libby urged gently.

"His name was George. He was a ranch hand, a drifter, like most of his lot." She smiled. *"Lord, he was a handsome brute. Tall and broad, with hair as gold as the sun and eyes as blue as any you've ever seen. I'd never seen the like of George Stratford. I guess I fell in love with him right there on the spot, first time I laid eyes on him, though I'd've never thought he'd notice me, as plain a girl as ever was."*

"That's not true, Aunt Amanda."

Amanda looked at her and laughed. "Don't go tryin' to deny what any fool can see. Don't matter anyway, Libby, 'cause George didn't see me with his eyes nohow." She shook her head. *"George saw me with his heart."*

Libby waited breathlessly for the story to continue.

"That was one of the prettiest summers I can remember.

The days were long and warm without bein' hot. The grass grew high and stayed green from the rainstorms that'd blow through in the evening, then be gone by morning."

Amanda's voice grew softer, causing Libby to lean forward, straining to hear.

"Sometimes he'd make love to me up on the hillside, right in the middle of the day. Sometimes he'd come to my bed in the wee hours of the night. He had the gentlest hands. There's no words for what the joinin' of a man and woman is like, but I understand why the good Lord meant for it t'be. Because it makes a woman one with her man. I can't ever lose George. He's a part of me."

Libby felt suddenly as if she were eavesdropping, as if she were seeing something too private. She turned her gaze toward the fireplace.

"I know you think you don't ever want a man in your life, Libby, because of your pa, but when you meet the right man, you won't be able to keep him out. I don't regret one minute of the time I spent with George. Not one minute."

"Why didn't you marry him then?"

"Because he died before we could."

"Oh, Aunt Amanda." She glanced at the woman again and was surprised to find her still smiling.

"Don't feel sorry for me. I never felt sorry. Not once. Unless it's 'cause I never got to have his children. I think I'd've been a good mother."

Libby rose from her place on the floor and went to sit beside Amanda. "You've been a good mother to me," she whispered as she took hold of the woman's hand.

Amanda's gaze was unwavering as it met Libby's. *"Don't you cheat yourself, girl. Don't you hide from life and never experience the good it's got in store for you. Don't you dry up inside and become a bitter old maid."*

*　　*　　*

Lost in the past, Libby was surprised when the wagon slowed and she saw they'd arrived at the ranch.

"There'll come a day when you'll want a man's kisses," she heard Amanda saying. *"Mark my words, Libby. The day will come when you'll want kisses and more besides."*

Turning her head, she looked at Remington and truly understood what Amanda had been trying to tell her years before. Libby wanted to be a part of Remington. She wanted to know him as she would never know another. Even if he was with her only for a summer, even if she were never to see him again, she wanted to be a part of him, wanted him to be a part of her. Mere kisses wouldn't be enough. She loved him too much, and when he left, she wanted her memories to be as full as Amanda's had been.

Remington climbed stiffly down from the wagon, then turned and reached to help her after him. She took hold of his hand but didn't follow him immediately.

He lifted his gaze. His mouth was set in a grim line. She felt him pulling away from her again, as he always did. Her fingers tightened, as if she thought she could take hold of his heart and force him to love her.

"You'd better get inside, Libby," he said in a firm, emotionless tone, pulling his hand away the moment her feet touched the ground. "I'll take care of the horses."

"I'll help you."

He turned his back to her and moved to stand in front of the horses, cutting himself off from her view. "I don't want your help." His sharp words were like a slap.

"Remington, don't—"

"Do as I tell you, Libby. Get inside."

She felt the blood rush from her face, felt herself grow cold. "Remington," she whispered, her voice shaking.

A moment passed, then he stepped out where she could see him again. Their gazes met. Her heart cracked as she sensed him pulling out of her reach.

"I told you to get inside, Libby. Now do it."

"But—"

"Damn it, when I tell you to do something, you do it without arguing with me."

Cold fury momentarily overcame her heartache.

He's just like my father. . . . The thought left a bitter taste in her mouth.

"Remington . . . "

He stared at her, waiting for her to continue.

"You can go straight to hell." She spun around and hurried away.

That night Libby sat on the floor beside her dresser and stared at the miniatures inside the locket. She studied the hard, ungiving expression on her father's face, and she knew she'd been unfair to think Remington was anything like the man who had sired her. Remington knew how to laugh and how to care about others. She didn't think Northrop Vanderhoff was even capable of such things.

At least, never with her.

Her gaze shifted to her mother, to the sad-sweet expression on her face. That was how Libby always remembered her, sad and wistful. She couldn't help wondering what was wrong with the Vanderhoff women, why they couldn't earn the affection of husband and father, why Northrop had forsaken them for another woman and her children.

Did her father love his mistress? Did he laugh with his sons? It was hard for Libby to imagine it. No, not just hard—it was impossible.

Pulling her legs up close to her chest, Libby rested her forehead atop her knees and closed her eyes. It was all so terribly confusing. She didn't know what she believed anymore. She'd thought she wanted never to fall in love, never to marry, never to lose her freedom. She'd wanted never to give a man dominion over her.

Yet she knew she did love Remington, that she did want to be with him, that she would give herself to him willingly, for either a night or forever.

She knew she should still be furious with him for ordering her about, but she wasn't. She understood why he'd pulled away from her. He didn't want to hurt her when the time came for him to leave. And because of it, she couldn't be angry with him. She could only love him more.

Straightening, she looked down at the locket one more time, at the faces of her parents, at her only link to the past. She brushed the miniature of Anna with the tip of her finger.

"What should I do now, Mama?" she whispered. "What should I do?" Then she closed the locket.

She wrapped the keepsake in the tissue paper, then placed it beneath the dresses. After closing the drawer, she left her bedroom to wander through the silent house.

The fire in the living room grate had burned low, and the red coals cast eerie shadows across the walls. The wind had risen, causing tree limbs to brush against the side of the house, whispering mournfully. It all seemed fitting for her odd mood.

It wasn't until she neared the sofa that she realized she wasn't alone. She drew in a quick breath of surprise as she stopped in her tracks, staring at the dark shadow in the overstuffed chair.

"Sorry," Remington said. "Didn't mean to startle you."

"I thought you were in bed."

"My leg was bothering me."

She felt a sting of guilt as she settled onto the sofa. "I'm sorry. I wish . . ." She let her voice drift into silence. She didn't know what she wished, except that he would stay with her even when he was well, except that he might learn to love her, too.

"I helped myself to the whiskey in the sideboard," he told her, filling the silence.

"Is the pain that bad?"

"No," he replied, his tone harsh and abrupt.

In truth, it wasn't his leg but his conscience that was bothering him. Even three shots of whiskey hadn't managed to blur the image in his head of Libby being taken away from the Blue Springs Ranch by her father. The image was so real, almost as if it had already happened. And it *would* happen as soon as he sent his telegram.

"Why did you leave your home to come here, Libby?" he asked softly, wondering if he'd get a different answer this time.

"I was running away from my father."

The truth . . . For some reason, he hadn't expected the truth. He blinked, trying to see her more clearly. The hot coals on the hearth cast a red glow over her profile. The darkened room seemed perfect for the sharing of confidences.

"He wanted me to marry someone I didn't love, someone who had something my father wanted. It was a business deal. If I'd stayed, I would have had no choice but to marry that man. My father never loses. He always gets what he wants."

Remington could taste his own bitterness as he listened to her. No one knew better than he about Northrop's relentless determination to get what he wanted.

"It was always that way," she continued, her voice soft and distant. "My father ran everything in my life. He chose my friends. He chose my clothes. He decided what I would do and where I would go, every minute of every day. If he could have loved me, maybe—"

Libby's voice broke. A moment later Remington heard her draw a deep, ragged breath.

"I saw what that life did to my mother. I didn't want the same thing to happen to me. So I ran away. I came here to live with Aunt Amanda. I learned how to take care of myself. I learned how to make my own decisions. That's why . . . that's why I was so angry with you for ordering me about. I want to take care of myself."

Remington set his glass on the floor, then leaned forward, found her hand, and clasped it within his own, squeezing gently. It wasn't his intent to draw her toward him, but that's what happened. With a gentle tug, he pulled her from the sofa and onto her knees on the floor before him. He cupped her face between his hands and claimed her mouth with his, wanting to wipe from her memory the pain he'd heard in her voice.

This was the daughter of his sworn enemy, and he cared for her far more than he should.

As his mouth continued to tease and taste hers, he drew his right hand from her cheek, following the curve of her neck down to the gentle swell of her breast. He heard her startled intake of breath as he rubbed his thumb across her nipple, felt his desire grow harder.

This was the daughter of his sworn enemy, and he wanted her with every fiber of his being.

He could smell the clean scent of her hair. With his left hand, he freed the ribbon that tied the end of her long braid, then loosened the plait until the thick tresses hung freely down her back. Releasing her mouth, he trailed kisses across her cheek to her ear, where he nibbled her tender lobe before burying his face in her abundant rose gold hair.

This was the daughter of his sworn enemy, and he meant to betray her.

Holding her by the shoulders, he gently pushed Libby away from him. "It's late. We'd better get to bed."

He rose from his chair, a bit unsteadily—and unsure if it was from the whiskey or the heady taste of Libby Blue.

"Good night," he added, then forced himself to walk away without a backward glance.

After he was gone, Libby leaned forward and laid her head in the chair where Remington had sat seconds before. She closed her eyes and allowed herself to recall the riot of emotions that had flooded through her at his touch. She felt again the rapid beating of her heart, the tingling of her skin. She felt a tightening in her loins, a strange wanting that she knew could be quenched only by Remington.

She wondered, as the coals died and the house grew cool and dark, if anyone had ever died from wanting someone as much as she wanted Remington Walker.

15

Anna Vanderhoff let the delicate yellow silk fabric slip through her fingers. "It *is* lovely, Mrs. Davenport, but I never wear this color. My husband prefers something more . . . subtle."

"But it would be perfect on you, Mrs. Vanderhoff. With your eyes and your hair . . . Why, you could find nothing better."

The woman was right, of course. The yellow would have been perfect. She had worn this particular shade often when she was a girl, before her marriage to Northrop. The first time she'd worn it after their wedding, he had demanded she remove the dress and destroy it.

A tiny sigh escaped her as she pushed away the bolt of fabric. "No, I'm sorry. Please show me something else."

"Of course, Mrs. Vanderhoff." The dressmaker turned toward the doorway leading to the workroom. "Jeanette," she said to the young woman standing there, "please bring out some of the other silks."

While she waited, Anna's gaze returned to the forbidden

fabric, and she felt bitterness burning hot in her chest. Why *shouldn't* she have a yellow dress if she wanted one?

But she knew why. Northrop would simply send it back to Mrs. Davenport. He would never allow her to wear it. The color was too frivolous and completely inappropriate, he would tell her, just as he'd told her before.

The shop door opened, causing a tinkling of bells to sound behind Anna. Before she could turn to see who had entered, she heard Mrs. Davenport's gasp of surprise.

Anna twisted on her chair. The woman was a stranger to her. Tall and attractive, she appeared to be no more than thirty years of age. She wore a graceful gown of India silk, the black fabric brightened with a pattern of pink and yellow blossoms. Her dark hair was mostly hidden beneath a large straw hat trimmed with pink ribbon and pink- and cream-colored flowers.

Mrs. Davenport hurried toward her. "Good afternoon, Mrs. Prine," she said softly.

Mrs. Prine? Anna continued to stare. Was this Northrop's Ellen? If so, the "Mrs." was a lie, for Anna knew Ellen Prine was neither married nor widowed.

"I'm afraid your gown won't be ready until tomorrow," the dressmaker said as she placed herself directly between Anna and the other woman.

"But you sent word that—"

"I'm sorry. It simply isn't ready."

The last of Anna's doubts disappeared. Mrs. Davenport would not have responded so curtly if she weren't anxious to get rid of the woman, who was obviously a well-known customer. And that could mean only one thing: the woman was Northrop's mistress and, as such, an embarrassment to the proprietress at this particular moment. Anna rose and turned to get a better look at her.

Ellen glanced in her direction. Her eyes widened, and her back stiffened.

Anna understood the reaction. She felt herself stiffening, too, knowing she was looking at the woman who had stolen her husband for the price of two sons.

"Mrs. Davenport, why don't you check on that fabric for me?" Anna suggested, never taking her gaze off Ellen.

"Well, I . . ." The dressmaker glanced from one to the other, then scurried from the room without another word.

Anna stepped around her chair. "You must be Ellen. I'm Mrs. Vanderhoff."

"I know who you are."

"For some reason, it never occurred to me you might patronize Mrs. Davenport's shop, but I suppose it makes sense. This way, Northrop has only one bill to pay at the end of each month."

Ellen didn't reply.

Anna moved closer, studying the younger woman. She was, indeed, quite pretty. Anna could see why Northrop had been attracted to her. She had pale, flawless skin and a generous mouth, a long, slender throat, and a narrow waist. Her hair was a deep umber shade, almost auburn, but without quite so much red. She could have been no more than eighteen when she'd given birth to Northrop's first son.

"I suppose it's surprising we've never met before this," Anna said at last. "After all, thirteen years is a long time."

"Yes."

"Do you love my husband, Miss Prine?"

Ellen looked surprised. "Love him?"

"I've always wondered, and this may be my only chance to ask. I may be dead and buried before another thirteen years pass. *Do* you love him?"

"Why else would I stay with him if I didn't?" Her tone was defensive, haughty.

Anna laughed, a bitter, hollow sound, understanding a great deal that hadn't been said. "Why, because there is nothing else you can do? You are trapped as surely as I am, Miss Prine."

"My sons will inherit Vanderhoff Shipping when their father dies. He's promised me."

"Yes, I suppose they shall. But you haven't answered my question. Do you love Northrop?"

Ellen's color was high. "You're not better than me, Mrs. Vanderhoff. Northrop would have married me if he could have. If it weren't for you, I'd be living at Rosegate as his wife. No one would look down their noses at me then."

Anna lowered her voice. "You've paid an enormous price, haven't you? I am sorry for you. I'm sorry for us both." She turned and glanced toward the workshop doorway, certain the dressmaker and all her seamstresses were standing just out of sight, straining to hear the exchange between Northrop Vanderhoff's women. "Mrs. Davenport?"

She appeared almost instantly.

"I've decided on the yellow silk after all. Please have the dress sent to Rosegate when it's finished." She glanced once more at Northrop's beautiful young mistress. "Good afternoon, Miss Prine."

As the shop door closed behind her, accompanied by the tinkling bells, Anna wondered if she would truly have the nerve ever to wear the yellow gown. Then she decided she didn't care. She'd bought it. That was all that mattered to her at the moment.

It was time Remington sent his telegram to Northrop. It wasn't fair to Libby, letting her think there might ever be more between them than a few kisses. It wasn't fair to either of them.

He told himself she would be better off away from the

cares of this ranch, away from Bevins's threats. Let her father find her a husband. Surely marriage could be no worse than what she was enduring here, and it might possibly be better.

Besides, he belonged back in New York, too. He should be back there now, taking Vanderhoff Shipping apart, one piece at a time, and using Vanderhoff's own money to do it with. He belonged in the city, amid the frantic activity and hubbub. That was where he'd made his new life after his father's death, after Sunnyvale was lost. That was where his friends were. He belonged there.

He'd do well to remember that revenge had brought him to Idaho, not Libby's happiness.

Yes, it was time he sent his telegram to Northrop. He needed to go into Weiser right away, and it didn't matter to him that travel by horseback would be painful for his leg. It was more painful staying where he was. Each time he and Libby were together, he felt the weight of his betrayal on his heart. He kept hearing her say, *"Remington, you can go straight to hell,"* and he didn't doubt for a moment that he would. In fact, he thought there was a good possibility he lees living there now.

Having made up his mind to ride into Weiser at once, Remington went looking for Libby. He'd just opened the back door when a wagon, carrying a man and a woman, entered the yard. He saw Libby leave the barn and hurry toward them.

"Lynette. Pete." She greeted them with a smile, the first smile Remington had seen her wear in two days. "It's good to see you."

The woman returned Libby's smile. "Pete's going into Weiser for supplies. I thought I'd come by for a visit, if I won't be in your way. Pete can pick up anything you need from town while he's there."

"Of course you won't be in the way. I'd love some

company." Libby glanced at Pete. "Thanks for the offer, but there isn't anything we need."

Remington stepped forward into the morning sunlight. "I could use a ride into town."

All eyes turned in Remington's direction.

"This is Mr. Walker," Libby said in a strained voice as he came toward them. "He . . . he's been helping me around the place."

The man on the wagon seat leaned down, holding out his hand toward Remington. "Howdy. I'm Pete Fisher, and this is my wife, Lynette."

"A pleasure to meet you." He shook Pete's hand. "Would you mind if I came along with you? I need to send a telegram."

"Don't mind at all. In fact, I'd be glad for the company. It's a long trip into town."

"Thanks." Remington glanced at Libby. Her eyes were filled with a great sadness, a sadness for which he knew he was responsible. He hardened his heart to it. "I'll get my hat."

Lynette Fisher leaned back against the side of the house and took a sip from the glass she held in her hand. "That boy has grown half a foot since the last time I saw him," she said as she watched Sawyer playing with Ringer. "You've taken real good care of him, Libby."

"I've tried."

"You haven't just tried, and you know it. Lots of folks would've sent him to an orphanage. You've become a mother to him."

Libby smiled. "I *feel* like his mother. I love him very much."

"And what about that Mr. Walker?"

Her smile vanished. Her gaze dropped to the glass she

held between her two hands. *I love him, too,* she thought, but she didn't dare say it aloud. Not after the way he'd walked away from her, his rejection so clear.

"I thought maybe that's how it was," Lynette said softly.

"Is it so obvious?"

Lynette patted Libby's knee. "I've loved Pete for over twenty years. I know a woman who feels the same about her man when I see her."

"I wish you were wrong."

"Why's that?"

"Because he's not going to stay. He's got a place back in Virginia. He'll have to return there soon."

"What's wrong with you going to Virginia with him?"

A cold wave of panic swept over Libby. "I couldn't leave the Blue Springs. This is my home."

"That's how I felt about leaving Iowa. That's where I grew up. It's where I met and fell in love with Pete. It's where we had our first farm." Her voice grew quiet. "It's where our only child is buried." She looked once again at Sawyer, playing with his puppy in the yard. "But Pete had a yearnin' to come west, and so I came with him. We made this our home. I've never been sorry for that." Her gaze returned to Libby. "You could do the same."

But you weren't hiding from anyone, Libby wanted to say. *You didn't have to worry about what your father might do if he found you.*

She'd been safe at the Blue Springs. Her father's detectives hadn't found her there. She remembered only too well her narrow escapes as she'd fled from Manhattan. Chicago. St. Louis. San Francisco. His detectives had tracked her to each of those cities.

But they hadn't tracked her here to Idaho. They hadn't found the Blue Springs.

What if Remington loved me and wanted to marry me

and take me to Sunnyvale? she asked herself. Would I go then?

Her pulse quickened and hope lightened her heart, but it was swiftly dashed. Her father wouldn't let something as trivial as her marriage stop him from taking her back to Manhattan. She'd known him to destroy men's fortunes and lives for little or no reason. He would do the same to Remington. He might even do something worse.

No, she couldn't leave the Blue Springs. Not even if Remington asked her to—and he hadn't asked her.

Sadly she gave her head another shake. "I don't think he'll ask me to go with him, so it doesn't really matter if I'd be willing or not."

She took a sip of the cold beverage in her glass, feeling trapped for the first time since she'd arrived in Idaho. Bitterly she realized her father was still controlling her life, even when he didn't know where to find her.

Northrop Vanderhoff had won yet again.

Northrop opened the front door of the fashionable house, located only a few blocks from his office. A maid appeared quickly to take his hat and walking stick.

"Tell Ellen I want to see her at once in the drawing room."

"Missus Prine isn't at home, sir," the maid said in a meek voice.

"Not at home?" He fixed a displeased glare on the girl. "Where is she?"

"I . . . I don't know, sir."

"It's Thursday. She knows I always come for lunch on Thursday."

"Yes, Mr. Vanderhoff. I know, sir."

He headed toward the drawing room. "Then send the boys down to see me."

"Right away, sir."

Northrop went immediately to the sideboard, where he lifted the top from a decanter and poured himself a brandy. Glass in hand, he turned and swept his gaze over the room, noting the thick carpets on the floor, the large oil paintings with gilded frames on the walls, the groupings of upholstered chairs and sofas. The room was bright and alive with color, very different from the somber tones of Rosegate. He'd never been sure how he felt about Ellen's decorating, but since he came to see her only two times a week, three at most, it didn't seem important enough to ponder for long.

The door to the drawing room opened, and Northrop turned to watch as his sons entered.

Cornelius, at twelve, was the taller of the two. He'd inherited his father's auburn hair, although Northrop's had long since turned stone gray. Unfortunately he'd inherited little else from either his father or his mother. Cornelius was a remarkably homely boy, thin as a rail, and meek. Nothing could make Northrop angrier than seeing his elder son shrinking back from him whenever Northrop raised his voice. The one bright spot was that Cornelius didn't seem to be dim-witted in addition to his other shortcomings.

Ward, who would have his tenth birthday in two weeks, was quite the opposite of his brother. Short and brawny, with a face that was almost too handsome for a boy, he had a quick temper and an even quicker fist. He seemed to think with his emotions rather than his head, which was a constant source of irritation for his father.

"You wanted to see us, sir?" Cornelius asked as the brothers stopped, side by side, just inside the doorway.

"Yes. Come in and sit down." Northrop pointed to a couple of chairs. As soon as they had obeyed, he strode across the room to stand in front of them, clasping his hands behind his back. "Boys, I have decided that it is time for you to leave this house and attend boarding school. As you know, you are my sons, but I am not married to your mother. You no doubt have already been called bastards by your schoolmates. While the circumstances of your birth are not your fault, it is the truth, and you know people shall try to make you suffer because of it. But money can make people forget many things, including the circumstances of your birth and your mother's unmarried state. You may be bastards, but you shall be rich ones if you do as I tell you."

Cornelius's face grew sickly pale. Ward's turned beet red.

"I cannot have sons who grow up hiding behind their mother's skirts. You must get out into the world, fight your own battles." Northrop fixed Ward with a harsh gaze. "But I mean fighting with your head"—he pressed his index finger against his temple—"not with your fists. Do you understand me?"

Cornelius swallowed, making his Adam's apple bob, then nodded. Ward's eyes narrowed and his mouth thinned into a stubborn line.

"Ward?" Northrop prompted.

"You can't make us leave Mother all alone."

"You'll do as I say."

The boy jumped to his feet. "You can't make us!"

Northrop's own temper flared, but he kept a tight rein on it. What the boy needed was the feel of a man's belt on his backside. That would be just what this sort of behavior would merit at the school he'd chosen for his youngest son.

At that moment the drawing room door swung open to reveal Ellen, her face flushed. "Northrop, I'm so sorry to have kept you waiting. I had an errand to run, but I thought I would be home before—"

"Another frock, I suppose," he interrupted.

Ellen glanced toward her sons, then back at Northrop as she freed her bonnet and removed it from her perfectly coifed curls. "Mrs. Davenport sent word my gown was ready. The one I ordered last month. The blue one you liked so much." She smiled at him, trying to hide her uncertainty. "Shall I have Cook serve our lunch?"

"In a moment. First, I must inform you of my decision about the boys. I've decided to send them away to school. I have a couple of good boarding schools in mind. They should be ready to leave next week."

"Next week? But Northrop—"

"On second thought, tell Cook to serve lunch at once. I must return to my office."

"Northrop, please," she said softly. "Can't we talk about this?" She stepped toward him and placed the palm of one hand against his chest. She looked up at him from beneath a fan of thick eyelashes and tipped her head in a coy fashion.

It seemed Ellen would never learn that sexual favors were useless in persuading Northrop to do or not do whatever he wanted. Ellen was his mistress. She belonged to him. He could have her whenever he wanted her. Therefore the silent offer she had made was meaningless to him.

He gripped her wrist, intentionally squeezing until he saw the pain in her eyes. "No, my dear Ellen, we cannot talk about this. If you want your sons to inherit Vanderhoff Shipping, then you shall not interfere in how I choose to educate them. Is that clear?" He released her hand and turned toward the dining room. "Now, tell Cook we are ready to eat. I have work to do at the office and can't be wasting my time here."

16

Pete Fisher was a friendly fellow who seemed willing enough to carry the conversation in between Remington's monosyllabic responses. Remington was actually glad of the distraction. It kept him from dwelling on the task before him. And by the time the two men reached Weiser, he knew considerably more about Pete and his wife, about Amanda Blue and the Blue Springs Ranch, about Timothy Bevins, and about the folks who lived at Pine Station than he had when he'd left the ranch that morning.

"Whoa," Pete called to the team of draft horses as he pulled back on the reins, halting the wagon in front of the telegraph office. He looked at Remington. "I'll be over at the mercantile. I'll just wait for you there."

Remington nodded. "I'll be along soon." He climbed down from the wagon, feeling a bit stiff and sore after sitting for so long. He waited in the street until Pete drove away, then stepped onto the boardwalk. He paused again, staring at the door before him.

It's the right thing to do. Get on with it.

Dragging in a deep breath, he reached for the doorknob and, after turning it, stepped inside.

The clerk looked up from beneath his green visor. "How do. Can I help you, sir?"

"I need to send a telegram."

The clerk slid a pencil and a piece of paper across the counter. "Write 'er down, just like you want 'er t'read."

Remington picked up the pencil and stared at the blank paper for a moment, then began to write.

"Have found your daughter. Send word of your date of arrival to . . . "

He stopped and scratched out what he'd written, then began again.

"Have found Olivia. Meet me in Weiser, Idaho, on July . . . "

Again he scratched out what he'd written.

"Some folks have a hard time gettin' their words on paper," the clerk interjected as he set another blank sheet in front of Remington.

He nodded and tried one more time:

"Have found Olivia. She is well and happy."

Libby was well and happy . . . but she wouldn't be when her father came for her.

He saw her as she'd been two nights before, captured in firelight. He heard her confession. *"He wanted me to marry someone I didn't love, someone who had something my father wanted. It was a business deal."*

Would she be forced to marry once she returned to New York? Would Northrop barter his daughter a second time?

The thought of her being unwillingly wed caused his heart to twist. She had fought hard for her liberty. Had he the right to strip it from her? Could he hand her back to her father for thirty pieces of silver?

Of course, his payment for finding Olivia Vanderhoff was far more than the infamous biblical story of betrayal, but it made his own treachery no less palatable. Not now. Not now that he knew her. Not now that he'd held her in his arms and tasted the sweetness of her lips and felt . . .

He crinkled the paper in his hand, wadding it into a tight ball. "Sorry," he said to the observant clerk, "I need to try one more time."

When he had the clean slip of paper on the counter in front of him, he wrote quickly, decisively:

"Have been unable to find Olivia. If your daughter was ever in Idaho Territory, she isn't any longer. I've found no clues to her whereabouts and believe it is pointless to continue the search. I suggest you save your time and money and accept that she has vanished for good. R. J. Walker."

He shoved the paper across the counter. "Send it immediately," he said, then paid the clerk and left the telegraph office before he could change his mind again.

Gil O'Reilly waited while the hotel clerk studied the photograph of Remington Walker. Finally the man set it on the counter and met his gaze. "Yes, I remember him. He stayed here in the Overland, but it's been some time ago. A couple of months, at least."

"Did he say what his business was in Boise City or where he was going from here?"

"Are you a bounty hunter? Is he a murderer or something?"

O'Reilly shook his head as he let out a chuckle. "Sure and there's no truth in that, sir. Mr. Walker is a friend of mine, and I've important news for him. Trouble is, the man loves to travel and he's not much at correspondence, so I'm unsure where t'find him."

"You know, you might try Mr. Wilen over at the bank.

Seems to me I recall Mr. Walker havin' supper with him one night in the restaurant."

"I do thank you for your advice, sir." O'Reilly picked up the photograph and slipped it into his pocket. "I'll do just that."

Remington was grateful that Pete didn't seem inclined to be as talkative during the trip back from Weiser. He was too busy trying to figure out why he'd just thrown away two hundred and fifty thousand dollars. It was a veritable fortune. He could have had his revenge against Vanderhoff. He could have kept the promise he'd made in Jefferson Walker's memory. With that kind of money, he might even have been able to buy back Sunnyvale, made it his own once more. There was so much he could have done with that money, but he'd thrown it all away.

Why?

The answer, of course, was actually quite simple, once he was willing to admit it.

He couldn't betray her. He couldn't send her back to her father, not for any amount of money.

He loved her.

It seemed an impossibility, given who she was, given who he was, but it had happened nonetheless. He'd thought himself incapable of falling in love. Although he'd enjoyed the companionship of many women over the years, none had ever made him think of love, perhaps because he'd been too filled with anger and bitterness.

Libby had broken through the anger, through the bitterness. Libby had not only made him think of love, she'd made him feel it.

But what did that mean for them? She wasn't really Libby Blue. Her name was Olivia Vanderhoff. She had a wealthy, powerful father who was looking for her.

Remington couldn't very well take her back to New York. If—*when*—Northrop learned the truth, Remington's reputation as a detective would be destroyed. What future would they have if he had no means to support her? He knew only too well how the inability to provide could wear away at a man until he gave up on life completely. He'd seen it happen to his father. He wasn't going to let it happen to him.

And there was the matter of the lies between them. Could he ever tell her the truth? What would she do if she knew what had brought him to the Blue Springs?

He couldn't help grinning. She'd probably shoot me again, he thought.

But his smile faded quickly. He couldn't tell her the truth. He was afraid to tell her. He was afraid if he did, she would despise him, and he wasn't willing to risk losing her. Not now that he'd found her. Not now that he'd found love. Perhaps one day, after they were married . . .

His smile returned. Married to Libby. He thought of her quick temper, of the passion in her kisses, of the laughter in her green eyes, of the way she looked in the men's clothing she wore, of her tenderness with Sawyer. Suddenly he was filled with optimism. He didn't know how, but he was certain they would work things through.

His gaze lifted to the road before them, and he willed the team of horses to hurry. He wanted to see Libby.

Watching Libby wave farewell to Pete and Lynette, Remington wondered why he hadn't before seen the vulnerability that lay just beneath her independent facade. Or if he had seen it, why he hadn't recognized it for what it was. But there it was, and he wanted to understand it. He wanted to understand it, and he wanted to make it go away.

And there was so much more he wanted besides. He wanted to share her hopes and dreams. He wanted to shoulder the heavy responsibility she'd been carrying for so long. He wanted to see her smile when she awakened in the morning and again when she lay down to sleep for the night. He wanted so much. . . .

Libby glanced over at him, then away. "They'll never make it home before dark. Look how late it is already."

"Pete didn't seem in any hurry getting back. He must not be worried about it. Besides, the moon will be up soon."

A long silence ensued.

"It was good having Lynette here for a visit."

"They're a nice couple."

More silence.

Finally, in a small voice, Libby asked, "Did you send your telegram?"

"Yes."

A tiny sigh escaped her. "I suppose that means you'll be leaving soon."

"I'm in no hurry."

She looked at him again, this time her gaze lingering, and he saw a spark of hope alight in her eyes.

What reason could he give her for not going back to Sunnyvale? What new lie should he use to cover the ones that had gone before? And as much as he hated lying to her, he couldn't tell her the truth. Not yet. Perhaps not ever.

He moved to the corral fence, leaning on it as he looked at the grove of trees, wanting to change the subject until he could sort things through in his head. "I think you ought to cut down some of those trees. It would give you a better view of the road. You'd know sooner if someone was approaching. With the trouble you've had this past year, it seems like a good idea." He glanced behind him at

Libby. "You mind if I do some clearing? It would only take me a couple of weeks to make a real difference."

Libby's heart quickened. A couple of weeks. At least a couple more weeks before he went away.

"No," she whispered as she moved to stand beside him. "No, I don't mind."

He turned slowly and gazed down at her, and she was sorry for the gathering darkness. She wanted to be able to see the blue of his eyes more clearly. She wanted him to be able to see what she was feeling. She wanted him to know how much she loved him.

He pushed loose strands of her hair over her shoulder, then cupped one side of her face with the palm of his hand. She closed her eyes and leaned into his touch, letting her emotions peak and swell, like a storm on the Atlantic.

"Of all the women in the world," he said softly, "why is it *you* I want?"

She opened her eyes. He wanted her!

"Trust me, Libby."

She could scarcely hear him over the hammering of her heart.

His lips brushed the tender flesh near her earlobe. His touch caused gooseflesh to rise along her arm. Her heart beat erratically, and she wondered briefly if it might stop altogether.

But she didn't wonder for long. The thought vanished the moment his mouth moved to capture hers. Her legs felt weak, and she reached up with her arms and clasped her hands behind his neck, hoping to steady herself. But the action drew their bodies closer together, and the jolt of heat that shot through her only made her feel more unsteady than before.

I love you, Remington. Stay with me forever.

She felt his fingers in her hair, felt them freeing her

braid, allowing her hair to tumble down her back. All the while his mouth continued to ply hers with deep, long, long kisses that made her feel as if she were afire, as if she were melting.

I trust you. With everything I am, Remington, I trust you.

He drew one hand down her spine to her waist. She felt the gentle tug as he pulled her cotton shirt free of her trousers, felt the rush of cool air against her skin as he reached beneath it and her chemise. She sucked in a breath of surprise as his hand drifted upward.

In the same moment that he cupped her breast in his hand, running his thumb gently back and forth over the nipple, he lifted his mouth from hers and stared into her eyes. She did stop breathing then.

Everything stopped. Even the earth and the sun, the stars and the moon. Everything stopped dead still and waited.

The small voice of Remington's conscience warned him he was going too fast, that he should tell Libby who he was before his touch grew more intimate, before his kisses became more demanding. But he couldn't heed the warning. He loved her, and he wouldn't let anything come between them. Not even the truth.

He felt a shudder of desire move through her, and his own passion burned hotter. He longed to remove her clothing and make love to her.

Here.

Now.

His conscience be damned.

With one swift, smooth motion, he swept her up into his arms and headed toward the house, the last ounce of his control gone. He wanted her. He needed her. He had to have her. He was afire with the need to have her, to bury himself inside her and make her his.

Scarcely rational enough even to be thankful Sawyer was already in bed and asleep, Remington carried Libby into his bedroom and closed the door. Gently he lowered her to her feet, then kissed her, caressed her, heard the soft moaning sounds she made in her throat.

Lifting his head, he whispered, "I don't want to hurt you, darling."

In the shadowed room he saw her look up at him. "I trust you, Remington. I know you won't hurt me."

She trusted him.

She touched his cheek with her fingertips. "I love you," she added softly.

She loved him.

That was when he knew he had to stop. That was when he knew he couldn't make love to her tonight.

She trusted him. She loved him. And because of it, he couldn't take her to his bed. Not now. Not until things were set right. And he needed a clear head to be able to figure out just how to set them right.

As he closed his hands around her shoulders, a groan of frustration slipped from his throat. "I think you'd better get out of here while you can," he said tightly.

Although he couldn't see her face clearly, he could still sense her confusion. "But I don't want to go. I don't want to stop."

"Libby . . ."

"I didn't want to fall in love with you, Remington. I was afraid to love, afraid to trust. Not just you. I was afraid to trust any man." Her voice grew softer. "There's so much about me you don't know. So much you couldn't possibly understand."

There's plenty more you don't know about me, he thought. And if he was lucky, she would never know.

"But I *do* love you, Remington. I want to stay with you. I want you to make love to me."

He felt his control slipping and knew he was running out of time. He stepped backward, allowing cool night air to sweep in between them, swirl around them. Then he turned and opened the door. Holding Libby by the wrist, he drew her with him into the hall, not stopping until they were standing in front of her bedroom door.

Mustering the last dregs of his will, he gave her a chaste kiss on the forehead. "Good night, Libby."

As he walked away, returning to his own room and the night filled with frustration that would follow, he couldn't remember ever doing anything more difficult in his life.

But at least it had been the right thing to do.

17

With hands behind his head, Remington lay in his bed and watched as early morning sunlight fanned out across the ceiling. He'd been awake much of the night, his thoughts too unsettled to find sleep, his body still frustrated by unquenched desire.

It would have been so easy to bring her to his bed and make love to her all night long. She trusted him. She loved him. She had been willing and eager, and he knew he would have found great pleasure as he'd shown her the delights of intimacy and love.

It was for those very reasons he'd kissed her good night outside her bedroom door and walked away, despite his body's urging to do otherwise. Her trust, her complete and total faith in him, had forced him to act worthy of that trust.

Before he could make love to her, before he could marry her, he had to settle things back east. He had to close the door on the past. He meant to return the fee Northrop had paid him. It wasn't going to be easy to come up with that much money. He would have to liquidate many of his assets to do it. But he would have no need for his agency or his home in Manhattan once he married Libby. He realized that he didn't need that life anymore. He wanted to live here at the Blue Springs. He wanted their children to be born and raised here.

He would sell the shares in Vanderhoff Shipping that he'd purchased before leaving New York City. He wouldn't need them. For all he cared, Northrop Vanderhoff could become the richest man in the world. With Libby as his wife, Remington would be the luckiest. Once he'd rid himself of the old ties, once the money he'd received to find Libby had been paid back, he could marry her with a clear conscience. Once that was done, as far as he was concerned, Olivia Vanderhoff would no longer exist. He and Libby would start fresh and new.

He thought of his father then, and for the first time in years he didn't feel the bitterness welling in his chest. It was time to let Jefferson Walker go, to let him rest in peace. It was almost as if he could hear his father telling him that loving Libby was more important than revenge, far more important.

He wished he could leave for New York today. The sooner he went, the sooner he could return and marry Libby. But there was much he needed to do here first. He wanted to hire on a few hands. He couldn't leave Libby and Sawyer alone. No one else seemed to think Bevins was a real threat—not even after what had happened earlier in the week—but Remington wasn't about to take any chances.

First he would have the new ranch hands begin clearing the trees that surrounded the ranch house and outbuildings. He didn't want Libby taken by surprise again.

Then he wanted to meet McGregor. Maybe the old sheepherder could tell him what needed to be done to get the Blue Springs on a firmer foundation. Maybe when Remington was back east he could buy more sheep or some equipment that would be of help.

But he wasn't going to worry about any of that today, he decided as he tossed aside the blankets and swung his legs over the side of the bed. Today he was going to ask Libby if she would marry him. The rest they could talk about later.

Whistling softly, he dressed and left his bedroom, heading for the kitchen. Within minutes he'd stoked the stove, found a frying pan, and sliced bacon from the side of pork that hung from a hook in the smokehouse. Then he went to collect eggs from the chicken coop.

Libby's dreams throughout the night had been filled with Remington. She had dreamed of lying in his arms, dreamed of the way his hands felt upon her breasts, of the way her body burned with wanting him, of the way he'd called her "darling." She'd dreamed he'd told her he loved her and wanted to stay.

It was a beautiful dream, and she resisted giving it up.

When she did awaken, it was to the smell of sizzling bacon. It took her a moment or two to realize she wasn't still dreaming.

She sat up and stared toward her door. Someone else was cooking breakfast?

She tossed aside the bedcovers and reached for her wrapper. She slipped her feet into a pair of house shoes, then hurried out of her room and down the hall to the kitchen, stopping in the doorway to stare at the unfamiliar sight.

Sawyer was setting the table with Amanda's best plates. Remington stood beside the stove, flipping bacon in the pan and trying to avoid the splattering grease.

Sawyer was the first to see her. "Mornin', Libby."

Remington turned and gave her one of his heart-stopping smiles. "Morning, Libby." He tipped his head toward the table. "Have a seat. The coffee's ready." He glanced at the boy. "Sawyer, pull out the lady's chair for her."

"Yes, sir," Sawyer replied with an enthusiastic grin.

Maybe she *was* dreaming, she thought as she moved forward.

"What's this all about?" she whispered to Sawyer once she was seated.

The boy shrugged. "Mr. Walker didn't tell me," he whispered back.

Remington delivered a steaming cup of coffee, placing it on the table in front of her. "Your breakfast will be ready soon."

"Remington, what on earth—"

He wagged a finger at her. "I'll bet you thought I couldn't cook anything but a simple stew."

"Well, I—"

"At Sunnyvale, we always had grits for breakfast, but I noticed the Blue Springs doesn't stock it in their pantry." He clucked his tongue. "Serious oversight, Miss Blue. We'll have to remedy the situation, although I don't suppose the general store carries them, either."

She'd never seen him like this, and she wasn't certain how to respond.

"I hope you like your eggs scrambled."

"Yes, I . . ." She let her sentence die unspoken as she watched him crack eggs over the hot skillet and whip them vigorously with a fork.

She resisted the urge to pinch herself just to make certain she was awake. If this was a dream, she preferred to keep on sleeping. She was enjoying it too much to cause it to end. She liked watching him as he worked. She liked listening to him whistling. She liked the merry twinkle in his eyes. She didn't know what had brought it all on, but she was more than willing to enjoy it while it lasted.

"Your breakfast, mademoiselle," he said a few minutes later, brandishing the plate with a flourish before setting it on the table before her.

She stared at the fluffy mound of yellow eggs and the crisp slices of bacon and the warm bread spread with huckleberry preserves, and her mouth began to water in earnest.

"It's wonderful," she said, glancing up at him again, waiting for some sort of explanation.

He didn't give one. Instead he motioned for Sawyer to sit down, then followed suit. He pointed to Libby's plate with his fork. "Go on. Eat."

With an amused sigh she did as she was told, taking a bite of eggs.

"Well?" Remington prompted.

She swallowed. "They're very good." Then she grinned. "In fact, they're so good, Mr. Walker, I'm willing to offer you the job as cook at the Blue Springs."

His smile broadened. "That's a kind offer, Miss Blue, but I think there are other jobs around here which I could do better."

Her heart beat a staccato rhythm beneath her breast. Was he going to stay? Was he really going to stay?

She wanted to tell him again that she loved him, but she felt a sudden shyness. The words seemed too intimate to say in the light of day, especially in front of Sawyer.

But she soon forgot to feel shy and unsure of herself as Remington regaled her and Sawyer with stories from his boyhood. Libby got swept up in the joyous mood that filled the kitchen. She laughed as he detailed some of the pranks he'd pulled on the old servant who had raised him, and she shook her head when he confessed to some of the trouble he'd made when he was at school.

Before she knew it, the kitchen was ablaze with morning sunlight, and she realized what time it had gotten to be.

"Oh, dear," she said aloud. "Melly must be miserable. I completely forgot about her." She started to rise from her chair.

"Wait, Libby. Let Sawyer take care of the milking this morning. We need to talk."

Even the memory of laughter seemed to vanish, and her heart began to pound as she settled back into her chair. What was he about to tell her? Had all of this just been his way of saying good-bye?

Remington jerked his head toward the back door. "Go on, Sawyer."

"Yes, sir."

Libby could hear her pulse pounding in her ears as she watched Sawyer leave the table. When he closed the door behind him, milk pail in hand, the sound seemed to rumble through the kitchen like thunder.

Nervously she touched a hand to her hair, remembering belatedly that it was as yet unbrushed and that she was still wearing her dressing gown and house slippers. She flushed when she realized Remington was staring at her, the twinkle of amusement gone from his eyes.

"I . . . I must look a sight," she stammered.

"Yes." A gentle smile returned briefly to the corners of his mouth. "You *are* a sight, Libby."

Her heart overturned.

"You're the sight I'd like to spend the rest of my life with."

She couldn't have drawn a breath to save her soul.

Remington chuckled softly. "I guess I could have planned this better." His gaze swept over the dirty dishes that cluttered the table. "I should have at least picked some wildflowers."

"Wildflowers?" she whispered, confused.

"When a man proposes, he should give his betrothed a bouquet of flowers, don't you think?"

"Proposes?" she echoed, still not certain this was happening.

How could it be? Only yesterday she had hoped for a much smaller miracle. Only yesterday she had prayed for the faith to believe a miracle could be possible. She would have been happy for him simply to stay, to make her his lover. Nothing more. She'd dared not hope for more.

And now he was proposing marriage?

Remington rose and came around to her. Favoring his bad leg only a little, he got down on one knee, then took hold of her right hand. His gaze searched her face. "Will you marry me, Libby Blue?"

She looked down at their joined hands. Can this really be happening? she wondered. Can it be real?

"I'm not a wealthy man, Libby, but I'm not impoverished, either. I'll be able to provide for you. Together we can make the Blue Springs strong again. I have some . . . debts and . . . and other obligations that I must clear up. I'll have to go back east and settle matters before we can marry." His hand tightened around hers. "But if you'll say yes, you'll make me a happy man. I won't fail you."

It was too wonderful to be true. She was afraid she would awaken from this exquisite dream any moment.

He drew her toward him until she, too, was kneeling on the floor. He threaded his fingers through her tousled hair, then said in a whisper, "Marry me, Libby."

Dear God, don't let me ever wake up, she prayed.

"Marry me," he repeated.

"We would live here? At the Blue Springs?"

"Unless you want to leave."

She shook her head. "No. No, I want to stay." She swallowed hard, still feeling breathless. "What about Sawyer?"

"We'll be a family, Libby. The three of us. If that's what you want."

"Yes. Oh, yes, Remington. It's what I want. Yes, I'll marry you."

Then they were kissing, and Libby knew she'd never been so incredibly happy in all her life. She had never wanted to find love. She had never dared hope she would know such joy as Remington had given her.

Surely nothing would ever break the bond of trust that had blossomed between them.

Anna knelt on the lush lawn and attacked the earth with her trowel, turning the soil, cutting the weeds. She enjoyed the feel of the mild sun on her back, the smell of the freshly turned earth, the buzz of the bees as they hovered over budding flowers.

In another month the temperature would climb and the humidity would make being outdoors miserable. June was Anna's favorite month of the year to work in the garden. That was when she could watch everything coming to life again. The vibrant colors. The promise of new beginnings. Renewed hope.

The yellow silk gown had arrived that afternoon. Anna had placed it under her bed, still in its box. What was she going to do with it now? she wondered as she sat back on her heels and looked up at the sky.

The heavens were dotted with cumulus clouds. Like giant pieces of cauliflower, she thought.

She smiled to herself as she returned to work. She and Olivia had often played that game, trying to decide what the clouds looked like. They would lie on the lawn, mindless of grass stains on their dresses, and stare up at the sky, Olivia's head on Anna's stomach. Olivia would point and call out an animal or a bird or a country, and

Anna would always agree with her, even if she couldn't see it.

Of course, they'd never played such games when Northrop was around. Northrop didn't believe in filling a child's head with nonsense.

Olivia would have liked her mother's new yellow gown. *It's just the color for your hair*, she would have said.

"Oh, Olivia, I miss you so very much."

She drove the trowel into the ground with sudden anger. How could she have been such a fool all those years? Why had she allowed Northrop to be so cruel to his daughter? She should have left him when Olivia was still a child. She should have taken her daughter and returned to her parents. They would have taken her in.

But, of course, she'd had too much pride to admit how dreadful things were between her and her husband. She hadn't even admitted it to herself, not until after Olivia ran away. Only then had she allowed herself to look at what she had become.

"What I still am," she muttered, pausing once again in her work.

After Olivia disappeared, it had been too late for Anna to go. She'd already lost her daughter. Her parents were long since dead and buried. She had no money of her own, no place to go, and no one to go to. And a lifetime of habits were not so easily changed. She had continued being the wife Northrop had so precisely molded.

Suddenly she dropped the garden tool into her basket, followed by her soil-stained gloves, then lay back on the lawn, her arms stretched above her head as she stared at the sky.

"There's a horse!" she shouted. "And there's a giant strawberry!" Then she laughed, but it was the laughter of an anguished heart.

Fleetingly she thought that if Northrop were to see her now, he would have her confined to an institution. Perhaps that was what he'd been after all these years. To drive her mad. Maybe he wanted to be rid of her, and this was his way of going about it.

But she knew it wasn't true. Northrop was proud of his wife. She had the background, the breeding, that a man needed in a wife. She was able to entertain and socialize with men and women who were important to Northrop, if only for his ego.

No, if he'd wanted to be rid of her, he would have done so. Northrop was ruthless in getting what he wanted. He always had been.

She thought of the telegram that had arrived from one of Northrop's detectives. He'd failed, the man had stated in it. He hadn't found Olivia. He'd advised Northrop to give up the search.

But she knew Northrop wouldn't give up. He was not a man who ever accepted defeat. He would keep searching for Olivia, until the day he died if it took him that long. The cost was irrelevant to him. It was only winning he cared about. Winning—and the blind submission of his wife and daughter.

"Good for you, Olivia," she said aloud as she stood up. "You've beaten him. Stay hidden. Don't ever let him find you."

I'd rather never see you again than have him hurt you, she finished silently.

Then she picked up the basket with her tools and gloves in it and walked back toward the house.

18

"*This is silly,*" *Libby protested* as she watched Remington toss the saddlebags over his shoulder. "Why should you move into the bunkhouse?"

"Because things have changed. I'm no longer an invalid who needs tending."

"But what difference does that make?"

Remington gave a humorless chuckle. "It makes a difference to me. I can resist temptation only so far."

As their gazes met, she could see the swirl of emotions in the stormy depths of his eyes.

"I want to do this right, Libby. I've done a lot of things over the years that maybe I'm not so proud of. This, I want to do right. I don't want Mrs. Jonas to be able to talk about you."

She let out an exasperated sigh, loving him for caring about her reputation even as she wanted to tell him she didn't care what Mrs. Jonas said. She wouldn't have been ashamed to take Remington to her bed. She wanted him to touch her, to ease the burning desire that swept through her whenever he was near. She wanted to discover all the wonderful intimacies that she was certain awaited her.

"I still say it's silly," she muttered, aching to touch him, to kiss him, to begin the discovery.

Remington dropped the things he was carrying and pulled her into his arms before she knew what was happening. He lowered his head until their gazes locked and their foreheads were nearly touching. "Go easy on me, Libby. I'm only a man."

Her mouth went dry, and the room started spinning around them.

He swore softly. "Don't look at me like that."

"Like what?" she whispered.

He swore again, then kissed her, crushing her up against him. Sensations exploded inside her, like a lightning storm on a hot summer night. She wrapped her arms around his neck, threaded her fingers through the hair at his nape, opened her mouth to his, reveled in the desire and passion.

Remington broke the kiss as quickly as he'd begun it, setting her away from him with a gentle but firm motion. "Miss Blue, we'll be married first," he said, his voice hoarse.

Suddenly Libby felt giddy with power. She couldn't help the smile that curved the corners of her mouth. "Then let's go to Weiser and get married. Today."

His eyes darkened. His voice strengthened. "We can't. I already told you I've got to settle my affairs back east before we can be married."

"But—"

"Libby, this is the way it needs to be."

There was something in his tone of voice, something in his eyes, that kept her from arguing with him anymore. "All right," she agreed. "If it's so important to you."

"It is."

She wanted to ask him why it was important. She wanted to ask what affairs he had to settle back east. She felt a sudden shiver of fear as a seed of doubt took root in her heart. There was so much she didn't know about him, so much he'd never told her, and now she was afraid to ask. What if he didn't return to the Blue Springs? What if his affairs back east kept him there, perhaps forever? What if his love for her wasn't strong enough to bring him back?

Drawing a deep breath and putting on a smile for courage, she said, "I'll get the bucket and mop. No one has stayed in the bunkhouse for two months. It's bound to be filthy out there."

Silently she pledged to make him love her so much that he couldn't stay away. Whatever was taking him from her wouldn't be able to hold him for long. She would make sure of that.

They spent several hours sweeping and dusting and mopping the bunkhouse. Libby doubted the single-room building had ever been this clean before, certainly not when the herders and shearers had been in residence.

When they were through and the bunk he'd chosen had been made up with fresh linens and a blanket, Remington suggested the three of them go for a ride so Libby and Sawyer could show him the rest of the ranch.

"It will do me good," he said before Libby could protest about his leg. "I've been idle too long."

With the sun high overhead, they saddled their horses and rode out together.

The slope of the mountain was steep, causing the horses to lunge as they made their way up to the plateau. Remington could feel the strain on his wound as he stood in his stirrups and leaned forward over Sundown's neck. But when they reached the top, he decided the climb had been worth a little discomfort.

The plateau, with its bluff that fell suddenly away, provided a panorama of the surrounding countryside. The lowlands were wide swaths of green grass, a ribbon of water winding down the center. The mountains were rugged and heavily wooded. From this vantage point he could see the rooftops of the house and barn at the Blue Springs.

"Look at the birds in that tree!" Sawyer shouted. "There must be a hundred of 'em."

Remington and Libby watched the boy as he ran across the clearing, stopping beneath the tall pine. The mossy arms of the tree danced as blue jays, dozens of them, hopped from limb to limb.

Remington's gaze shifted to Libby. She was wearing a soft expression, one of tender loving, one that reminded him of her mother. Anna Vanderhoff had worn a similar expression when she'd told Remington about her missing daughter.

He suddenly wished he could tell Libby what her mother had said, about the love that had shone so clearly in her eyes, about how much Anna longed to see her daughter.

She turned her head and found him watching her. Smiling, she gave a little shrug. "I guess that isn't why we rode up here, but I've always liked watching Sawyer play." She faced the bluff and pointed with her arm. "That's Bevins's spread over there. The house doesn't look like much from here, but it's as close as a person gets to a mansion in these parts. I think Bevins fancied himself a country gentleman when he had it designed. You'd never guess it was built for a bachelor with no children."

Far in the distance he found the large white house, set up against a hillside.

Turning and pointing again, Libby continued, "That's the Fisher farm down there, near the creek, and over that ridge is Pine Station."

"How much of this land belongs to the Blue Springs?"

"From there"—once more she pointed—"on up to the pass through those mountains is officially our land. But the flocks are only here for a few months of the year. Mostly at lambing and shearing time. We summer in the upper valleys toward the lake country. For a good portion of the winter, we take them farther south. Not that we have to worry as much about the feed situation, now that our flock's so small."

"We'll buy more sheep."

"There's no money for that. Not after losing the wool crop. We'll just have to stop selling lambs to be butchered and rebuild the flock that way."

Remington heard the weariness in her voice. Tenderly he laid his arm around her shoulder and drew her up against his side. "We'll work it out."

She looked up at him, and he could see realization dawning in her eyes. "I don't have to do this alone, do I?"

He shook his head.

Her expression was puzzled. "I never wanted anyone's help. I planned on running this ranch alone for the rest of my life. I planned on making all my own decisions."

"I'm not going to take over," he reassured her, understanding what had gone unsaid. "It's still your ranch. We'll do it together."

Libby laid her head against his shoulder. "I wish you didn't have to go. I don't want to be here without you. Not even for a few weeks."

He heard the uncertainty in her voice, knew that she was wondering what was so important for him to return to. But there wasn't anything he could tell her. At least not yet. The time wasn't right. Maybe it would never be right.

Tightening his arm, he said, "You won't be here alone. I plan to hire some more help before I go."

"We can't afford any more hands."

"You let me worry about that for now. I've got enough to pay their wages for a few months. That includes McGregor and the other shepherd."

"Ronald Aberdeen," she supplied. "But Remington, I can't let you—"

This time he pulled her around to face him, tipping her head back so their eyes could meet. "Maybe *you* can't, Libby, but *we* can. This is our future. Yours and mine and Sawyer's. We're in this together, and we'll make it work together."

Tears glistened in her eyes, and it was as if he could look into her past, could see how frightened she'd been at times, how lonely. He wanted to make her forget it all. He wanted to make everything perfect for her from this day forward.

She gave him a tremulous smile.

He kissed the tip of her freckled nose. When he straightened, he said, "Now, Miss Blue, we've got some plans to make. When is it we need to take those supplies up to McGregor?"

"Soon . . . but, Remington, your leg. Are you sure you should—"

He grinned. "Are you always going to fuss over me like this, Libby?"

Whatever she might have answered was silenced by a sudden cry of alarm from Sawyer. Remington and Libby whirled toward the sound and saw a cloud of dust rising above the rim of the bluff.

"Sawyer!" Libby raced toward the edge.

Remington was only a step behind her. He grabbed hold of her arm, then looked down. His gaze quickly found Sawyer. The boy was clinging to a large tree root that protruded from the cliff, and it looked as though he'd found a toehold on a narrow ridge just below him.

"Sawyer! Are you hurt?" he called down.

It took the boy a moment to tip his head back and look up. "N-no. I . . . I d-don't think s-so."

"Hang on. We'll get you out of there." He glanced at Libby. She was as pale as bleached sheeting. "Sit down," he told her, afraid that if she didn't, she would be the next one to tumble over the side of the cliff. Once she'd obeyed, he hurried toward Sundown. He removed the rope from the saddle, then led his horse back to the ridge.

"Sawyer, I'm going to make a loop in the rope and lower it down to you. You grab hold of it and put it around you, under your arms. Okay? Do you understand?"

"Uh-huh."

"Remington," Libby whispered, fear crystallizing in her voice.

He didn't allow himself to look at her as he twisted the rope, tightening the knots, testing them several times. He secured one end around the pommel of Sundown's saddle, then stepped toward the edge again and looked over.

"Here comes the rope, Sawyer. Don't try to grab for it. Let it come to you. . . . Okay. It's just above your right shoulder. Let go with one hand and take hold of it. . . . Sawyer? Can you hear me?"

"I . . . I can't l-let go."

As if to accentuate the problem, the ledge holding Sawyer's feet began to crumble, tiny pebbles tumbling away.

Libby reached out and grabbed hold of Remington's hand. "He's too frightened. He can't move." She got to her feet. "Bring up the rope, Remington. You'll have to lower me down after him."

"You!" He turned his gaze on her.

"Yes, me," she replied, the fear gone entirely from both her expression and her voice. "Whether you admit it or not, you still need to be careful with your leg. Besides, I'm a good deal smaller and lighter than you. It'll be easier for you and Sundown to pull Sawyer and me up."

He wanted to refuse her. He wanted to tell her he forbade her to go down the side of that cliff, risking her life. But he couldn't because he knew she was right.

Libby leaned forward. "Hang on, Sawyer. I'm coming down for you. Just hold tight."

The hemp rope pinched the flesh beneath her arms through her shirt as Libby was lowered over the side of the bluff. Her heart pounded in her ears, and she felt short of breath. And if she was this frightened with a rope tied safely around her, she could just imagine how much more terrified Sawyer must be, clinging tenaciously to that insubstantial root.

She forced herself to sound calm. "I'm almost there, Sawyer. Can you see me?"

"Yeah. Yeah, I c-can s-see you, Libby."

"Good. Just keep your eyes on me and don't be afraid."

She continued to walk down the face of the rocky cliff, her hands tight fists around the rope. It had never occurred to her before what a slender thing a hemp rope was. How could it be expected to support not only her weight, but Sawyer's, too? She reminded herself that a rope like this could stop an angry steer or a wild stallion, but it didn't help much.

Again she managed to disguise her own fear when she spoke. "Here I am, Sawyer. I'm right beside you."

The boy stared at her, bravely trying to make a joke. "I've just been waitin' for you, Libby."

"I know you have." She gave him an encouraging smile. "Now, I'll tell you what we're going to do. I'm going to wrap my arms around you like this." She slipped her arms around his chest, clasping her wrists at his back. "Now, you let go of that root and grab hold of the rope. . . . Go on. Let go. I've got you."

She'd just begun to wonder if he would do it when she felt his weight shift into her arms. Without her instructing him to do so, he grabbed her around her waist with his legs, easing some of the strain on her arms.

"Pull us up, Remington!" she shouted.

She forced herself not to look at the rope, knowing how weak it would seem to her. Nor would she allow herself to look up, because she knew the distance to the rim would seem at least twice as far as it actually was.

An eternity later, her gaze moved from the rocky face of the bluff onto the flat surface of the plateau. She saw Remington as he led Sundown away from the ridge and knew no sight had ever looked more wonderful to her.

"We're here, Sawyer," she whispered, giving the boy a little push to shove him onto the ground. A moment later she lay beside him, hugging him to her, this time in relief. "Don't you ever frighten me like that again, Sawyer Deevers. You understand me?"

"I won't."

She freed her iron grip on him and sat up. Remington had joined them and was kneeling on the ground nearby.

"You all right, Sawyer?" he asked.

The boy nodded.

Remington turned his gaze on Libby. "You?"

"I'm fine."

Then he pulled her into his embrace, whispering, "You're an amazing woman, Libby Blue." He kissed her, then added, "Let's go home."

19

"*Damnation!*" *Northrop bellowed* as he stared at the telegram in his hand. Then he stormed out of his office, striding quickly to the sitting room. He found Anna with her needlework in hand.

"When did this come?" he demanded.

Her eyes widened. "What is it, Northrop?"

"Don't play innocent with me, Anna. You know damn good and well what it is. It's a telegram from Mr. Walker, and it was buried beneath the papers on my desk. Papers I placed there days ago."

Her voice softened to a weak whisper, but her gaze never wavered from his. "I'm sorry, Northrop, but I really don't know what you're talking about. Perhaps it arrived while I was in the rose garden."

His eyes narrowed. There had been a time when he'd known if she was hiding the truth from him. And if she was hiding the truth, he could frighten it out of her with a raised voice alone. But lately . . .

"All women be damned!" he hollered, thinking not just of Anna, but of Ellen and Olivia.

He folded the telegram in half, then folded it again. She wouldn't beat him at this game, he thought as he turned his back on her. Anna was mistaken if she thought she could best him.

And so was Olivia.

His daughter would return to this house, and she would do the dutiful thing as his daughter. Her disobedience had cost him a small fortune in fees to incompetent detectives. It had cost him the railroad he had so desperately coveted. Worse yet, it had made him the laughingstock of his peers, although they were wise enough never to let him see their amusement.

He swung around to face his wife. "I *will* be obeyed," he growled at her.

Anna shrank back in her chair, as if fearing he would strike her. But there were more enjoyable ways to torture Anna than with the back of his hand.

He took a few more steps toward her and waved the folded telegram in her direction. "Don't fool yourself, Anna. Olivia will be found, and she'll be sorry she defied me." He shoved the paper into his pocket.

Anna's cheeks lost all color. "Let her go, Northrop. Let her be happy."

"Happy?" He laughed sharply but without humor. "Are you saying I can't make my own daughter happy?"

Two more steps carried him to her chair. He reached down and pulled her to her feet. When he gripped her by the upper arms, he could feel her tension.

"Are you saying I don't make *you* happy, Anna dear?"

Her eyes teared as his grip on her arms tightened. Triumph made him feel hot, powerful. Lust flared suddenly to life. He would take her up to her bedchamber and teach her a lesson about how a wife was meant to find happiness.

"Northrop." She looked straight into his eyes, not trying to pull away, her shoulders squared, her tears gone, her voice calm but firm. "Let go. You're hurting me."

He was taken aback by her demeanor. It was unlike Anna to stand up to him. Surprising even himself, he released his hold on her arms.

She stepped away from him immediately. "Good night, Northrop. It's late and I'm tired." With calm elegance she picked up her embroidery basket. "Don't come to my room tonight. I have a dreadful headache and shall be fast asleep by the time you retire."

Don't go to her room? He couldn't believe she'd had the gall to say that to him. If he wanted to, he damn well *would* go to her room. He would damn well do whatever he wanted in his own home and with his own wife. It was his right. And it was her role to do as he bade her, when he bade her.

But for some reason the desire to bed his wife left him. Another time, perhaps, he would teach her the lesson she so badly needed to learn, but not tonight.

Remington, Libby, and Sawyer set out for the sheep camp early in the morning, a few days after Sawyer's fall. While they were gone Pete Fisher had agreed to keep an eye on the place, milking Melly and feeding Misty and her puppies.

They rode hard, leading pack horses loaded with supplies for the herders. Remington had insisted his leg was well enough to withstand the ride, but by late afternoon Libby could see the discomfort etched in his face when she glanced his way. She knew he would never be the one to decide to stop for the night. He would say to continue, hoping to reach the camp before nightfall. But Libby doubted they would. It had been nearly a month since her last trip up here, and the flock would have pushed farther north and east by this time.

Her mind made up, Libby reined Lightning to a halt. "I think we'd better stop for the night."

"How much farther is it?" Remington asked as he drew up beside her.

"At least another five hours. We can't make it before nightfall, and I don't want to attempt to find McGregor after dark, not even with a full moon."

Remington's gaze swept the area. Then he pointed to a spot not far off the trail. "That looks like a good place to make camp."

With a nod, Libby nudged her gelding forward, leading the way up the gentle slope of hillside to the chosen campsite. She dismounted as soon as she reached the level area, sheltered by an outcropping of rocks on one side and offering a vista of the valley below. With easy, practiced motions she unsaddled Lightning.

Out of the corner of her eye, she noticed the way Remington favored his leg as he stepped down from the saddle. She saw him grimace as he rubbed his thigh.

She shouldn't have let him come, she thought. She should have ridden up to the camp alone.

But then she imagined the argument they would have had if she'd tried to tell him he couldn't come with her, and she shook her head. He was a determined man. If she'd learned nothing else about Remington, she'd learned that much. She supposed it was even one of the things she loved about him.

As she pulled two cans of beans from the saddlebag on the pack horse, she allowed her thoughts to drift back over the past six weeks, marveling at all that had happened to change her life. Did love happen like this for everyone? she wondered. Did it take them by surprise, almost against their will? Did it swallow them up, consume them, make them forget everything else?

That's what it was like for her. It was a glorious discovery, a miracle, that she could feel this way about a man. Even Remington couldn't possibly understand just how amazing it was.

She glanced across the camp and watched Remington and Sawyer hobble the horses and turn them out to graze.

Perhaps one day she would be able to tell Remington everything. Perhaps one day she would be able to tell him about her father and mother, about a girl named Olivia Vanderhoff who no longer existed. About how he'd taught her to love and to trust.

Perhaps one day . . . but not now. She didn't want to spoil the present with old memories and heartaches.

Later that night, with a full moon rising over the eastern mountains and the heavens scattered with winking stars, Remington lay on the ground with an arm behind his head, staring upward. He didn't think he'd ever seen a sky as beautiful as this one. Looking at it, he could believe anything was possible.

Long ago, when he was about seven years old, he and his father had camped out under the stars. Jefferson had been home from the war only about two months, and Remington had been so excited about the excursion with his father.

There were little things he remembered so clearly about that night. The sweet smell of jasmine and the croaking of bullfrogs. The honey cake Naomi, their cook, had baked for him. The musty smell of the tent his father had pitched, just in case it rained. How thin his father had been, and the sadness in Jefferson's eyes as he'd looked at Sunnyvale and commented on how it needed a coat of paint.

He wished he'd spent more nights like that with his father. He wished he'd let his father know that he'd loved him before it was too late. Their time together had been so brief, and he could never get any of that time back again.

He wouldn't make that mistake with Libby. He wanted to tell her every morning that he loved her. He wanted to tell her every night how much she meant to him. Once he'd settled things with her father, he would be free to do so. He'd be free to make her his wife, to hold her and love her, to watch her grow large with his child inside her, to maybe slip away and lie with her under the stars on a summer night just like tonight.

He turned his head and looked at her. She was sleeping on her side, her head resting on her arm, her knees drawn up toward her chest. Soft moonlight caressed her face, erasing the freckles on her nose and the worry that so often filled her eyes. Her rose gold hair was silvered by the moonlight. Wisps had pulled free from her braid and curled about her ears and face.

Lord, she was beautiful.

He longed to pull her into his embrace, shelter her from the night chill by nestling her against the curve of his body. He wanted to hold her and protect her.

And he wanted to love her.

Desire flared to life with surprising swiftness, burning hot in his loins. He knew she would welcome his lovemaking. He had seen it in her eyes many times, her willingness, her love.

Her love . . .

That was the reason he wouldn't take her now. And not just because of her love for him, but also because of his own love for her. He wanted things right between them when he took her to his bed. He didn't want Northrop's specter hanging over them when the time came to make her his own.

Libby opened her eyes and met his gaze, as if she'd known he lay there watching her. A gentle smile bowed her mouth. A provocative mouth, he realized now. A mouth that was made for kissing.

Unable to keep himself from it, he reached out and drew her toward him. She came willingly, sliding across the blankets spread on the ground, moving from hers and onto his. She lay against him, both of them fully clothed, her head on his shoulder.

"What were you thinking?" she whispered.

"I was thinking how beautiful you are."

She tipped her head back, bringing her mouth a hairbreadth from his own. "I never wanted to be beautiful. Not until I met you." She let out a soft breath, almost a sigh but not quite. "You've taken away so many fears, Remington. I will love you forever, if only for that alone."

His lips brushed hers as he said, "You don't have to be afraid, Libby. Not ever again. I promise."

Then he kissed her, silently swearing to himself that this was one promise he would never break.

20

Remington liked Alistair McGregor from the moment they first shook hands. Short of stature and wiry, McGregor had a tanned face, weathered by years out in the elements, thinning dark hair streaked with gray, and an ironlike grip. His gaze was direct, unwavering.

"So ye're still here, Mr. Walker," McGregor said. "I thought ye'd be gone when yer leg was mended." The shepherd sounded like a suspicious father.

"No," Remington answered. "I plan to stay."

"Is that so? And why is that, if I might ask?"

Remington glanced at Libby, then back at McGregor. "I've asked Miss Blue to marry me."

McGregor's expression didn't change in the least as he turned toward Libby. "And ye've said aye, lass?"

She nodded.

"Would ye mind tellin' me why?"

"Because, McGregor, I love him."

The smile curving the shepherd's mouth was infinitesimal. "Then I'm glad for ye. 'Tis a celebration we'll have tonight. Can ye tell me when the blessed union is t'take place?"

Remington put his arm around Libby's shoulders. "I've got business to settle back east, but I hope it won't take me more than a couple of weeks. Then I'll be on the next train headed west. We'll marry upon my return."

"'Tis good news. I've longed t'see this lass happy, and it seems ye've done it. Come an' rest a moment an' tell me all about yerself, Mr. Walker."

In the next few minutes Remington told the Scot what he could, then ended by saying, "I'm open to suggestions on what I can do to be of help to Libby. How can we keep the Blue Springs the best sheep ranch in the territory?"

"Ye could stop that thievin' coward of a man, for starters," McGregor said with a frown. "'Tis a string of bad luck we've had this year. 'Twill take time and a change of that luck t'make the Blue Springs strong again."

McGregor didn't need to explain who the "thievin' coward of a man" was. Remington knew.

McGregor grinned as he looked at Libby. "But 'tis not the time for such talk now. Ronald will be wantin' t'hear yer news, lass. He willna forgive us if we tarry any longer."

The proprietress of the Pine Station general store took only a quick glance at the photograph before handing it back to Gil O'Reilly. "Yes, I've seen him. He was here in my store not more than a week ago. Stood right there where you're standing now." She lifted her chin, her expression disapproving. "I wouldn't be at all surprised to learn Mr. Walker's in trouble with the law. Is that why you're here?"

"No, madam, 'tis not. Mr. Walker is a friend of mine." O'Reilly offered a friendly smile. "Would it be too much trouble t'ask where I might find him?"

"He's at the Blue Springs Ranch. And heaven only knows what he's doing there." She clucked her tongue. "And her with that boy living under her roof, too. It's disgraceful. Positively disgraceful. That's what it is."

O'Reilly did nothing to stop the flow of information. Since Mrs. Jonas seemed in the mood to talk, he would let her.

"Shameful." She shook her head. "Libby Blue should have sold that ranch after her aunt died. It's not proper for a young, unmarried woman to be living out there without another woman present, not with all those men working for her. Not that there's so many men around these days, you see, not with the hard times she's had." She pursed her lips for a moment, as if she'd suddenly sucked on a lemon. "And she doesn't fool me that Mr. Walker is working for her, either. I've been told he's livin' in that house with her. Not in the bunkhouse, mind you, but livin' right in that house with her and doing God only knows what."

O'Reilly shook his head and made some sounds of agreement.

"Well." The woman drew herself up stiff as a board. "You can surely see why I don't think much of your friend."

"That I can, madam, and I'll see what I can do t'spirit him away from this Jezebel's clutches." Again he gave her a smile. "Now, if you'll be good enough t'tell me how t'find this ranch, I'll be on my way."

A few minutes later O'Reilly walked out of the general store with a definite lightness in his step. If his instincts were right—and they usually were—he'd not only found Remington Walker, he'd found Vanderhoff's missing daughter.

But Remington had found her first. So why hadn't he sent word to Vanderhoff? From all O'Reilly had been able to ascertain, Remington had been in the area for nigh onto two months. Surely he hadn't only just discovered Olivia Vanderhoff.

Maybe he was wrong. Maybe this woman, this Libby Blue, wasn't actually the Vanderhoff girl after all. But if she was, why had Walker remained silent?

O'Reilly stepped up into the small black buggy he'd rented in Boise City. Once settled on the seat, he picked up the reins and clucked to the horse, starting down the road in the direction of the Blue Springs Ranch, curious to see what he would find when he got there.

Remington frowned thoughtfully as he listened to McGregor telling him about the business of sheep ranching. He wondered if he would get enough money from the sale of his home and other assets to clear himself with Vanderhoff and still have the necessary funds to help put the Blue Springs back on firm footing. He'd better have enough. He'd promised Libby he would take care of her, and he was bound and determined to keep that promise.

"Teddy!" Libby shouted, drawing Remington's attention.

She was standing on the opposite side of the meadow where the sheep were grazing. Her hat had been pushed off her head and was hanging against her back from its leather string around her neck.

She whistled and motioned with an outstretched arm, and a dog took off in that direction. Remington's gaze followed the black collie as it raced quickly up the hillside after several recalcitrant ewes. Teddy darted back and forth, keeping the sheep together, pushing them just enough to move them down the hillside, but not so much he caused them to bolt, his actions precise and lightning quick.

When the ewes had rejoined the flock, Remington's attention returned to Libby. He heard her words of praise to the sheepdog, but it was Libby herself who earned his own silent admiration.

It couldn't have been easy for her, these past years. She had been raised in ease and opulence. One of her ball gowns would have probably paid a sheepherder's salary for an entire year, if not for two. There had to have been many times of adversity, of hardship. But through the years she had molded herself into the woman he saw before him—capable, independent, determined.

Her father would be scandalized if he could see her now.

The thought made him grin. He'd grown so used to seeing Libby in trousers and boots, her hair in a braid, a wide-brimmed hat flopping against her back, that he thought nothing of it. Northrop Vanderhoff and all the Knickerbockers be damned! She was exquisite just as she was. God knew, he would do anything to keep her safe, to protect her, cherish her. He would love her until his dying day and beyond. Of that there was no question.

As if she'd read his thoughts, Libby looked up, her gaze catching his from across the meadow. She smiled when she found him watching her. Even across the distance that separated them, he could see the trust and love in her eyes.

A spark of dread ignited in his heart. If ever she should learn what had brought him here . . .

He shoved the thought away and returned her smile. The moment he'd fallen in love with Libby, he'd become someone else. She needn't know why he'd come to the Blue Springs. It wasn't important. Only the future mattered. His future with Libby.

Pete Fisher sat astride his draft horse. The animal's pace was plodding at best, and Pete's mind wandered aimlessly, as if keeping time with the horse's gait.

Pete was tired after a long day in the fields. All that was left was to milk Libby's cow and feed the dog and her pups. Then he could go home, sit down to supper, and call it a day. Of course, tomorrow morning, before dawn, he would be riding back to the Blue Springs to repeat the chore, but he didn't really mind. He owed a lot to Libby Blue—and to her aunt before her. Without the water from the springs, the Fishers wouldn't have a farm to work. And he knew if Bevins ever got hold of Libby's ranch, the creek would dry up quicker than a keg of cider at a barn raising.

After meeting Remington Walker, he suspected he needn't worry about Bevins. Remington seemed the sort of man who rarely failed in what he set out to do. Bevins wouldn't be able to make any more trouble at the Blue Springs, not now that Remington and Libby were getting married. Pete would bet the farm on it.

"Guess that's exactly what I'm doing," he muttered. "Betting the farm."

As he crested a rise, he could see the rooftops of the house and barn above the grove of trees that surrounded the Blue Springs Ranch. He also heard the muffled but persistent barking of the dog, and he knew instantly something was wrong.

He kneed his horse, forcing the animal into a bone-jarring trot, and rode down the hillside and into the trees. Just as he broke into the clearing, he saw a man leave the house.

"Hey!" he shouted.

The stranger looked over his shoulder, then hopped into the buggy and whipped the horse into a gallop, disappearing almost instantly around the side of the house. Pete gave chase, but he knew it was pointless. The intruder's horse had already carried the buggy beyond view.

He returned to the yard. Misty, shut up inside the barn, was still barking. He dismounted, then opened the barn door.

"Misty, quiet," he commanded, hoping the dog would recognize his voice. When she obeyed, he reached down and patted her head. "Come on. Let's see what he was up to."

Pete searched the house but found nothing out of order, beyond the broken latch on the back door. He had no way of knowing if anything was missing; that would have to wait until Libby and Remington returned. But he had no doubt that Bevins had had something to do with the break-in.

He couldn't know how wrong he was.

The campfire had burned low and Remington had just drifted off to sleep when the dogs began to howl and bay. Remington and Libby were on their feet instantly. They exchanged a quick look, then reached for their rifles.

The rising moon was cresting the mountains in the east, spilling a soft white light over the grazing land, but Remington couldn't see anything except sheep and trees as he moved cautiously forward. Then, above the din of barking dogs and bleating sheep, he heard an unfamiliar sound that made the hairs on the back of his neck stand on end.

Suddenly Libby bolted past him at a dead run.

"Libby, wait!" he shouted, but she didn't even break her stride. He took off after her.

The sheep parted before them like water breaking before the bow of a ship. From across the meadow he saw McGregor running, too.

Another bloodcurdling cry split the night air just as Libby came to an abrupt halt. She raised her rifle and took aim. Remington's gaze followed the direction of the weapon's barrel.

Although he'd never seen one, he knew immediately that the animal crouched over a dead ewe was a cougar.

He'd heard stories about the great mountain lion of the American West. Now he knew those stories were true.

As the dogs darted toward the cougar, it swiped with its mighty paw, barely missing them. At the same time it let loose another scream of protest.

"Teddy, get back!" Libby shouted at the most persistent of the dogs, but Teddy didn't obey. Time and time again the collie rushed forward, and time and again he narrowly escaped the giant cat's deadly claws. "Teddy, get back! You're in the way!"

Sensing Libby's anxiety for the dog's safety, Remington raised his own rifle, closed one eye, and stared down the barrel. He waited until Teddy had darted forward and backed away again, and then he fired. His aim was sure. The mountain lion fell with a thud onto its side.

Teddy's barking ceased as he eased forward, sniffing suspiciously. Remington understood just how the dog felt. He wouldn't relax until he was certain the cougar was dead. He moved forward slowly until he reached the mountain lion. He poked it with the barrel of his rifle, then lifted its head by the scruff of its neck and let it fall back to the ground. Reassured that the danger was over, he turned around.

By this time Libby was kneeling on the ground, hugging Teddy and another of the dogs. Her gaze fell on the sheep near Remington's left foot. The ewe's throat had been torn open, and blood had turned its fleece a bright red.

Libby looked up at him, and he could see the moon's reflection in her eyes. "Life is so very fragile out here," she said softly.

"Life is fragile everywhere, Libby." He knelt beside her.

She laid her head against his shoulder. "Sometimes I don't think I'm strong enough to handle it."

He placed his finger beneath her chin and forced her to look up at him. "You're the strongest woman I've ever known, Libby Blue." He kissed her forehead. "Don't ever doubt that about yourself."

She was silent for several heartbeats before she said, "I won't doubt it, Remington. Not as long as you're with me."

"I'm with you. I always will be."

As she stared up at him, Libby couldn't help thinking that this was no hapless eastern dude, as she'd thought on the day she'd shot him. This was a man who could fell a mountain lion with a single shot. This was a man who showed no fear, even when in danger.

Who are you really, Remington Walker?

The thought was sudden, unexpected, but valid.

He could be loving, passionate, stubborn, infuriating, tender. He had a wonderful laugh and a heart-stopping smile. He was a gentleman, a businessman, a man with polish and style, yet a man completely at ease as he milked a cow, whipped up breakfast in a crude kitchen, or helped build a chicken coop.

Who was he really?

Libby realized how little either of them had talked about their pasts. She knew why she had kept silent, but what were his reasons? Did he have secrets of his own?

As quickly as the doubts and questions had come, she pushed them away. There was only one thing she needed to know—that he loved her.

And she loved him.

Nothing else mattered to her now. Nothing else would ever matter to her.

So she told herself.

21

Weary and dusty, Remington and Libby returned to the ranch four days later. Sawyer had asked Libby to let him stay with the sheepherders for a few weeks, and since McGregor hadn't minded, Libby had given her permission. Remington might have voiced an objection if he hadn't intended to hire a couple of hands before leaving for New York. He didn't want Libby alone at the ranch while he was away.

Lengthy shadows spread before them as they rode into the yard at the Blue Springs. Remington had just spied Pete Fisher's big black draft horse when Pete came walking out of the barn, milk pail in hand.

"Glad to see you back," he called to them as he set the pail on the ground. Coming toward them, he removed his hat and wiped the sweat from his brow. "Did you have any trouble on the trail?"

"No trouble," Remington responded, guessing by their neighbor's expression that Pete didn't have the same thing to report. "What about here?"

"I'm not sure."

Remington dismounted. "What does that mean?"

"Someone broke into the house. As far as I can tell, nothin's gone. I'd take credit for runnin' the intruder off, but he was already leavin' when I got here."

"Was it Bevins?" Libby asked as she stepped down from her saddle.

"No, wasn't Bevins. But I didn't get a good look at his face. Nobody I knew, from what I could see. He was wearin' a hat pulled kinda low and he was gone soon as he saw me." He shrugged. "Wasn't any way I could catch him."

Remington glanced at Libby. "You'd better check inside, see if you can tell what he was after." As Libby walked away, he turned back to Pete and asked, "Could it have been a drifter just after something to eat?"

"Could have been, I suppose, but I haven't seen many drifters drivin' buggies around the country."

"A buggy," Remington murmured. A buggy was an odd choice of transportation for someone intent on breaking into a house. He was fairly certain neither Bevins nor any of his cowpokes would come by buggy to perform mischief.

Pete tugged on his hat brim. "Well, I'm gonna head on back to my place. Lynette's probably got supper on by this time." He pointed to the pail on the ground where he'd left it. "I got the milkin' done and fed the stock. Dogs, too."

"Thanks, Pete. We're grateful for your help."

"Nothin' Libby wouldn't have done for me if I needed it. Always been good neighbors, the Blues. Amanda was the salt of the earth, and Libby's a lot like her. Like I said, glad to help. Just let me know if you need me again."

"We'll do that."

Remington waited until the farmer had mounted his big workhorse and ridden away, then picked up the milk pail and carried it into the house. Libby was standing in the kitchen, hands on her hips. She was frowning, deep in thought.

"Nothing," she muttered. "There's no evidence that anyone was here. I've checked all the valuables. Nothing's missing. And nothing seems to be gone from the pantry, either." She turned to face him. "Why would someone break in and then take nothing? Pete said he was already leaving, so it wasn't like the man was surprised or chased away. What could he have wanted?"

"I don't know." Remington placed a hand on her shoulder, his own gaze moving around the room. "But I don't like it."

Northrop looked down at the telegram in his hand. It was dated June 25, 1890, three days before. He'd read the message many times since receiving it, each time relishing the information more than the time before. And tomorrow he would be on a train bound for Idaho. Until then he savored the sweet taste of victory.

His eyes skimmed the telegram again, picking out what was most important to him.

"*. . . have located not only Mr. Walker but your daughter . . . will remain in Weiser, Idaho, until you arrive . . . send any instructions to me, in care of the Weiser Hotel . . . Gil O'Reilly.*"

Northrop folded the telegram and returned it to his breast pocket. At dinner tonight he would break the news to Anna. Then he would see how defiant she felt.

A chorus of crickets greeted the night as darkness spread its blanket over the Blue Springs. Inside the house, Libby stood beside her bedroom window, staring in the direction of the bunkhouse, her arms crossed over her breasts as she tried to ward off the eerie feeling that had lingered throughout the evening.

Someone had been in her room. Someone had gone through her things. She could find no evidence that he'd been there, but she knew he had. Not simply because Pete Fisher had seen him leaving, but because of an unsettling aura within the house, within her room. She couldn't explain what she was feeling. She only knew it was real—and frightening.

She'd hated it when Remington had gone out to the bunkhouse for the night. She'd wanted to ask him to stay with her. She'd wanted to plead with him not to leave her alone. What difference could it make? she'd wanted to ask him. They'd just spent several nights on the trail together. What could it matter if he stayed with her now?

But she hadn't asked him, because she'd begun to sense how important it was to him that they marry before he made love to her. And if he'd stayed in the house, without Sawyer there to serve as a deterrent, she'd known she would have gone to his room and joined him in his bed. A sixth sense warned her she would have regretted that. Not for herself, but for Remington.

But, oh, how she missed him. She'd grown used to having his arm around her. She'd grown used to having him pull her close during the wee hours of the night. She'd even grown used to the feelings of longing and frustration that had accompanied those sleepy embraces. They'd been worth it just to be so near him.

An uneasiness enveloped her heart, a dark foreboding. She remembered how this very same foreboding used to come upon her, the sense that she would soon be discovered, the urge to run, to change her identity, to conceal herself. It had been years since she'd felt it, yet it was as familiar as hunger pangs in the morning or the need to yawn when she was sleepy. Only years ago she'd been able to run. She'd been able to find a new place to hide. But she couldn't run any longer. Whatever the danger, she wasn't going to run again.

She closed the window and let the curtains fall into place, then turned around. For what must have been the twentieth time, she searched the room with her gaze, trying to find some clue, something out of place, but everything seemed as it had always been.

Why had he been here, the intruder? Why had he come if not to steal something of value, either real or sentimental? All of Amanda's costly paintings were in their proper places. The coins in the earthenware jar hadn't been taken. Nothing was out of place in her bureau drawers.

It was as if he'd never been there.

But he *had* been there. She felt his presence still, and she was afraid of what it meant.

Standing against the wall of the bunkhouse, Remington watched as Libby shut her bedroom window, then saw the curtains close, hiding her from view. He let out his breath, not realizing until that moment that he'd been holding it.

It had taken all his resolve to leave the house. He'd known she'd wanted to ask him to stay with her. He was glad she hadn't asked. He wasn't sure he'd have been able to deny her.

Maybe he should forget going back to New York. Maybe he should just keep Northrop Vanderhoff's money. Maybe he should marry Libby now. What difference would it make?

His gaze moved over the moonswept landscape, looking for any sort of movement that would indicate something amiss.

What difference would it make? he asked himself again.

But the answer wasn't easily explained. He simply knew that he had to be clean of Northrop's money before he could make Libby his wife. He didn't want to owe Northrop anything when he made love to Libby for the first time.

Making love to Libby.

He'd imagined it so many times, it had nearly become a reality to him. He could see her rose gold hair fanning across the white pillow. He could see her perfect breasts—small, rounded, and firm. He could see the curve of her narrow waist, the swell of her hips, the creaminess of her skin, the length of her legs. He could taste the desire in her kisses, see the passion burning in eyes of pale green.

Remington swore as he pushed away from the wall and paced to the other corner of the bunkhouse.

He hadn't lived as a monk. He'd known the favors of the gentler sex over the years. But never had thoughts of a woman possessed him as thoughts of Libby did now. She was like a fever in his blood, and it angered him. He needed his thoughts to be clear. He needed his wits about him if he was to protect her. He couldn't be imagining her body beneath his when he was supposed to be watching out for her safety.

He swore again as his gaze searched the black shadows that were the trees surrounding the house and yard. He couldn't make out a thing in their inky midst. Anyone could be out there, even now. As soon as they hired more hands for this place, he was going to set them to work felling trees. He wanted to be able to see trouble coming, not be taken by surprise.

A wave of uneasiness swept through him.

Someone had been at the Blue Springs while they were gone. Someone had broken into the house. Why? What had he been after? And who was he? The most likely suspect was Timothy Bevins, even though Pete had said it

wasn't. He hoped Pete was wrong about that. He hoped
Bevins was behind the break-in, because if he wasn't . . .

Remington set his mouth in determination and looked
at the house again. A light still burned in Libby's room,
and he wondered if she was as sleepless as he. Then he
sank onto the bench near the bunkhouse door, resting his
rifle on his thighs, and prepared to watch through the
night.

Anna's eyes felt like sandpaper. After Northrop had left
her bedroom, wearing that ugly, triumphant smile of his,
she had wept until her tears were used up. She felt empty
and beaten.

He'd found her. He'd found Olivia, and tomorrow he
would go for her. He would go bring her back—drag her
back in chains if he had to—and God only knew what he
would do then.

For several weeks Anna had been able to imagine she,
too, could break free of Northrop. Her daughter's victory
had given her hope. But hope for what? She had no
money of her own, no other family, no place to go. She
had spent her life seeing to Northrop's every need,
responding to his every whim. Being the proper, obedient
wife of Northrop Vanderhoff was all she knew how to do.

She tossed aside the bedcovers and sat up. She wished
it weren't so late. She wanted a bath. She wanted to try to
wash away Northrop's touch. She wanted to rid herself of
the feel of him, the smell of him.

She knelt on the floor and reached beneath the bed,
drawing out a large box. She removed the lid and stared at
her yellow gown, still wrapped in tissue paper.

For a brief time she'd believed she could wear the
dress. For a brief time she'd believed she could defy
Northrop.

She felt like crying again, but there were no more tears. She was dried up, like a well in a drought. She was dried up and about to blow away in a wind.

She leaned down until her face was hidden in the folds of the yellow dress. "Run, Olivia. Please run." Her voice fell to a whisper. "God, help her."

But faith was buried beneath despair, and she couldn't find the strength to believe her prayer would be answered.

22

With a hot summer sun burning overhead, Remington cantered Sundown toward the Bevins spread. The three-story whitewashed house, set up against the rise of a mountain, was easy to see in the distance. He suspected he was just as easily seen and was no doubt being watched.

The valley that cradled the Bevins ranch was long and wide, with thickly treed mountains forming the borders. Blue Creek cut a winding swath through the center of the valley floor. Brown-and-white cattle grazed peacefully in the tall yellow-green grass, creating a picturesque scene right out of an artist's rendering.

As Remington drew near the house and outbuildings, Bevins stepped onto the wide veranda that bordered two sides of the house. Remington reined Sundown to a walk, guiding the horse up close to the covered porch. He didn't dismount after stopping. Instead he tipped his hat slightly back on his head so Bevins could see his eyes. He wanted to make sure the man understood what Remington was about to tell him.

Bevins spoke first. "I'm surprised to see you here, Walker."

"I thought it was about time I paid you a visit." Out of the corner of his eye, he saw a couple of men step out of the barn and lean against the corral fence, watching and listening. "I wanted to ask your help."

"My help?" Bevins was clearly surprised.

"Yes. You know Miss Blue's been having a rough time of it this past year, but lately she seems to have had more than her share of trouble."

Bevins's face grew dark. "What's that got to do with me?"

"Nothing"—Remington leaned on his saddle horn—"I hope." He paused a couple of heartbeats, then continued, "I just thought you might keep an eye out for strangers, vagrants. You know the type. Troublemakers."

"You're takin' a mighty personal interest in that ranch of Miss Blue's."

"That's because it's about to become my ranch. Miss Blue and I are getting married." Any pretense at polite conversation disappeared from his voice. "And as her husband, I mean to protect both her and what's ours. I'm not going to stand for any more sheep mysteriously disappearing. There won't be any sheds burning down in the middle of the night. There won't be any runaway horses on the Pine Station road. And I won't tolerate anyone lying about my wife. Whoever's behind the trouble she's had in the past had best stop or it'll be me they answer to."

Bevins's hands closed into fists at his sides, and his face grew red with anger. "What're you accusin' me of, Walker?"

Remington raised an eyebrow, feigning innocence. "I'm not accusing you of anything. Just passing along some information to a neighbor."

"Yeah, well, you can pass it along to someone else. It don't mean anything to me."

Remington straightened in the saddle. "I guess it's time

I got back to the Blue Springs, anyway. There's plenty of work to do. Too much for one man, as a matter of fact. That's why I went down to Weiser last week and hired on some extra hands. They'll be helping me keep a close eye on the place." He backed Sundown away from the porch, then tugged his hat brim, shading his eyes once more. "Good day, Bevins."

He touched his spurs to Sundown's sides and rode away at a lope, confident that Bevins had received his warning and hopeful he would heed it.

Libby stood outside the front door and watched as the hired hands felled another tree in the grove. The tall lodgepole pine fell to the ground not quietly, but with a great deal of cracking and splintering and a jarring thump at the end. A cloud of dirt rose from the dry earth, briefly obscuring the men from view.

She knew Remington was right about thinning out the trees for a better view of the surrounding valley, but it still hurt to watch them fall. The grove of aspens, cottonwoods, lodgepoles, and tamaracks had always made her feel more protected than endangered. They had been her shelter from the world when she'd first come to the Blue Springs. They had hidden her from view, not kept her from seeing out.

The sounds of axes biting into another trunk filled the air, and with a sigh Libby turned and reentered the house. She made her way back to the kitchen and began preparations for supper. The new ranch hands would be hungry after putting in such a hard day. Besides, she wanted to prepare something special for Remington. This might well be his last night at the Blue Springs for some time.

He hadn't actually told her he would be leaving tomorrow, but she knew it would be soon. He'd had his talk with McGregor, obtained the sheepherder's advice. He'd hired on more men, both to work around the ranch and, she knew, to keep an eye on her in case there was trouble while he was gone. And now he'd paid his visit to Bevins.

Her hands stilled in midair as a shiver ran up her spine. She'd dreamed of Bevins last night. She'd dreamed he'd grabbed hold of her arm and wouldn't let her pull away. He'd told her she'd lost, that everything was his. His fingers had pinched the flesh on her arms, and he'd laughed as she'd tried to pull free. "You can't escape me," he'd said. "You can't get away."

And then the face and the laughter had changed, and she'd found herself looking into the face of her father. "You can't escape me," Northrop had repeated. "You can't get away."

She closed her eyes and leaned against the worktable, trying to drive the image from her mind. It was a silly dream. Bevins couldn't hurt her and her father couldn't find her, and she wouldn't allow either of them to give her any more nightmares.

Outside, another tree came crashing down, and Libby felt a second shiver of fear, the cause of it nameless, faceless, and, therefore, all the more potent.

Northrop settled back in the plush, velvet-covered chair of the Vanderhoff car, listening to the now familiar *clackety-clackety-clackety* of wheels upon rails. There was something satisfying in the sound. Or perhaps the satisfaction came from knowing where the train was taking him.

If the train kept on schedule, he would be in Weiser by nightfall. Tomorrow he would confront his daughter for the first time in nearly seven years.

Olivia would be surprised when she saw him, but only a little. She had to know he'd been searching for her all these years. She had to have feared the day of discovery, almost from the moment she'd bolted. She couldn't have forgotten that her father had never been bested, not in his business affairs or in his personal ones. And he sure as hell wasn't going to be bested by his daughter.

He struck a match and lit his cigar, holding it between thumb and forefinger as he drew on it.

By damn! He loved winning.

He exhaled a long breath of bluish gray air, watching the smoke curl in thin wisps as it rose toward the ceiling of the rail car. Then he frowned, his thoughts turning to Remington Walker, the detective he'd hired over ten months before. He wondered again why Walker had failed to report finding Olivia. Had he thought to hold out for more money? If so, he was about to regret it, for now he wouldn't receive a penny of the bonus Northrop had agreed to pay him, nor would he get the remainder of his quite sizable fee.

"Let her go, Northrop. Let her be happy. . . ."

His frown deepened to a scowl as he remembered the night Anna had made that plea. Only it wasn't her words that angered him. It was the spark of defiance he'd seen in her eyes.

Let Olivia be happy? By the gods, she'd be happy when he damn well told her to be happy. He wouldn't allow disorder or rebellion. Not in his business life. Not in his personal life. He *would* be obeyed.

His frown turned to a smug grin.

He had taught Anna a new lesson of obedience before he'd left New York City. He expected it was a lesson his wife wouldn't soon forget.

A night breeze moved softly amid the treetops. A branch from a tall pine swept its needles back and forth against a windowpane. The house creaked, then was silent; creaked, then was silent. A log in the stove shifted and crumbled, stirring up new flames, and the sound filled the kitchen like a boom.

Libby looked across the table at Remington, feeling that same, unshakable fear squeezing her chest. "Tomorrow?" she whispered.

"The sooner I go, the sooner I get back." He took hold of her right hand and held it between both of his.

She swallowed the lump in her throat. "I know. It's just that . . . " *It's just that I'm not ready for you to go yet.*

"I'll return as soon as I can," he said gently. "It shouldn't take long for me to take care of my business affairs. A few weeks at most."

I'm afraid, Remington. Stay with me. Love me.

Still holding her hand with one of his, he rose from his chair and came around the table, drawing Libby up to stand before him. With his free hand, he caressed the side of her face. Then he kissed her, and she tasted her own longing on his lips.

When the kiss was broken, Libby pressed her cheek against his chest and whispered, "How shall I bear it when you're gone?"

His reply was simply to tighten his arms around her.

Again she heard tree branches brushing against a window, heard the creaking of the house, heard the sizzle of the fire in the stove. All familiar sounds, but lonely. So terribly lonely.

Stay with me, she wanted to plead, but she knew she couldn't. She knew he had to go. She knew she had to let him go. This trip was important to him, although he hadn't told her why, so she kept silent.

"I'd better get some sleep." He tipped her head with his index finger and planted one more kiss on her mouth. "I'll leave at first light."

"At first light." Her heart ached as she repeated the words.

Remington drew away from her, and she found herself staring hard at his face, memorizing the cut of his jaw, the slight cleft in his chin, the shape of his dark brows, the midnight blue shadows in his inky black hair. She could not rid herself of the terrible fear that she would never see him again, that he would go away and not return, and she wanted to remember everything about him if memories were all she would have.

He touched her cheek with his fingertips one more time, then turned and left the house, closing the door softly behind him.

Stay with me! her heart cried, but her throat was too tight to speak, and now it was too late.

She put out the lamp burning in the center of the kitchen table, then turned and walked through the darkened house to her bedroom.

He loves you. He'll be back. He wants to marry you. There's no reason to be afraid.

No, there wasn't any reason to be afraid, yet fear latched hold of her heart and refused to let go. It was a feeling that had stayed with her from the moment she'd learned someone had been in her house, going through her things. She couldn't shake it, no matter how often she told herself it was foolish.

She opened the door and stepped inside her bedroom. A gentle breeze rippled the curtains at the window, and a sheen of moonlight lightened the shadows. As she walked across the room, she tugged her shirt free from the waist of her trousers, then freed the buttons at the neck and pulled the shirt over her head.

He'll come back, she promised herself. There's nothing to fear. Remington's going to return.

If only she'd asked him why he had to go back. If only she'd asked him to tell her more about his home, about his friends, about his life.

But it doesn't matter. He's chosen to be with you.

She sat on the edge of the bed and pulled off her boots and socks.

What if he returned to Sunnyvale and found he couldn't leave it? What if he found it was too difficult to give up his plantation and the life he'd always known?

Would he have taken me with him if I'd asked? she wondered.

She closed her eyes a moment. It didn't matter if he would have taken her. She couldn't go. She couldn't leave the Blue Springs.

With a sound of frustration, she freed her trousers and slid them down her legs, leaving them in a pool on the floor. Clad in her chemise and drawers, she reached for her nightgown.

A hand covered her mouth, and she was jerked backward so suddenly that there was no chance to scream, no chance to realize what was happening before another arm gripped her around the waist, pulling her tight against a rock-hard chest.

"Very pretty, Miss Blue."

Bevins!

"A pity there ain't more light. I'd like to have seen more."

How had he gotten into her room? How had he gotten into the house unseen?

As if he'd heard her thoughts, he answered, "Your new hired hand's gonna have a lump on his head for a few days." His fingers pressed tightly against her mouth. "And if you give me trouble, you're gonna have the same. You hear me?"

She nodded, her heart pounding, her breathing rapid.

Bevins forced her to her knees, then with surprisingly deft movements replaced the hand over her mouth with a gag. The taste of the fabric was foul, and she tried to force it out with her tongue, making noises of objection.

"Quiet," he ordered gruffly.

He jerked her arms behind her back and tied her wrists together. The rope pinched her skin, making her eyes water. Again she protested, trying her best to scream through the gag.

This time he cuffed her into silence. The blow knocked her onto her side on the floor and left her ears ringing.

Bevins leaned over her. "Don't cause me no trouble, and maybe you won't suffer."

She'd known Bevins was a troublemaker, a thief, even a bully. She hadn't suspected he was insane.

"Walker thought he'd scare me off. He thought he could tell me to keep away from you and this ranch. Well, you're not gonna marry him. This ranch is gonna be mine, and I'm not waitin' any longer to get it."

In the pale moonlight she could see the madness in his eyes, and her blood turned to ice in her veins. He meant what he'd said. He would kill her. She didn't doubt it for a second.

"Shame this house has gotta go. I might've been able to use it. 'Course, it's not as big as mine, but there's plenty of nice things here. Too bad I can't save 'em."

She tried to rise, but he pushed her back onto her side with his foot.

"Fire's gotta start where you are," Bevins said to himself as he looked around. "Otherwise they just might get you out in time. This room's no good. The window faces the bunkhouse."

Fire.

Blind terror consumed her.

"Guess I could put you on the sofa. Have the fire start out there. Yeah, I think that's what I better do. Start the fire out there where it won't be seen so soon."

Remington!

23

Remington lay on his bunk, staring up at the ceiling, waiting for sleep. Across the room, he could hear Jimmy Collins snoring softly. He supposed he should be thankful. He'd discovered that Fred Miller sounded like a grizzly bear when he slept, his snores shaking the rafters of the bunkhouse. But Fred had the first watch tonight, and with any luck Remington would be asleep before he came in to trade places with Jimmy.

Except he knew he wouldn't sleep, no matter how silent the room. Whether his eyes were open or closed, he kept envisioning the way Libby had looked at him tonight, trying to be brave yet unable to hide her sadness, her uncertainty. He kept hearing her whisper, *"How shall I bear it when you're gone? . . . "*

"How will *I* bear it?" he wondered aloud.

He wouldn't be away for long. Only for a few weeks.

How *would* he bear it?

He sat up, lowering his feet over the side of the bed; then, with elbows resting on his thighs, he cradled his head in his hands. His deceit lay like a stone on his heart.

But what choice did he have?

He should take her with him. He should tell her the truth about what had brought him to Idaho. He should tell her the truth and then he should marry her and take his wife with him to New York while he settled his affairs. He shouldn't be away from her, not even for one night.

But what if she hated him when she learned the truth? What if she refused to marry him? What if . . .

He stood and reached for his trousers.

She wouldn't hate him. She loved him. She'd forgive him for his deception once he'd explained things to her. And then she'd marry him.

He didn't bother to put on his shirt or his boots. He was in too much of a hurry.

Swift strides carried him across the yard to the back door. He entered the kitchen and stepped toward the table with the intention of lighting the lamp. Just as he reached for it, a sound stopped him. A sound so soft he shouldn't have heard it. A sound that was out of place with this house, with this night.

All his senses went on alert. He eased back from the table, peering down the dark hallway toward Libby's room, listening, waiting. Then he heard it again. A moan. A sigh. He couldn't be certain which. He knew only that something was amiss.

The door to Libby's room flew open, and Remington drew back into the kitchen, waiting breathlessly. Then he heard a deep voice mutter a curse.

Bevins. Bevins was with Libby.

Remington clenched and unclenched his hands. He forced himself to breathe. He concentrated on each sound, each shifting shadow.

"Get out there," he heard Bevins order. "On the sofa."

Libby's white cotton undergarments made her easy to follow as she stumbled out of the room, as if pushed from behind. He heard her muffled protest and knew she was gagged.

He controlled his white-hot fury, biding his time, waiting for the right moment. He could make no mistakes, not when Libby's life was hanging in the balance. Not after she'd touched his heart and changed him. Not after she'd shown him that loving her was more important than revenge, more important than anything. Even his own life.

The shadow that was Bevins came out of the bedroom, following Libby into the living room. Remington began to inch his way down the hall. He wished he had his revolver, but he couldn't go for it now. He couldn't even look for Libby's shotgun. His only hope was surprise.

He paused at the corner, listening once again. He heard logs being tossed onto the grate, heard Bevins muttering to himself. He eased himself forward, peering into the room.

Libby was on the sofa. Bevins was crouched at the fireplace, his back to the entry. He knew there wasn't likely to be a better opportunity than this one. The time to act was now.

Remington sent up a silent prayer that his leg wouldn't fail him, then he lunged into the room, hurling himself at the hunched figure.

Libby's eyes flew open at the sound of a grunt. She saw the darkened shapes of the two men as they rolled on the floor. Bevins shouted a vile curse as the fire tongs clattered onto the hearth.

Remington!

She heard the sound of knuckles hitting flesh, heard a sharp intake of breath and another grunt. She tried to scream Remington's name through the gag, but all that came out was a muffled moan.

"Libby, get out of here! Run!"

She pushed off the sofa, struggling against the rope that bound her wrists as she rushed for the doorway.

"Oomph!"

She stopped and turned at the sound, knowing it was Remington who'd made it, wondering if he was hurt. But she couldn't help him this way. She turned again and ran down the hall into the kitchen. With her back to the kitchen door, she fumbled with the knob, trying desperately to open it. Above the pounding of her heart, she heard something in the living room crash to the floor and shatter. She heard swearing and groans. She heard the sounds of bodies hitting the floor and the furniture.

Please. Oh, please open, she prayed as she tried to grip the knob. Tears of frustration pooled in her eyes as her fingers slipped away again and again. She had to get out to the bunkhouse. She had to get help for Remington.

It was useless. Her hands were bound too tightly. She couldn't get a good grip on the knob. She couldn't open the door.

A knife. Perhaps she could cut the rope and—

The sudden silence seemed louder than the fighting had been. She pressed her back against the door, waiting.

God, let him be all right, she prayed.

She heard the strike of the match, saw a pale flicker of light at the end of the hall. The light brightened as a lamp's wick caught flame.

She couldn't breathe. She couldn't move.

Remington.

He stepped into view, lamp in hand.

A choked sob escaped her. She pushed away from the door, stumbling, nearly falling. And then he was there, holding her in his arms, murmuring her name as he freed her wrists and removed the foul gag from her mouth.

"You're all right," she whispered. "You're all right."

"I'm all right." Remington cradled her face with his

hands and stared into her eyes. "What about you? Did he hurt you?"

She shook her head. "No. No, he didn't hurt me." She touched a cut on the corner of his mouth, then brushed his hair back from his forehead. His left eye would be bruised and swollen tomorrow. She could see signs of it already. But he was all right. He was alive. That was all that mattered to her.

He gave her another tight hug, then said, "You'd better sit down."

Realizing her legs were shaking uncontrollably, Libby did as he'd told her. She clenched her hands in her lap and stared down the hallway as he walked back to the living room, disappearing from view.

Bevins had planned to burn down the house with her in it. He'd planned to murder her.

The horror of it returned tenfold. She clutched her abdomen as the shaking spread through her, making her weak, leaving her sick.

She heard footsteps and looked up. Terror blazed in her chest at the sight of Bevins walking toward her. A scream was strangled in a throat too tight to allow its escape. Then she realized Bevins's arms were behind his back, as if tied, and that Remington was right behind him. Bevins's face was bloodied and bruised.

"Stop," Remington ordered when they reached the table. Then he lit a second lamp and picked it up. To Libby he said, "Wait here. I'll be back."

She nodded, still unable to speak, knowing she wouldn't be able to stand, either.

Remington took Bevins to the barn. He opened the door to the small storage room and shoved the man inside. He found a stout rope and bound Bevins's ankles, then ordered his prisoner to lie on his side on the horse blanket he'd spread on the floor. Once Bevins had obeyed, Remington tied another rope between his ankles and wrists.

"You can't leave me like this," Bevins cried.

Remington grabbed him by his shirt collar and brought their faces close together. "I wouldn't complain if I were you. You're lucky I don't hang you here and now." He let Bevins drop back to the floor with a thud.

Swiftly he cleared the storage room of tack and hoes and shovels. He would leave nothing that might be used to cut the ropes, nothing the man could use as a weapon in the unlikely event he were to get loose. Then, taking the lamp with him, Remington closed and secured the storage room door.

He was impatient to return to Libby, but first he had to find out what had happened to Fred Miller. He awakened Jimmy Collins and sent him to the barn to guard Bevins. A few minutes later Remington located Fred just as he was regaining consciousness. He lay in the midst of the grove, the back of his head covered with drying blood.

Remington knelt beside the hired hand and helped him to sit up.

Fred tenderly touched the back of his head. "Goll durn," he muttered. "I'd like t'get my hands on whoever done this."

"It was Bevins. He's trussed up in the barn now." Remington quickly told Fred what had happened, then offered to help him back to the bunkhouse.

"I'm okay, boss. I can make it to the bunkhouse on my own. You go see about Miss Blue."

Remington didn't waste time arguing. He was only too happy to comply.

He found Libby seated where he'd left her. She turned toward the door as it opened. Her face was pale, her eyes wide with lingering fear. Even from the doorway he could see her body shaking.

He should have killed the bastard, he thought as he moved toward her.

Wordlessly he drew her up from the chair and into his arms. She seemed to melt against him.

"It's all right," he whispered, stroking her back.

"He was going to burn down the house."

"He can't do anything now. He's tied up and locked in the storeroom in the barn."

She shook her head, her forehead touching his chest. "He was going to kill me."

"He won't be killing anybody. We'll hand him over to the sheriff tomorrow."

She looked up at him. "I thought . . . I thought . . . "

"I know." He turned, still holding her with one arm. "Come on. Let's get you to bed." He took up the lamp with his other hand.

She leaned on him, letting him guide her down the hall and into her bedroom. When they reached the bed, she grabbed hold of his hand, gripping him as if her life depended on it. "Don't leave me, Remington." Quiet desperation filled each word, each syllable. "Please."

"I won't leave you." He set the lamp on the nearby stand, then gently urged her to sit on the edge of the bed. "Lie down, Libby," he said softly.

"Don't go."

"I won't." He pressed her shoulders back until her head touched her pillow. "I'm going to stay right here with you."

"I was so afraid."

"I'm here, Libby. No one can hurt you now. You mean too much to me to let anyone harm you."

Tears fell onto her cheeks. "Stay with me, Remington. Hold me, please."

"I'll hold you," he promised. He turned the lamp down to a gentle glow, knowing instinctively she wouldn't welcome the dark. Then he lay down on the bed, gathered her into his arms, and held her close against him.

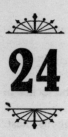

24

Libby wasn't sure how long she'd slept, but when she awakened she found herself still held in the safety of Remington's comforting embrace. She opened her eyes, tipping her head back to look at him. He was awake and watching her, and she knew instinctively that he'd been like that from the moment he'd lain down beside her on the bed.

"You stayed," she whispered.

"Where would I go?" he asked softly. "Everything I want is here."

As love swelled in her heart, the last dregs of her fear vanished. She placed her hand on his bare chest. His skin was warm, and the heat seemed to spread to her hand and up her arm. She felt his steady heartbeat beneath her palm.

"You mean too much to me to let anyone harm you." She heard his words again in her head, relived the declaration of love in her heart.

"Remington." Longing filled her voice.

His blue eyes appeared almost black in the dim lamp-light, an ebony gaze that held hers captive with unspoken warnings and promises.

The air became charged with emotions, and a strange ache filled her. Lacing her fingers through the hair at his nape, she drew his head down toward hers, breathlessly awaiting the moment their mouths would touch. The kiss was whisper soft at first, a touch barely perceived yet one that rocked her to her very soul.

She closed her eyes and let the kiss deepen. She pressed her body closer to his, felt the warmth of his chest through the thin fabric of her chemise. Her skin tingled in anticipation.

Remington's tongue traced the line of her lips. She opened her mouth and gave him entry. He tasted masculine, warm, wonderful.

He lifted his mouth from hers. She opened her eyes.

Make love to me, Remington, she pleaded silently. *I've been waiting so long for you to make love to me. Don't go away without making me yours.*

"Ah, Libby," he whispered as if he'd heard her thoughts, "I'm not strong enough for both of us. I can't resist you if you don't stop me."

"I don't want to stop you. I won't be able to bear it if you stop now."

He groaned, a sound of resignation to the inevitable, and her heart fluttered. She waited, breathless, wanting, hopeful.

Kissing her again, he drew his hand up along her ribs until it reached her breast. Gently he kneaded the soft flesh, circling the now taut nipple with his thumb. She pressed forward, filling his hand, wanting more, needing more. A strange moan slipped from her mouth into his.

He rose up onto his knees in an easy, fluid motion, bringing her with him. Once there, face-to-face, knees to knees, he cupped her face in his hands and stared into her eyes with a look of adoration.

"You're so beautiful," he said.

She experienced no regret, no fear, as she once had when she'd heard those words. Instead she rejoiced. She was glad to be beautiful for Remington.

He kissed her forehead, her eyelids, the tip of her nose, the pulse point beneath her jaw, the hollow of her throat. Her breath came in tiny, quick gulps. Gooseflesh rose on her arms and legs, and a sigh was forced from her lips.

Then he straightened and looked down at her once again while he gently untwined her braid, then combed his fingers through the freed tresses, spreading her hair over her shoulders, allowing it to fall down her back in thick, rose gold waves.

"I love your hair down, wild and free."

She felt his gaze upon her like a caress, real, warm, alive. A shiver of virginal uncertainty spread through her.

Deftly, with one hand, he freed the tiny ribbons at the front of her chemise. Then he drew the garment upward. She raised her arms, allowing him to pull it over her head. Her hair tumbled down the bare skin of her back.

He paused, and their gazes locked.

Are you sure? his eyes seemed to ask her.

Don't stop. Please, don't stop, hers replied.

His gaze moved from her eyes down to her breasts. Suddenly shy, she moved to cover herself from his view.

"Don't." The word was abrupt, gruff, irresistible.

She lowered her arms to her sides, feeling his gaze warming her skin.

With both hands this time, flesh upon flesh, he caressed her breasts, kneading, circling, lifting. Strangely, she seemed to feel his touch more in the apex of her thighs than where he actually fondled her.

As if he read her thoughts, he lowered one hand to the

waist of her underdrawers. With a gentle tug he loosened the tie that secured them.

Cool night air from the open window swept over her naked skin. Yet she wasn't cool. She burned with a fever of wanting. She closed her eyes, reveling in the unfamiliar sensations.

Remington laid her back on the bed with care, then slid the underdrawers from her legs. A moment later he lay stretched out along her right side. Though their bodies didn't yet touch, a sixth sense told her he was as naked as she, and she was glad, eager to unravel the mysteries of love, to discover for herself that special union that bound a man and woman together.

Again he touched her breast, this time with his mouth. She sucked in a gasp of surprise at the new sensations that exploded within, turning her insides to molten fire. His right hand touched her right leg, moving slowly upward, ever upward, white heat following the caress.

As his fingers reached the place of her desire, he trailed kisses up from her breast until their mouths were joined once again. He stroked her, wondrous and tender, and she moved to meet each touch. Her skin tingled until she knew she would soon burst into a thousand pieces.

Then he was poised above her. His distended flesh pressed against the place of her greatest need. She waited in eager anticipation, all remnants of uncertainty and shyness gone.

It was a resplendent thing, that moment of joining, that instant they became one. She received him with joy, her heart thrumming a song of love. He moved with a rhythm as old and as natural as time itself, and she moved with him. She listened to his harsh breathing and knew that it matched her own.

His body lowered as his thrusts grew quicker, harder. She heard his soft sounds of desire, heard her own throaty gasps. She tipped her head backward, pressing it into the pillow. His mouth followed the arch of her neck. His tongue pressed against the sensitive skin in the hollow of her throat.

A thousand needles of pleasure pierced through her. She shuddered, and a rapturous cry tore from her lips. For a heartbeat she was suspended in air, but he didn't let her fall. He held her, lifted her, drew her back from passion's precipice and into a whirlpool of feverish ecstasy. The rhythm of their ancient dance pounded, quickened, deepened.

Building . . . building . . . building . . .

Soaring higher . . . ever higher.

And when she thought she could bear the pleasure no more, she felt them topple over the edge together. Another cry escaped her, mingling with his throaty exclamation.

Suddenly all was still except for their quickened breathing.

After a long while, Libby opened her eyes and found Remington watching her. "I didn't know." Her words, softly spoken, were filled with awe.

His smile was tender, as tender as the touch of his fingertips as he brushed damp tendrils of hair off her forehead.

"Will it always be like this between us?" she asked, hardly daring to hope it could be true.

"Always, Libby."

She sighed and allowed her eyes to close. "Then I think I shall want to live forever."

Remington rolled onto his side, taking her with him, their bodies still joined. "Forever," he whispered, almost like a prayer.

She closed her eyes, content with tonight and with all her tomorrows, then drifted off to sleep.

25

As dawn spilled through the window, Remington leaned on his elbow, bracing the side of his head with the heel of his hand, and stared at Libby. He found there was great pleasure in watching her sleep, her lips still looking lush and well kissed, her pale, rose gold hair fanned out across the pillows, tiny wisps curling near her temples.

Slowly he tugged the sheet downward until he could feast his eyes on her firm, perfectly shaped breasts. Dark areola surrounded her nipples, the skin slightly puckered. He knew if he kissed her breast, the tiny bumps would grow pronounced and the nipples would harden into stiff peaks.

The image made his own body grow hard.

Unable to resist the temptation, he leaned forward and laved her nipple with his tongue, delighting in the changes his loving wrought. She wriggled slightly. A tiny moan sounded deep in her throat.

He raised his head and looked at her face, watching as her eyes opened. She gave him a sleepy, innocently seductive smile.

"Good morning," he said.

"Mmm." She stretched, catlike.

"It's about time you woke up."

"I didn't want to wake up. My dreams were too"—again she stretched—"mmm . . . delicious."

He rose above her, bracing himself with his forearms and knees. "Reality can be even more delicious, my dear."

She blushed but didn't look away. "I know." She moved her hips beneath him, causing a spasm of desire to rush from his engorged member through his entire body.

He cleared his throat, fighting for control as he reminded himself that she'd been a virgin until last night. "We should probably wait."

This time there was no innocence in the smile she gave him. "I don't want to wait." Her voice was husky, breathless. Again she moved beneath him, this time with purpose.

Control shattered.

"As you wish, Libby Blue," he whispered just before claiming her mouth in a searing kiss.

A long while later Libby watched as Remington rose from the bed. She studied him unabashedly as he moved across the room. While she had seen the more intimate parts of his anatomy during the days she'd nursed him, this was different. Entirely different.

She found she loved every plane, every contour, of his body. She liked the dark hair on his chest and on his legs. She liked the shape of his calves and the taut muscles of his thighs. She liked the firm roundness of his buttocks. She even liked the morning stubble on his chin and jaw, though her cheeks were burned because of it.

She watched as he washed himself, then shaved with the razor she'd provided during his recovery. She was glad he didn't dress immediately—and felt shamefully wicked because she was glad. She enjoyed observing the way his muscles flexed and relaxed as he stroked the razor this way and that.

When he was finished shaving and had rinsed his face in the wash basin, he turned toward her and said, "Madam, if you don't stop looking at me like that, our hired hands will think both of us have died and will come into the house looking for us. I'm not sure it would be wise for them to see you just now."

Heat rose in her cheeks again, but she smiled anyway.

Remington laughed. "I'd better check on our prisoner. Then I could use some breakfast. I don't know about you, but I've worked up a tremendous appetite."

"I'll fix something," she said as she sat up.

He strode across the room, grabbed her by the shoulders, and drew her up onto her knees, then kissed her thoroughly, leaving her breathless and remembering every wonderful thing he had done to her last night and again this morning. When he released her, she sank back onto the bed, flushed and limp.

"I won't be long," he promised as he put on his trousers. Then barefoot and bare chested, as he'd been when he'd come to the house last night, he left her bedroom.

Staring up at the ceiling, Libby whispered, "You were right, Aunt Amanda. You were right about everything." She grinned and let out a delighted moan, wishing she'd coaxed Remington back to bed for just a little longer.

But he was gone, and it was time she arose. Although Remington hadn't mentioned it, she knew they would have to take Bevins into Weiser and turn him over to the sheriff. She would have to give her statement regarding the events of last night. It wasn't apt to be a pleasant day.

Then there was the matter of Remington's departure. But maybe he wouldn't leave just yet, she thought, remembering the pleasure they'd just shared. Maybe she could entice him to delay his trip, perhaps for another week or two. Perhaps even longer.

Feeling wonderfully female, she tossed aside the tangled sheets and rose, almost eager to test her newly awakened powers of persuasion.

Northrop studied the surrounding terrain, finding it difficult to imagine Olivia living here. He hadn't seen another buggy or horseback rider or even a farmhouse since they'd left Weiser at daybreak. He couldn't fathom his daughter living in such a remote area, without even the simplest necessities to make life enjoyable.

Harder still was absorbing the information O'Reilly had gleaned just prior to Northrop's arrival in Idaho. According to the detective, Remington Walker and Olivia—or rather, Libby Blue, as she called herself—were engaged to be married.

He frowned. Walker was no fool. He couldn't possibly think he could marry Northrop's daughter and hope to inherit the Vanderhoff fortunes.

O'Reilly didn't think such was the case, either. "Sure but I think he's marryin' her for herself and herself alone," the Irishman had told Northrop last night. "Looks to me as if he loves her, sir."

Love? It was a highly overrated emotion, in Northrop's estimation. He'd seen intelligent men do many foolish things in the name of love, but he had never fallen victim to it. He never would. Remington Walker, it seemed, had.

And Walker, like others before him, would regret it.

Northrop's mouth curved in a knowing smile. He hadn't built the Vanderhoff fortunes without understanding basic human nature and how to use that nature to his own advantage. If his instincts proved correct, Olivia would be more than willing to return with him to New York before this day was over.

He looked at O'Reilly. "How much longer before we reach this ranch?"

"Not long, sir. We're nearly there."

Libby whipped up a breakfast of biscuits and gravy, pork sausage, and fried eggs and set a pitcher of chilled milk, brought up from the springs, in the center of the table. When all was ready, she rang the bell outside the back door.

Moments later Remington and Fred entered the kitchen. Libby listened as Fred apologized for letting Bevins sneak up on him, then she made a fuss over the lump and scab on the back of his head. After the two men sat down to eat, she dished up another plate and took it out to Jimmy, who was on his second turn at guard duty.

"What about him?" Jimmy asked, jerking his head toward the closed door of Bevins's temporary jail.

A cold chill seeped into her veins as she recalled less pleasant images of last night. "Remington will bring out food for the prisoner when he's through with his own breakfast," she answered hurriedly, then stepped outside into the warming rays of the morning sunlight.

She had nearly reached the kitchen door when she saw a buggy approaching, her view of the road unimpeded now that the trees had been cleared. She raised a hand to her brows, shading her eyes as she tried to make out who their visitors might be, but the black top of the surrey cast deep shadows over the faces of the two men who sat side by side on the carriage seat.

Misty ran to the edge of the yard and barked a quick warning. In a higher, sharper pitch, Ringer mimicked his mother, and the rest of the puppies followed suit. Misty looked back at her mistress, waiting for a command.

Libby stepped away from the house as the buggy drew closer, the horse traveling at a brisk trot. The driver didn't slow the animal to a walk until the carriage was passing through the break in the trees.

Libby felt a strange wariness as she waited. She knew she should order Misty back, but she couldn't seem to do it. She couldn't seem to take her eyes off the passenger in the fine black surrey with its red carriage stripe and the green cloth trimmings, watching as sunlight climbed from his chest . . . to his neck . . . to his face.

Her heart stopped. Her throat went dry. Her body stiffened and refused to move.

Not now. Oh, God. Not now.

The buggy drew to a halt in front of her, and Northrop descended. His steely gaze studied her for what seemed an eternity.

Not now . . . not now . . . not now.

"Well, Olivia, I am here at last." He lifted an iron gray eyebrow. "Have you no greeting for your father after so many years?"

Not now.

She opened her mouth to speak, but the words wouldn't come out. She remembered the dream she'd had only two nights ago, heard her father saying, *"You can't escape me,"* felt her own helplessness choking her.

Then she heard the door open. She saw her father's gaze shift to a place over her shoulder, and she knew Remington stood in the doorway to the kitchen.

Remington's here.

Those two simple words gave her courage. Everything was all right because Remington was there. She could face her father with Remington beside her. She could face anything as long as he was near. Her father had no more power over her. Not now. Not ever again.

She turned, watched Remington's approach, saw the flinty expression in his eyes, the hard set of his mouth.

"It's good to see you again, Mr. Walker," her father said.

Libby's breathing became shallow, difficult.

Remington glanced at her, tried to hold her gaze, but she had to turn, had to look at her father once again.

"I'm glad your search was successful," Northrop continued, still speaking to Remington. "I'm certain you are, too, considering the tidy sum you've made for less than a year's work."

A groan caught in her chest. No, it's not true, she told herself. Father can't possibly know him. It's not true.

"Libby," Remington said softly.

"I never expected you to find Olivia in Idaho, and judging by the telegram you sent me a few weeks ago, neither did you. I'm sorry I wasn't able to let you know when I would be arriving, but I felt it would be better to surprise Olivia." He pulled a bank draft from his breast pocket. "This is only the bonus we agreed upon. As you can see, I'm a man of my word. You found Olivia before your year was over." He held the draft at arm's length. "When you return to Manhattan, send round an invoice for your expenses and the remainder of your agency fee. I'll have my man at the bank issue the payment at once."

Libby took the draft from her father's hand before Remington could move. She stared at it, but the numbers blurred together. She blinked to clear her vision, then blinked again.

It was made out to Remington Walker. She read his name over and over, trying to see something else, but it remained unchanged.

Her father had known Remington was here. He'd brought the bank draft with him. He knew Remington. He knew him. He—

Remington's hand alighted on her shoulder. "Libby, listen to me."

Her eyes refocused on the amount of the draft. She read it aloud. "Two hundred and fifty thousand dollars." She shook her head, disbelieving. "A quarter of a million dollars." She glanced up, stared into the unflinching gaze of Northrop Vanderhoff. "Is that what I'm worth, Father? So very much? I didn't know. I never imagined how much you valued me."

"Libby," Remington tried again.

She turned and stared at Remington, wanting—*needing*—to see something in his expression that wasn't there. "Tell me it isn't true, Remington. Tell me Father didn't hire you to find me. Tell me."

But he didn't deny it. She saw the truth in eyes that for so long had been inscrutable, eyes that she wished desperately would hide the truth from her now. "I can explain," was all he said.

"Explain what, young man?" Northrop interrupted in a loud, cheerful voice. He stepped forward to take hold of Libby's arm, drawing her away from Remington. "You've confirmed your reputation as the best detective in Manhattan. Hell, on the entire eastern seaboard. You've done what no one else could do, and believe me, there are plenty who've tried." Northrop turned Libby to face him, taking the bank draft from her fingers as he spoke to her again. "I can't imagine that there's anything you want to take with you from this wretched place, Olivia, but if there is, get it now. We've a train to catch."

She waited for Remington to say something, anything, to end the nightmare, but he didn't. He couldn't, she realized, because everything her father had said was true. Remington had been hired to find her. Remington had arrived at the Blue Springs because he'd been doing what he'd been paid to do. Remington had known her name, known her secrets. Remington had sent a telegram to her father. And now Remington had been handsomely paid for his betrayal.

"You mean too much to me to let anyone harm you."

His words, only last night thought to be a declaration of love, now took on a different meaning.

Too much to let anyone harm her?

She might have laughed if the pain in her chest hadn't prevented it. What man wouldn't move heaven and earth to keep her safe in order to collect the reward her father had offered for her return? Yes, she'd meant a lot to Remington. She'd meant a veritable fortune. He'd even proposed marriage in order to protect it.

He'd lied to her. It had all been a lie. Even last night.

"There's nothing here that I want," she said, although the voice didn't sound like her own.

"Good. Then we'll be on our way." With a firm grip on her elbow, Northrop helped her into the surrey.

Remington stepped quickly forward. "You don't have to go with him, Libby. If you'll only give me a chance to explain . . . "

A blessed numbness blanketed her, pulling her back into a small place where no one could touch her, where no one could hurt her. "Explain what?" she said, unconsciously echoing her father. "It's all true, isn't it?"

"Yes, but—"

"You've done an admirable job, young man," Northrop interrupted, placing the draft in Remington's hand. Then he got into the buggy beside Libby.

"What about Sawyer?"

Remington's words pricked her shield, but not enough to break through it. "McGregor will take care of Sawyer. Tell him I'll send him the deed to the ranch. Tell him . . ." She shook her head and lowered her eyes. "Tell them both good-bye."

"Let's go, O'Reilly," Northrop ordered.

Libby never looked back as the surrey sped away from the Blue Springs.

26

September 1890
New York City

The drawing room of the Alexander Harrison home on Fifth Avenue was crowded and stuffy. From one end of the vast room to the other, the cream of New York society shared gossip and exchanged opinions, their individual conversations merging into one noisy hum of voices. Across the hall, in the music room, a small orchestra played the "Blue Danube" waltz, the sweet strains of the violins drifting above the general din.

Remington stood near the fireplace with three other men, acquaintances from his private club. Like them, he was dressed in evening attire—a white shirt with high stiff collar and cuffs, a black bow tie, a white waistcoat with a shawl collar and two pockets, and a gold watch and chain. His jacket and trousers were the color of soot, his cotton gloves a contrasting white. And like the men around him, he'd been made welcome in the Harrison home because he had the proper resources, breeding, and connections—despite his father's suicide—to make him suitable company for the unmarried young women who were present this evening.

But Remington was there to see only one young woman. He was waiting for Libby Blue.

The story of the disappearance of Northrop's daughter had been whispered in parlors and drawing rooms for a number of years. It had been no secret that the shipping magnate had hired detectives to find her, although it had never been discussed in Northrop's presence. Yet now everyone seemed to calmly accept the story that Olivia Vanderhoff had been selflessly nursing an ailing friend all these years.

It never ceased to amaze him, he thought as he listened to Charlton Bernard's voice droning on, the way power and wealth could alter the truth, the way facts and memories, even history itself, could be changed in the blink of an eye—or at the will of a man like Vanderhoff.

Charlton brought his rendition of the story of Olivia Vanderhoff to a close, ending, "I've heard she was quite overcome by the death of her friend and hasn't left Rosegate since her return to New York."

George Webster glanced toward the host and hostess, standing on the far side of the room. "Penelope must be beside herself that Miss Vanderhoff chose her soiree to make her first public appearance since her return. Mother is positively green with envy. She'll take to her bed with a sick headache for the next three days, if I know Mother."

The other men laughed. All but Remington.

"I hear Miss Vanderhoff is a real beauty," Michael Worthington commented.

As Charlton and George gave their hearty concurrence, Remington thought of Libby as she'd looked the last morning he'd seen her, over two months before. He remembered the sparkle in her apple green eyes, the inviting curve of her bowed mouth, the luster of her rose gold hair as it spilled across the sheet, the softness of her creamy white skin. He could still hear her laughter, innocent and seductive at the same time.

Charlton chuckled. "You can be sure there will be plenty of suitors leaving their cards at Rosegate after this night. Now that she's come back into society, Miss Vanderhoff will have no lack of men seeking her hand in marriage."

Remington's fingers tightened around his glass.

"And do you plan to be one of them?" George elbowed his friend in the ribs.

"If I want to make my parents happy, I will," came Charlton's reply. "Have you any idea how much Vanderhoff is worth? And his daughter is his only legitimate heir."

Remington excused himself, unable to bear listening to them another moment. He wondered what they would think if he were to tell them he was the detective who'd found Libby, what they would think if they knew Remington had seen far more of the woman they blithely discussed than their mamas would think proper.

He weaved through the crowd, exchanging a word here and there but managing to avoid being drawn into any lengthy conversations. Finally he took up a spot in a corner of the room beside a giant porcelain vase overflowing with American Beauty roses. He fixed his eyes on the doorway and waited for a glimpse of Libby, just as he'd waited outside Rosegate, hoping for a glimpse of her. He'd been there daily, without success, for almost an entire month. Tonight would be different.

Half an hour later his wait was rewarded—but not by Libby Blue.

It was Olivia Vanderhoff who stood framed in the

doorway of the drawing room. Her hair was worn high on her head, exposing the length of her slender neck. Her throat and ears sparkled with brilliant diamonds. There wasn't so much as a hint of a smile on her mouth, and her eyes seemed to stare ahead with cool disregard, as if she didn't actually see the people around her. She wore an elegant gown of dusty rose—draped, pleated, and bustled—that set off her narrow waist and her high, rounded breasts.

She looked exquisite, but Remington would have preferred to see her in flannel shirt and denim trousers. He would have preferred to see Libby.

Penelope Harrison, Alexander's second wife, had been a classmate of Olivia's at finishing school. They had never been especially close, but no one would have guessed, given the welcome her hostess gave her.

"Olivia, dearest! I'm so delighted you came this evening." Penelope clasped Olivia's hands, then leaned forward and kissed both of her cheeks. She turned toward the gentleman at her right. "Olivia, this is my husband, Alexander Harrison. I don't believe the two of you have been introduced. Mr. Harrison was in Europe when you . . . when you went away."

Alexander, a handsome man in his midforties, bowed at the waist. "A pleasure, Miss Vanderhoff. My wife has been awaiting your arrival with great anticipation."

Olivia inclined her head ever so slightly. "Thank you, sir. It's a pleasure to make your acquaintance."

Northrop stepped forward to shake Alexander's hand, apologizing for their tardiness. "My wife took suddenly ill, and we were waiting for the doctor."

"I hope it's nothing serious," Penelope said with what sounded like genuine concern.

Northrop shook his head. "No. Nothing more than a cold, I suspect. My wife suffers from a rather delicate constitution."

That was a lie, of course. Anna had neither a cold nor a delicate constitution. Northrop had forbidden her mother to come to the Harrison soiree. He'd done it to punish her.

"It's bad enough that I have a daughter who looks as cheerful as a corpse," he'd shouted at Anna earlier that evening, his voice ringing through the house. "I'll not have you dragging about as if you're in mourning. I'll make your excuses."

Poor Mama.

Penelope slipped her arm through Olivia's. "You've been gone so very long, Olivia. Let me introduce you to my guests. I'm sure your father won't mind if I steal you away."

It mattered little to Olivia whether or not she was stolen away from her father or whether or not she met any of the other guests. Nothing had mattered to Olivia since the moment she'd stepped into that surrey and left—

With cool precision she cut off the rest of that thought. She was all right now, as long as she didn't allow herself to remember. She could survive as long as she didn't think about what had been. In the past weeks she'd become an expert at excising memories, at blacking them out, cutting them off before they could take hold and hurt her again.

Because nothing mattered to her, she could be and do whatever her father wanted. And tonight he'd wanted her to come to the Harrisons' soiree.

She wondered who her prospective bridegroom might be from among the men in this room. Gregory James had found another heiress to wed, but there were many others in need of a rich bride. Marriage had to be the reason her father had insisted she attend the party. Northrop did nothing without reason or purpose.

"Gentlemen, look who I've brought to you," Penelope

said, drawing Olivia's attention back to the present. "Olivia, you remember Mr. Bernard and Mr. Webster."

She gave them each a cool smile. Charlton Bernard's grandfather had made his fortune in real estate. It was possible, but not likely, that he was her chosen suitor. George Webster's family owned fabric mills in upstate New York. Probably not the right sort of money for her father. Northrop would prefer a son-in-law with the proper pedigree in addition to his other assets.

"And this is Michael Worthington. He moved to New York from Atlanta several years ago, and he's quite taken us all with his southern charm."

"A pleasure, Miss Vanderhoff." Michael took her gloved hand and kissed her knuckles. "May I offer my condolences? I understand you lost someone close to you recently."

A picture flashed in her head—rugged mountains, golden aspens, and green pines, pastures dotted with woolly sheep, black-and-white puppies tumbling in grassy fields, a log house, Sawyer, and—

She stiffened. "Thank you."

"May I also say that word of your beauty failed to prepare me for the stunning reality?"

"You're so beautiful. . . ."

Olivia swallowed, refusing to envision the face she had adored, refusing to see again the moment he'd spoken those words to her.

She pulled the cold, protective shell tight around her heart. "Thank you again, Mr. Worthington."

Penelope tapped his arm with her fan. "Behave yourself, Michael Worthington. Mr. Vanderhoff might not approve of you speaking so boldly to his daughter on your first meeting." Then, with a laugh, she drew Olivia away from the three bachelors.

Olivia moved by rote, allowing her hand to be kissed without feeling touched, saying the proper words without really hearing what was said to her, looking into people's eyes without seeing anything. She forced a smile when she knew one was expected from her. She held herself straight and regal.

She performed perfectly, just as Northrop Vanderhoff's daughter was expected to perform.

Remington watched the charade with an aching heart. He saw beneath the practiced facade, saw the brittle woman within, and knew that he was the cause of it.

I'm sorry, Libby.

He would do anything, give anything, to win her forgiveness, to earn back her love. That's what had brought him to New York. That's what had brought him to this house tonight.

After Libby left the Blue Springs, Remington had been swamped by guilt. For a brief time he'd thought about staying on at the ranch, forgetting everything else and just staying where he could remember Libby in so many ways. Memories of her had been everywhere. In the house. In the barn. In the paddock. Up on the trail. At the summer range. Everywhere.

But it hadn't been enough. Not for him. And not for Sawyer, either. That's why the two of them had come to New York. They'd come to get Libby, and they weren't going back without her.

Through the crush, he saw Libby break away from Penelope Harrison and make her way toward the glass doors that led out to the courtyard. Slipping unobtrusively from his corner, he followed her, knowing that his chance had, at last, arrived.

Olivia drew in a deep breath of air, thankful to have escaped the crowd. She wasn't used to having so many people around. It had been years since she'd attended such a gathering. She'd forgotten what it was like—the noise, the heat, everyone pressed together, leaving no room to move with ease.

After a few more breaths she proceeded across the stone courtyard toward a break in the tall shrubs, away from the glaring light spilling through the glass doors. But even in the garden beyond the shrubbery and courtyard, she found no peace, perhaps because it was so small. Another tall house rose to the left and another to the right and still another across the alley. She felt trapped, confined. She longed for wide vistas and sweeping valleys and—

No, don't remember.

Sinking onto a marble bench, she tipped her face upward. Such a tiny patch of black velvet sky. So few stars. There was a place where the sky seemed to go on for eternity. A place—

Don't remember.

She squeezed her eyes closed and let her head fall forward again. Why was she so plagued with these thoughts tonight? It didn't matter anymore. None of it mattered anymore.

Better to forget. It was so much better to forget.

There was an advantage to being caught in a crowd of laughing, talking people. It made it more difficult to think. She should go back inside before—

"Hello, Libby."

Her breath caught. A heavy weight pressed in upon her chest.

"I've missed you."

Oh, God, have mercy on me.

"Libby?"

She turned as he stepped toward her. In the shadows of the tall shrubs, he was little more than a shadow himself, yet her mind saw him with great clarity. She saw his devastating smile, the light in his blue eyes, the slight wave in his shaggy black hair. She saw the breadth of his shoulders, the length of his legs.

She saw his deception. She heard his lies.

Olivia rose from the bench. "I didn't know you were in New York, Mr. Walker."

"I've been here a few weeks. It took me some time to clear up the matter of Bevins with the authorities. He won't be back to bother you again, Libby. He'll be in jail until he's an old man. Maybe until he dies." He took another step toward her. "I've wanted to see you ever since I arrived. I've been waiting for an opportunity when we could talk in private."

Like a heavy woolen cloak, she pulled indifference about her, shielding her heart. "I can't imagine we have anything to say to each other."

She moved to step around him, but he caught hold of her arm in a gentle grasp.

"Libby . . . "

She looked up into his eyes. "I'd rather you didn't call me that."

"But—"

"Leave me alone, Mr. Walker. There is nothing for either of us to say. The past is best forgotten."

"I brought your locket with me. You left it behind when you—"

"I don't want it."

"Libby—"

"*I don't want it.*"

A lengthy silence followed. Then, without resistance from Remington, she pulled her arm free and moved toward the courtyard.

"Libby, Sawyer is with me. He'd like to see you."

A tiny gasp of surprise rushed through her parted lips as she turned. "You brought Sawyer to New York?" she asked, barely above a whisper.

"Yes."

Don't be a fool. It's too late. You can't be anything to Sawyer. Not anymore.

Remington held out his hand. "Here's my card. Sawyer is always there in the morning, with his tutor. If you won't come to see me, at least come to see Sawyer."

Despite her better judgment, Olivia took the calling card from him. She stared down without seeing, trying so hard not to see, not to care.

From within the house, she heard the sweet strains of a Tchaikovsky waltz begin to play.

"Remember the night we danced?" Remington asked, his voice low. "Dance with me again, Libby."

"No," she whispered.

"I never meant to hurt you. I love you."

She stepped backward as if he'd slapped her. "Mr. Walker," she said, her throat tight, "of all the lies you ever told me, that was the cruelest one of all." Then she whirled about and hastened into the house.

In her wake, Remington's calling card fluttered to the ground.

27

Remington stared at the amber liquid in his glass, thinking he would love to get drunk. He would love to drown all his regrets, all his guilt, all his self-recriminations, in a bottle of brandy. But drinking himself into oblivion wasn't the answer, and he knew it.

He set the glass aside and turned his gaze toward the fireplace, watching flames lick at the logs on the grate.

It had been nearly a week since he'd seen Libby at the Harrison party, and still she hadn't come to visit Sawyer. He'd been so sure she wouldn't be able to resist seeing the boy. He knew she loved Sawyer as if he were her own son. He'd been certain she wouldn't be able to stay away.

He leaned against the padded back of the leather-upholstered chair, closing his eyes against the grim truth: she hated Remington more than she loved Sawyer.

That was a lot of hate.

And how could he overcome it if he couldn't see her, talk to her, explain what had happened? Explain that he didn't want her father's money, that the telegram he'd sent to her father wasn't what she thought it was, wasn't what Northrop had made it sound like?

What a fool he'd been! He should have done something to cover his own tracks. He should have known there would be other detectives. He should have led Northrop and his hired lackeys away from Libby. Hell, he should have done a lot of things differently.

He sat forward, his forearms resting on his thighs.

It got him nowhere to sit and think of the things he should have done, the things he shouldn't have done. That wasn't going to win Libby back. That wasn't going to break her free of her father's stranglehold.

He couldn't just walk up to the door and present his card to see her. He knew, without even trying, that he'd be forbidden entrance. And even if he were to get in, Libby would refuse to talk to him. No, his best course of action was to seek her out away from Rosegate. Which meant he had to increase his social activities. Which meant he had to play the part of the marriageable bachelor. He had to receive invitations to all the right homes and suppers and soirees and balls.

Remington rose and strode across the room to the fireplace. He leaned an arm on the mantel, staring once again into the fire.

His family connections had always allowed him to move in the circles of proper New York society, but he'd never cared to venture there. He'd concentrated, instead, on increasing his personal fortunes slowly and steadily. He'd mingled with the right men on Wall Street, and with their help he'd invested wisely. Occasionally he'd dined at their homes and met their wives and their daughters, but he'd never shown any interest in matrimony. He'd had only one goal: to find a way to destroy Northrop Vanderhoff.

He struck the mantel with his fist. What a fool he'd been! he thought again. What a blind, ignorant fool!

"I'm not going to give up, Libby," he swore. "I'm not ever going to give up."

The supper party at Rosegate was a small affair—a select thirty guests, many of them descendants of the original Knickerbocker families that had been the nucleus of Manhattan society since the beginning of the century. There were, however, a few exceptions, most notably the guest of honor, the Honorable Spencer Lambert, Viscount Chelsea and heir to the tenth earl of Northcliffe.

The viscount, seated on Olivia's left, had been extremely attentive to her throughout the first ten courses. He had sought to entertain her with stories of his adventures in the American West, bemoaning his failure to encounter an American bison but pleased about both the grizzly bear and the elk he'd managed to bring down.

Spencer was, of course, the man her father had selected to be her husband. Olivia knew it even though nothing had been said to her. She wondered if the viscount would care that she wasn't the lily white maiden a future earl should expect. But then, when an English lord was in need of a fortune to bolster his coffers, perhaps he was not necessarily as choosy.

"I must tell you, Lord Lambert," Penelope Harrison chimed in from across the table, "we are delighted you have returned to Manhattan."

"So am I," he replied, his gaze on Olivia. "Indeed, so am I."

She tried to make herself smile, but it was a half-hearted attempt. She knew it mattered not what she did or said. Her marriage had little to do with charming Spencer Lambert and everything to do with the dowry her father would offer.

Olivia turned her head to look down the length of the

table. Northrop sat at the head, his face mostly obscured by glittering candelabra. How much would he pay to marry her off to this Englishman? He had spent a great deal to find and bring her back. How much more would he spend to send her away?

It was rumored it had cost Anson Stager a million dollars to make his daughter, Ellen, Lady Arthur Butler. Lily Hammersley had become the duchess of Marlborough, it was said, at the price of four million dollars. The former Anita Murphy had joined the ranks of American heiresses in England for two million dollars.

How much for me, Father?

She turned her attention back to Spencer, looking at him with a cool, detached eye. He was handsome enough, she supposed, with his golden hair and pale brown eyes. His face was narrow and clean shaven. He was a few years older than she, perhaps not yet thirty.

He would want an heir. After money to replenish drained coffers, that's what these marriages were all about, really, begetting a son to carry on the title.

Unexpectedly she thought of a boy with tousled coffee-colored hair and dark brown eyes full of mischief, and her heart ached. Sawyer was here in Manhattan. She remembered the Madison Avenue address of Remington's home as if it had been engraved on her mind instead of on his card. A memory that teased and tempted her, inviting her to go to see him.

It must have hurt Sawyer, her leaving the way she had, without so much as a note good-bye. He'd already lost both his parents. Was it right for her to abandon him this way?

If she could go to him . . . If she could try to explain why she'd had to go away . . . If she could let him know she loved him and would always be thinking of him, even if there was an ocean or an entire continent between them . . .

If only she could go to see Sawyer.

But to do so would mean seeing Remington, too, and that she didn't think she was ready to do.

Anna Vanderhoff sat at the opposite end of the table from her husband, playing her part as hostess with the ease born of years of practice. The guests to her right and to her left never felt neglected. She engaged them in conversation, encouraging them to talk about themselves, laughing when appropriate, all the while keeping an eye on the servants as they brought out each course, watching to see that wineglasses were filled and no one looked in want of anything.

But it was her daughter who captured her thoughts.

Looking at Olivia now, Anna felt as though her heart were breaking in two. She remembered the way her beloved child had looked upon her return to Rosegate. She'd seen the utter desolation in her eyes of green. Anna knew something had happened to Olivia in Idaho, something that had sent her back to New York without a fight, something beyond simply being found by Northrop's detectives.

And Anna was helpless to do anything for her. If only Olivia would talk about it, tell her what had happened. But her daughter had retreated within herself, and nothing Anna said or did seemed to help.

Again she looked down the length of the long table, the white tablecloth covered with fine china and silver, crystal goblets and candelabra with long, tapered candles. She looked at her husband and asked him silently, *What have you done, Northrop? What have you done to Olivia?*

"It appears the viscount is quite taken with your daughter, Mrs. Vanderhoff," the guest at her right hand commented, intruding on her private thoughts.

Her gaze returned to Olivia, this time taking in
Spencer Lambert. "Yes, it does," she replied.

If Northrop had his way—and when did he not?—their
daughter would be a countess one day. Olivia Lambert,
countess of Northcliffe. But would she be happy? Anna
wondered, knowing that Olivia's happiness mattered
more to her than titles or castles in England.

If only you would tell me what happened.

Remington opened the door to Sawyer's bedroom. Light
from the hallway spilled across the ornate carpet beside
the bed. Remington followed the path of light into the
room.

"Sawyer?"

The boy immediately opened his eyes.

"Sorry to wake you."

"I wasn't asleep yet."

Remington sat on the edge of the bed. "Sawyer, I've
got an idea on how we might be able to get Libby to at
least talk to us. Will you help me?"

"That's what we came for, isn't it?" he answered
quickly. "What do you need me to do?"

"Well, it isn't you Libby's mad at. It's me. She wants to
see you. I could tell. We just need to remind her that
you're not back at the Blue Springs but right here in New
York—"

"And then she'd come for a visit," Sawyer finished for
him.

"Exactly."

"And then maybe she'd want to see you, too."

"With luck."

Sawyer put his hand on Remington's shoulder. "She
will. I know it."

Remington hoped the boy was right.

28

"*What about the emerald gown,* Miss Olivia? It sets off your hair real nice."

Olivia glanced over her shoulder as her maid drew the dark green velvet gown from the wardrobe. "It doesn't matter, Sophie. Choose whatever you like."

Sophie clucked her tongue. "Doesn't matter, she says. And you going out in the viscount's carriage for one and all to see. I can't imagine there's an unmarried girl in all of New York who doesn't wish she was in your shoes, and you saying it doesn't matter what you wear. Why, you've got more new gowns than you could wear in a month. There must be something that catches your fancy."

Without reply, Olivia turned again and stared at the changing leaves in the trees beyond the window. If she closed her eyes, she could see aspens cloaked in gold. But she didn't close her eyes because she didn't want to see aspens. She refused to see them.

"You'd better hurry, Miss Olivia. His Lordship will be here soon, and you know what your father will be like if you keep the viscount waiting."

"Yes, Sophie. I know."

"And come back from that window. Have you forgotten you're wearing only your corset and petticoats?"

Olivia was about to do as the maid had bid when a small figure caught her attention. A boy with dark brown hair, his hands shoved in his pockets. He stood across the street from the Vanderhoff mansion, staring up at the house. She leaned forward, nearly touching her forehead to the glass.

"Sawyer," she whispered.

Almost as if he'd heard her, he raised his arm and waved at her. She waved back, then placed her hand on the window, wishing . . .

Suddenly she whirled away. "Hurry, Sophie. Help me into my gown at once."

The maid looked surprised by Olivia's sudden change of mood, but she did as she was told, lifting up the gown and slipping it over her mistress's head, then quickly fastening it up the back.

Olivia reached for the matching hat that waited on the bed. She smashed it onto her head, tucking up loose strands of hair and tying a hasty bow beneath her right ear.

"Your hair, miss. We haven't—"

"It doesn't matter, Sophie. My hat will hide it."

"But Miss Olivia—"

She grabbed the green reticule Sophie had set out, not bothering to see if a handkerchief had been placed inside. Then she slipped her feet into her new walking shoes and rushed toward the door.

She moved as quickly as possible along the hall and down the stairs, praying her father wasn't waiting for her in the front parlor. Givens, the butler, was passing through the entry hall just as Olivia reached the bottom of the stairs. With a finger to her lips, she begged him for silence, then hurried toward the front door, not stopping until she was outside.

Her eyes quickly sought the familiar figure across the street. But all she saw was Spencer Lambert's spider phaeton coming down Seventy-second Street toward Rosegate. Olivia scarcely spared the viscount a glance as she searched up and then down the street, but Sawyer was nowhere to be seen.

Her heart sank. She was too late. She'd missed him. He'd gone away before she could get dressed and down the stairs. He must think she didn't want to see him. He was gone, and heaven only knew when another opportunity would present itself. She'd been lucky to get out the door this time without being stopped by her father.

As Spencer's phaeton drew to a halt, the groom jumped down from the skeleton rumble and hurried forward to hold the reins while the viscount descended from the driver's seat.

"Miss Vanderhoff, what a surprise to find you waiting for me," he said with a brilliant smile. "I never cease to be amazed by the freedom you American girls enjoy."

You pompous jackass.

It was the first spark of anger she'd felt in over two months, but she hid her irritation behind a look of wide-eyed innocence. Meeting the viscount's gaze, she said, "To be honest, Lord Lambert, I'd forgotten you were calling. Did we have an engagement?"

Her remark removed the self-satisfied smirk from his mouth. "Indeed we did. We were to go for a drive in Central Park. I hope you have not made other plans."

Sudden inspiration made her swallow the comment that would have sent him away. Instead she offered what she hoped was a conciliatory smile. "Not at all, Lord Lambert. I was only going to take a bit of air. I'd much rather go for a drive in your carriage . . . with you." She took hold of his arm. "Come into the house and say hello to Father while I get my muff. Then we can be on our way."

Olivia endured the drive through Central Park with impatience, although she never let on to Spencer about her feelings. It wasn't until the carriage was headed back to Rosegate that she touched the viscount's arm with gloved fingers.

"Lord Lambert, would you do me a tremendous favor?"

"Of course, Miss Vanderhoff. Anything within my power."

"Might we stop by a friend's house? Just for a moment. I promise not to tarry long."

"Naturally. I'll be glad to oblige. And you needn't hurry. Nothing could please me more than to prolong our time together." He covered her hand with his own. "Just point the way. I'm still not well acquainted with the streets of your fair city."

Remington frowned when he saw Libby sitting beside the English dandy, her cheeks and nose pink from the crisp fall air. He hadn't expected her to come calling with Lord Lambert in tow.

But at least she'd come, as he'd hoped she would. He'd figure out what to do about the viscount later.

"Sawyer, Libby's here."

The boy descended the stairs like a stampeding herd of wild horses and raced over to stand beside Remington at the parlor window. He frowned when he saw Libby wasn't alone. "Who's he?" He sounded as displeased about the viscount as Remington felt.

"An English lord looking for a wife." The plain fact tasted sour on his tongue.

"He's gonna marry Libby?"

Remington watched the viscount assist her from the carriage. "Not if I can help it," he muttered. Then he looked at Sawyer. "You know what to do?"

Sawyer nodded.

"All right." He squeezed the boy's shoulder. "Good luck." He headed toward the door at the back of his home, calling as he went, "Mrs. Blake, I'll be out for the afternoon."

Perhaps I shouldn't have come, Olivia thought just before the door opened.

"Yes?" asked the plump woman with rosy red cheeks and a crisp white apron.

"Is this"—the question caught in her throat for a moment, and she felt a familiar sting in her heart—"the Walker residence?"

"Yes, it is, but Mr. Walker isn't in. He went out only a moment ago. I'm Mrs. Blake, the housekeeper. May I leave a message for him?"

She was glad he wasn't in, of course. She hadn't wanted him to be in. "I've come to see Sawyer Deevers. Is he at home?"

The door opened wider. "He is, ma'am. May I tell him who's calling?"

She opened her mouth to say "Libby," then stopped herself. She glanced over her shoulder, thankful that Spencer had agreed to wait for her in the carriage, knowing she would owe him some sort of explanation later. "I'm Miss Vanderhoff. Tell him I'm a friend of Libby Blue's."

"Please, come in, Miss Vanderhoff." Mrs. Blake showed Olivia into the parlor. "I'll tell Master Sawyer you're here." Then she left the room.

I shouldn't have come.

She let her gaze wander over the furniture. This was Remington's home. This was where he lived, where he slept, where he ate.

I shouldn't have come.

"Libby!"

She whirled around and stared at the boy in the doorway. It seemed Sawyer had shot up another six inches since she'd seen him last. His hair had been trimmed, and he was wearing new clothes. He looked well and strong and wonderful.

Her throat was hot with tears, and she swallowed hard. She hadn't cried. Not in all these weeks. Not even once. She wasn't going to let herself cry now.

"Hello, Sawyer," she said, barely above a whisper. "Was that you I saw outside my window this morning?"

He nodded. "I wanted to see you."

"I wanted to see you, too."

He shot across the room and threw himself into her arms, hugging her tightly. "I've missed you, Libby."

She couldn't stop the tears after all. "I've missed you, too."

Sawyer pulled back and looked into her eyes. Then he reached up and brushed the tears from her cheeks with his thumb. "You oughta come back to the Blue Springs. You ain't happy here."

"Aren't happy," she corrected out of habit.

"Aren't happy." His gaze was wise beyond his years. "You *aren't* happy . . . are you?" But it wasn't really a question.

Olivia forced a tiny smile. "You don't understand, Sawyer. It's so very complicated."

"Remington wants you to come home."

She straightened, turned away. *Home.* She mouthed the word but no sound came out. Her chest hurt.

"I want you t'come home, too."

She walked over to the window and gazed down at the carriage waiting for her at the curb. She looked at Spencer Lambert, the man her father intended for her to marry. And so she would marry him, because she wasn't strong enough to fight her father any longer. The last time she'd fought him . . .

It had hurt. It had hurt so very deeply. And she couldn't bear to be hurt like that again. "I can't go home with you, Sawyer."

"You're wrong, Libby," a deep, familiar voice said from behind her. "You could go with him. Your father couldn't stop you."

She closed her eyes. She wouldn't feel. She wouldn't think. She wouldn't let him touch her, hurt her.

She didn't have to turn around to know Remington had moved closer. She could feel him entering the room.

"I'm glad you came today, Libby."

Her throat burned. "This was all a trick, wasn't it? Sawyer standing outside my window. It was just a trick to get me here." She turned slowly, holding herself stiff and straight.

Remington stood in Sawyer's place. His blue eyes were as dark as storm clouds, his expression determined. "I just need to explain, Libby. You owe me a chance to explain."

"I don't *owe* you anything, Mr. Walker."

"I didn't tell your father I'd found you. I sent him a telegram saying he should give up the search, that I couldn't find you. I didn't want his money. Not after I fell in love with you."

A sudden fury sprang to life. She longed to hit him. She didn't want to think. She didn't want to remember. She didn't want to be sad or angry or confused or lonely. All she wanted was to feel nothing, to care for nothing. He and Sawyer were making her feel again, and she hated Remington for it.

"You, Mr. Walker," she said softly, "are an accomplished liar."

"I never lied about loving you."

"You never said you loved me until last week. I only thought you had."

"I wanted to make things right first."

"And just how were you going to do that?" Not waiting

for an answer, she stepped around him and walked toward the entry.

"I'm not going to give up," Remington called after her. "We have something between us that is too special to lose."

She stopped and turned. "*We* have nothing between us."

"Ask your father to show you my telegram."

He'd lied to her about who he was, about why he'd come to the Blue Springs. He'd lied about his home in Virginia. He'd even lied about wanting to marry her, artfully postponing the deed itself until her father could arrive and prevent it. Why did he persist in heaping more lies on top of those that had gone before? Why couldn't he let it be? He had his money. What more did he want?

The anger drained out of her, leaving her tired, so tired she wondered if she could make it out to the phaeton. Her shoulders drooped, and her reticule felt like a heavy weight, pulling on her arm.

"If you really loved me," she said softly, "you would leave me in peace." She turned again. "Tell Sawyer I'm sorry. Try to help him understand."

Northrop was in a dark fury when he descended from his carriage that evening and strode up the front steps at Rosegate. Slinging the door open before him, he bellowed, "Olivia!"

Anna appeared in the doorway of the parlor, looking pale and alarmed. "Northrop, what is it?"

"Where's that daughter of mine?"

"I believe she's in her room. But what in heaven's name is—"

"Olivia!" He stared up the dark-paneled staircase. "Get down here." Turning to his wife, he said, "Send her to my study. I'll wait for her there."

"But, Northrop—"

He ignored her, striding angrily down the hallway to his private office.

He would not allow it. He would not allow her to defy him again. If he had to lock her in the house, in her room, then so be it. He would make a prisoner of her if he must.

Olivia arrived in the doorway just as he settled into the chair behind his desk. "You wanted to see me, Father?"

"Come in and sit down."

She did as she was told.

Northrop leaned forward in his chair. "Is it true?"

"Is what true, Father?"

"Has that detective returned to New York? Have you seen Walker?"

There wasn't so much as a flicker of emotion on her face. "Yes."

Northrop slammed his hands on his desk and rose from his chair. "By Gawd, Olivia, I won't have it! You'll not jeopardize your marriage prospects by consorting with that man. Do you want the whole world to know how I found you? Don't think I don't know what you were doing with him there. You're going to stay away from him. Do you hear me?"

"You needn't shout, Father." She stood, looking cool and regal and remote. "I have no interest in *consorting* with Mr. Walker." Without waiting for his dismissal, she turned and walked toward the door. Just before reaching it, she paused and glanced behind her. "Has Lord Lambert asked for your permission to marry me?"

Her question surprised him. "Not yet, but I expect he will soon."

"I see. Will it be necessary for us to have a long engagement?"

"I suppose not."

"Good," she said, then disappeared into the hallway.

Frowning, Northrop stared after her. The interview had not turned out as he'd expected. When he'd heard today that Remington Walker was back in the city and that he'd been seen talking to Olivia at the Harrisons' soiree, he'd suspected trouble was afoot.

He sank onto his chair, steepling his hands in front of his face.

He wasn't a fool. He'd known the moment he'd seen her at that miserable ranch that his daughter wasn't the innocent girl who'd run away nearly seven years ago. He supposed he should be glad she hadn't produced a bastard child for him to deal with. She did seem earnest in her disinterest in Walker, but Northrop wasn't convinced it would last. Not when the man was here in New York and apparently allowed to move in the same social circle as the Vanderhoffs.

It was possible he could do something to discredit Walker, but it would be risky. He didn't want to ruin Olivia's reputation at the same time, not when it was entirely possible others might learn it was Walker who had found her, not when the carefully fabricated story of her sick friend could be exposed for the fiction it was. Society had politely turned its head and ignored what Northrop wanted it to ignore. But not even his most stalwart friends would be able to ignore the truth should it come out. The truth would ruin all his plans.

He tapped his forefingers together, staring off into space.

It seemed Olivia's plan was the best. Get her married to the viscount and packed off to London as quickly as possible. There was much to be gained from an alliance with the Lambert family and the influence it would bring the Vanderhoffs in England and throughout the British Empire. The value would be far greater than the railroad he'd lost seven years ago. And once they were wed, Remington Walker could be dealt with in an appropriate manner.

Yes, he would have to speed along Spencer Lambert's courtship of Olivia. The quicker the two of them were married, the better.

29

The last of the season's roses bloomed in the Rosegate gardens even as sharp autumn winds rattled drying leaves loose from tree branches and sent them rolling across the ground. But Anna noticed neither the wind nor the fading blossoms as she strolled among the rosebushes late in the afternoon a week after Northrop's angry interview with Olivia.

Anna's concern for her daughter had mounted with each passing day. The coveted proposal from the future earl had been received two days before, and Olivia had accepted without hesitation. The news had been proclaimed in *The New York Times* in yesterday's edition. Today there had been a steady stream of well-wishers arriving at Rosegate, many of them expressing envy for the brilliant match that had been made. Olivia seemed content with the decision, but Anna's troubled heart wasn't eased by the appearance of contentment.

Olivia wasn't in love with Spencer Lambert. Nor, Anna suspected, did the viscount love Olivia. And Anna so wanted her daughter to be in love. Happily in love. She wanted

Olivia to have so much more than an arranged marriage based upon the exchange of wealth or property or position.

She stopped and stared toward the house. Rosegate had been one of the first large mansions built in Manhattan at a time when most Knickerbockers were still content to reside in their modest, comfortably uniform brownstones and live their lives with quiet dignity.

But Northrop had always wanted more and more. He had wanted great wealth and power, beyond what his family already had. And he had achieved it, too, thanks more than a little to the hardship that had befallen others during the Civil War.

It had been during those war years that Anna first met the dashing Mr. Vanderhoff. They'd been introduced at a ball to benefit the wounded soldiers of the Union Army. Within days of Northrop's first call at her home, she'd thought herself in love with him. During their few chaperoned meetings together, she had fallen completely under his spell.

It had been a wonderful period in Anna's life. She'd had no idea then that their brief courtship would be the last truly happy time she could remember.

Except, of course, for the birth of their daughter. Anna had been happy when Olivia arrived. Happy to have someone to love who would love her in return. But even that Northrop had tried to spoil. He'd insisted on a nurse to care for the child when she was little, a governess for when she was older, and finally upon sending her to finishing school.

Now, Anna wanted more of a life than that for Olivia. She wanted Olivia to love and be loved by the man she married. She wanted her to share the same quiet devotion with her husband that Anna had seen between her parents, as Anna had wanted for herself and Northrop.

She pulled her cloak more tightly about her, suddenly feeling the wind as it cut through the wool cloth, chilling her to the bone. She remembered the yellow gown, wrapped in tissue and hidden in a box beneath her bed. That dress seemed to symbolize all that was wrong with her marriage and with her life. Somehow she had to protect Olivia from the same future, from the same failure.

As happened so often of late, Olivia found herself standing at her third-story bedroom window. A delivery wagon moved along Seventy-second Street, headed toward Madison Avenue.

Madison Avenue. Where Remington lived.

"I never lied about loving you. . . ."

But he had. He had lied.

"I'm not going to give up. We have something between us that is too special to lose. . . ."

But there wasn't anything between them. Not anymore. She was going to marry Spencer Lambert. She was going to leave America and live in England, where everything was different and she could forget.

A shiver ran through her as the memory of Remington's mouth upon her breast returned, as if to mock her silent arguments. Heat flared in her belly and loins, a desire to be touched, stroked, kissed.

"Damn you, Remington," she whispered as tears came to her eyes. She hated him for making her remember. She hated him for making her cry. It had been so much better when she'd been numb, when she'd been stone cold inside, bereft of feeling. This was torture. Slow torture. And she hated him because of it.

"Ask your father to show you my telegram. . . ."

She covered her ears with her hands and squeezed her eyes closed. "Leave me alone. Please, just leave me alone."

But he was still there, in her head, in her heart. *"I never lied about loving you. . . ."*

She heard the knock on her door but ignored it. She

didn't want to see anyone. She wanted no more congratulations, no more comments about her good fortune. And she didn't want to see her intended, either.

"Olivia?" The door opened. "Olivia?"

She lowered her hands from her ears and turned to face her mother.

"May I come in, dear?"

She held back a sigh and nodded. "Of course, Mama."

Anna closed the door behind her, then crossed the room to stand before her daughter. She took hold of Olivia's hand. "Sit down with me for a moment, will you? I think we need to talk."

"Oh, Mama . . . "

"Please, dear."

Reluctantly she allowed her mother to draw her across the room to the sofa and chairs grouped near one of the two fireplaces in her bedchamber. Anna sat on the sofa, Olivia beside her.

Her mother's light blue eyes searched Olivia's face for a long while before she spoke. "I want you to tell me what happened while you were gone from New York."

"It isn't important."

"Yes, it is," Anna replied forcefully. "I think it's very important."

Olivia glanced off toward the window.

Her mother's grip tightened on her hand. "Olivia, don't do this to yourself. Don't hide from the truth." Her voice grew soft. "Don't be like me."

She looked at her mother again, surprised and saddened by her words.

Anna leaned forward. "Listen to me. I know what it means to withdraw inside yourself. I've hidden from the truth for so many years, it's become second nature to me. But that's no way to live. You were meant to have more. So much more."

Olivia kissed her mother's cheek but remained silent.

"Who is he?" Anna asked. "The man you love."

She shook her head, as if to deny such a man existed.

"Tell me about him, Olivia."

She wasn't aware at first of the tears that trickled down her cheeks.

"It might help to talk about him," her mother encouraged.

"It won't help. Nothing will help."

Anna gathered her into her arms, pressing Olivia's head against her chest. "Oh, my darling daughter, tell me what has happened. Tell me what has hurt you so deeply."

And suddenly the words began to pour out of her, just as the tears streamed down her cheeks. She told her mother about Amanda Blue and the Blue Springs Ranch, about Dan and Sawyer Deevers, about Alistair McGregor and Ronald Aberdeen, about old Lightning and Misty and her pups, about Pete and Lynette Fisher, even about Timothy Bevins.

Then, in a halting voice, she told her mother about Remington Walker, about falling in love with him, about his betrayal.

For a long time after Olivia fell silent, after her tears were dry, Anna continued to hold her, rocking her gently. Finally she took Olivia by the shoulders and held her away, forcing her daughter to meet her gaze.

"You must tell the viscount you cannot marry him," she said. "You must break it off before it's too late."

"It's already too late. I'm going to marry him and go to England."

Anna grabbed Olivia's chin between thumb and forefinger. "Olivia, Mr. Walker didn't lie to you about the telegram. I saw it. He told your father to give up looking for you. He told Northrop you couldn't be found."

A breathless "No" escaped her parted lips.

"It's true. I swear to you, it's true."

*   *   *

From his office in the Vanderhoff Shipping warehouse on
the East River, Northrop could see Governors Island, the
Statue of Liberty, and Ellis Island. Churning its way
through the choppy, whitecapped river, the Fulton ferry
headed toward its slip on South Street. Tall masts waved
over ships that were docked at piers lining the riverbank,
and smoke belched from chimneys rising above the many
low, steep-roofed loft buildings of lower Manhattan.

Northrop rarely visited the warehouse these days, but
when he was a lad he'd often joined his grandfather here.
Even then he'd dreamed of Vanderhoff warehouses in
ports around the world, and he'd seen those dreams come
true through the years. Now, with Olivia's marriage to
Lord Lambert, he would expand his empire even farther.
The earl of Northcliffe's sphere of influence was great.
The union of their families would open many doors previ-
ously closed to Northrop.

He laughed softly. To think he'd been willing to settle
for a railroad from Gregory James. A railroad was something he could buy. In fact, he now owned all the railroads
he needed in America.

It seemed Olivia had done him a favor by bolting all
those years ago. It hadn't occurred to him back then to
look beyond New York for a son-in-law, not until he'd
witnessed for himself the number of American heiresses
marrying titled Englishmen. Now his daughter was joining
their ranks. She would be a countess and the mother of
earls, and Northrop would profit by it, he was certain.

He frowned as his thoughts turned suddenly to
Remington Walker. Why had Walker sought out Olivia at
the Harrisons' soiree? he wondered, not for the first time.
Northrop didn't doubt for a moment that Olivia had fancied herself in love with the detective. He was certain the

two of them had become lovers. Had Walker hoped to continue the alliance upon his return to New York? Had he really hoped to marry Olivia and get himself a piece of Vanderhoff Shipping?

Well, it didn't matter now. Olivia was engaged and would soon be wed. With the money Northrop had paid Walker, the younger man would be comfortably set for the rest of his life. Unless he was a fool, he would keep silent about the part he'd played in Olivia Vanderhoff's return to New York. And if he was a fool, Northrop would find a way to silence him.

Turning away from the grimy window, he reached for his hat and walking stick, then headed for the door. He considered going to see Ellen, but he quickly discarded the idea. There was little pleasure to be found there these days. Even after all these weeks, his mistress had yet to forgive him for sending his sons away to school. Her anger was evident in her eyes, in her words, even in her bed.

And Anna was no more pleasant to be around than Ellen. Something about his wife had changed over the summer months, although he wasn't quite sure what it was. Certainly he found no satisfaction when he joined her in her chamber.

He clenched his jaw as he settled back against the plush seat of his carriage. Why was it women seemed determined to make his life miserable? he wondered, then cursed them all.

Olivia stared at her mother, still not believing what she'd heard. Not daring to believe it.

Anna took hold of Olivia's hands and squeezed them tightly. "Go talk to him. He loves you. And you love him, Olivia, or you wouldn't be suffering so."

She shook her head.

"You can deny it all you like, but it's true. You can't marry Lord Lambert, not if you love another man. Go talk to Mr. Walker."

Her throat burned, and she found it difficult to speak. "Father has forbidden me to see Remington."

"To hell with your father."

Olivia drew back and stared at her mother in surprise. She had never heard words of defiance from Anna. Never in all her life.

Her mother rose from the sofa, allowing Olivia's hands to slip through her fingers. "At least think about what I've said." Then she walked toward the door, accompanied by a whisper of rustling petticoats.

After the door closed behind her mother, Olivia turned her gaze upon the fire blazing on the hearth, a small voice of hope whispering in her ear, *Remington didn't tell him where you were. Remington didn't lie about that.*

But how did he find you, then? the voice of doubt countered. *Why did he pay Remington all that money, if not because Remington had found you and told him so?*

Her mother was right. She had to talk to Remington. She had to listen to what he had to say. She had to know the truth.

She closed her eyes and allowed herself a moment to remember. For months now she'd refused every thought about Remington, about Sawyer and the Blue Springs Ranch. She'd refused them to keep the pain and hurt away. But now she let them come. She allowed the memories to flood over her, indulging in every image.

If it were true . . . if Remington hadn't betrayed her . . . if he truly did love her . . .

She hugged herself, wanting so to believe.

"Please let it be true," she whispered. "Oh God, please let it be true."

30

Remington set the latest edition of *The New York Times* on the table and looked about the large room of his private club. Both businessmen and the idle rich sat in comfortable chairs, most of them reading their newspapers and smoking their pipes or cigars. He wondered how many of them were well enough connected to receive an invitation to Libby's wedding.

The thought set his teeth on edge.

During the past week he'd tried everything short of storming the doors of Rosegate itself in order to see her, but their paths had not crossed again. Now that her engagement to Lord Lambert had been formally announced, he wondered if it might be too late already.

"If you really loved me, you would leave me in peace. . . ."

His heart tightened as he heard her words again in his head, saw the weariness in the way she'd carried herself. He'd done that to her. He'd put the sadness in her beautiful eyes. If only . . .

"Remington Walker. What luck!"

He glanced up to find Charlton Bernard standing before him.

"This is going to sound terribly gauche, my friend, but I was wondering if you might do me a favor." Charlton sat on a nearby chair. "My sister—you remember Lillian—is having a supper tonight for a few friends, and she has come up short one gentleman. She made me swear on my life that I wouldn't return without someone to round out her guest list. Do say you'll come."

Remington was all set to decline, but Charlton didn't give him a chance.

"This is Lillian's first night to shine since her wedding last summer. She and her husband have just moved into their new home, and Lillian has been running the servants into the ground in preparation for her debut as a hostess. You may have heard that Lord Lambert and his fiancée, Olivia Vanderhoff, will be there. Quite an accomplishment for my baby sister. Of course, Mother was none too pleased that Miss Vanderhoff chose to marry that viscount instead of me, her darling son"—Charlton grinned—"but the old girl's putting up a good front for Lillian's sake." His smile disappeared. "Listen, I know this is terribly poor form to invite you like this, but it would be a tremendous help."

Remington only half heard what the man said. He'd stopped listening the moment he'd learned Libby would be there. "I'd be glad to help out," he said when Charlton stopped talking.

"Splendid! Here's Lillian's address." He handed Remington a card. "Dinner will be at eight. See you then." Charlton rose and walked away.

Remington stared down at the card. He'd been given one more chance to see Libby. He wasn't about to let anything go wrong this time.

*   *   *

As usual, Olivia let her maid select what she would wear for the evening, but now the reason for her indifference had altered. Why should she care about clothes when all that mattered was to see Remington, to talk to him, to listen to what he had tried more than once to tell her? But first she had to find a way to slip out from under her father's watchful eye.

As if he'd known she'd had a change of heart, Northrop hadn't left Rosegate for the past twenty-four hours. It seemed he was always nearby, watching and listening. The only sanctuary was in her own room.

"You'll look lovely in this gown, Miss Olivia," Sophie said as she carried it across the room. "Green really is the best color for you. And it's a Worth, you know. It's no wonder every lady wants her gowns ordered from Paris. Even Mrs. Davenport cannot equal this, and your mother's sworn by her dressmaker for years."

Olivia didn't even spare the dress a glance. She simply raised her arms and allowed the maid to lift it over her head and drop it down. The fabric, cool and smooth, whispered over her corset and linen chemise, her cotton drawers, and her dark green stockings. Then she turned and faced the cheval glass, which reflected her lack of interest as Sophie fastened the closing up her back.

It was a graceful gown of Nile green China crepe, with a sash of black watered ribbon. A garniture of pink blossoms adorned her waist. The low, square corsage, revealing just a hint of cleavage, was covered by shirred gauze, and an epaulet of pink flowers rode her left shoulder. It was new, flattering, and fashionable.

How she missed her trousers and boots! And she hated the pinch of the corset around her rib cage. She longed to be able to draw a deep breath without feeling hindered.

"Your shoes, Miss Olivia," Sophie prompted as she scooted the green evening slippers closer to her feet.

She put on the shoes, then moved to the stool in front of her vanity table and sat down so Sophie could dress her hair.

Twisting a ring on her finger, she remained silent, her thoughts on Remington. How was she to see him if her father continued to watch her like a hawk? She couldn't ask Spencer to take her to Remington's house again. He might suspect something and mention it to her father. And she wasn't sure whom she could trust among the servants. They all knew how ruthless their employer could be. Could she ask any of them to risk their position for her by taking a note to Remington? Would she trust the wrong person and find she'd been reported to her father?

"Miss Olivia, I wonder if I might ask something of you."

She refocused her thoughts and met Sophie's gaze in the mirror. "What is it?"

"When you go to England after the wedding? I was wondering if you might take me along as your maid. You see, my grandmother still lives there. I haven't seen her since I was a little girl. Now that my parents have both passed on, I'd like very much to see her again. She's all the family I've got left in the world."

Maybe she could trust Sophie with a message to Remington, in exchange for helping her get to England. Maybe this was the opportunity she'd been hoping for. Maybe . . .

"I'll do what I can, Sophie," she told the maid. "I promise." *But with any luck,* she added silently, *you won't be going to England with me because I won't be going at all.*

*   *   *

Upon Alfred and Lillian Cameron's return from their European honeymoon, they had set up housekeeping in a modest four-story brownstone on Lexington Avenue, only a few blocks from the Episcopal Church of the Epiphany.

Eighteen and pretty, Lillian welcomed her guests to the Cameron house with a nervous smile and the look of a new bride who feared she might not be able to pull the evening off. She grew especially anxious upon the arrival of the viscount and his intended.

At the moment Libby appeared in the doorway, her hand on Spencer Lambert's arm, Remington chanced to find himself alone, which gave him the opportunity to watch her with an unfettered gaze.

She seemed to grow more beautiful every time he saw her. The gown she wore was exquisite, as was the emerald necklace gracing her throat. Her complexion was milk white, without even a hint of freckles on her nose and cheeks.

I miss your freckles, Libby.

As if she'd heard him, she lifted her eyes. Their gazes met and, for a breathless moment, held. Remington expected her to turn away with a look of cool disregard or one of pain and betrayal. He did not expect a tentative smile.

But there it was, curving her mouth upward at the corners.

She whispered something to the viscount, then drew him across the room. "Mr. Walker," she said softly, "it's a pleasure to see you again."

Was this some sort of joke? he wondered.

"May I introduce Spencer Lambert, Viscount Chelsea."

Was this how she intended to punish him for his perfidy, by flaunting her fiancé in front of him?

She glanced at the man beside her. "Spencer, this is Remington Walker. His father, I've heard, raised some of the finest horses in the South before the war. Mr. Walker has continued the tradition since his move to New York.

I've seen the gelding he rides and can tell you it is quite the best-looking horse I've ever seen."

Remington scarcely looked at the viscount as the two men shook hands.

"It's always a pleasure to meet one of Olivia's friends," Spencer said. "Perhaps you'll show me your livestock one day."

"Yes. To be sure," he murmured in response, still watching Libby and trying to guess what it was he saw in her expression.

She swept her gaze over the room. "Oh, look, Spencer. There's Penelope and Alexander." She faced Remington again. "Please excuse us, Mr. Walker, but we must say hello to the Harrisons."

"Of course."

The couple started away, but Libby stopped and turned back, whispering, "I must talk to you. Alone."

Their opportunity came when the gentlemen went off to smoke after supper and the ladies retired to the parlor to await their return. With only a glance exchanged between them, both Remington and Olivia knew what they should do. Within minutes each had slipped away and up the stairs. They met in a small sitting room on the second floor. A gas lamp, turned low, provided a source of light as they faced each other.

Olivia, her stomach aflutter with nerves, was suddenly uncertain as to what she should say, how she should begin. Finally she asked, "How is Sawyer?"

"He's fine. He misses you." His blue eyes, looking almost black in the dim light of the sitting room, studied her with increasing intensity.

"Remington, I . . ." She licked her dry lips with her tongue, then began again. "Remington, I . . . I want you to tell me what happened. Between you and my father. I . . . I want to know the truth. I want to know everything. I *need* to know everything."

He reached for her hand, but she took a step backward, out of reach. She wasn't yet ready for any physical contact with him. She was still afraid that her fragile hope could crumble, shatter into a thousand pieces.

When he spoke, his tone was gentle. "All right, Libby. I won't touch you." He motioned toward two chairs. "Come and sit down. It's a long story."

She led the way, settling onto the edge of a carved rosewood chair. Her heart was thumping crazily in her chest.

Remington raked the fingers of one hand through his hair, a small frown drawing his brows together. "It's hard to know where to begin."

Tell me you love me. Begin there. But that would be the wrong place to start, and she knew it. She wasn't able to deal with proclamations of love just yet.

"Did you know our fathers were friends, years ago?" He didn't wait for a reply. "That was before the war."

She listened as he recounted the story of Northrop and Jefferson, about the years both before and after the Civil War, about Jefferson's despair and suicide. She wasn't shocked by the part her father had played in the ruination of Jefferson Walker and the JW Railroad; she'd known him to do the same sort of thing too often through the years.

"When your father called me to Rosegate and asked me to find you, I thought at first it was because he knew who I was. I thought it might be his way of making some sort of amends. But he didn't know me. He'd forgotten my father as if he'd never existed. When I demanded the bonus if I found you before the end of a year, I never expected him to agree, but once he did, I knew this was my only real chance to have my revenge. I couldn't destroy him as he had my father, but I could hurt him, at least a little."

There was a tight band around her chest, making each breath she drew painful.

Remington stared off into a dark corner of the room.

"When I awakened in that bedroom at the Blue Springs and saw you for the first time, I knew even then that it was going to be hard to send you back to your father. I could see you were happy there. But I'd promised *my* father I would seek retribution. I wanted to get well and send that telegram and return to New York. I wanted to get out of Idaho as quickly as possible." He brought his eyes back to meet hers. "But I fell in love with you, Libby, and the money didn't matter anymore. Revenge didn't matter. Nothing mattered except being with you. When I went to Weiser with Pete Fisher, I sent your father a telegram saying I'd failed, that you couldn't be found. I told him to give up his search."

"How did he find me, then? Why did he pay you that money?"

"He had me followed. He hired another detective to find me when I didn't send my usual report." His eyes narrowed, sparking with anger. "And he paid me that bonus money to make sure you wouldn't stay with me. He's a shrewd man, your father."

It sounded plausible. It could be true. But how was she to be sure?

"Why wouldn't you marry me right away?" she whispered, then swallowed the sudden tears that burned the back of her throat. "Why did you put it off?"

"Because I didn't want your father to come between us. I didn't want to owe him anything, not even the portion of my fee he'd paid me before I left New York. I wanted things to be right before we married."

"But you didn't tell me the truth. You didn't tell me who you really were. You let me believe you still lived at Sunnyvale. You let me believe so many things that weren't true."

He leaned forward. "No, I didn't tell you the truth, and I was wrong not to. I shouldn't have kept silent. I should have explained everything. But there were so many lies between us, and I was afraid you would hate me when you learned the truth."

"You were afraid?"

"Afraid I'd lose you." He took hold of her hand, and this time she didn't pull away. "Maybe I have after all, but I hope not."

She closed her eyes. "I'm afraid, too."

His fingers tightened. "I love you, Libby. I want to marry you. I want to take you back to the Blue Springs. We were happy there. We could be happy again."

She looked at him. Was he telling the truth? Could they be happy again? Did she dare believe him? He'd lied to her about so much, but then, she was guilty of lying, too. Wasn't she as much at fault as he? Could they put everything behind them? Could she learn to trust him again?

She slipped her hand free of his and rose from the chair. "I'd better return before I'm missed. We don't want people to talk."

"Libby, wait!" He reached for her again.

She shook her head, raising a hand to stop him. "I need some time to think, Remington. It's all so confusing. I'm engaged to Spencer, and—"

"Don't let your father force you into a marriage you don't want. Even if you can't love me, Libby, don't let him do this to you."

I do love you, her heart confessed. But she couldn't tell him so. She was still afraid. Afraid to believe.

Olivia shook her head slowly, then turned away and left the room.

Rosegate was quiet, the windows darkened, by the time the Lambert carriage brought Olivia home. Spencer escorted her into the entry, where he helped her out of her cloak.

"Is something troubling you, Olivia?" he asked as he

took hold of her elbows and turned her to face him. "You've been inordinately quiet this evening."

She couldn't quite meet his gaze. "No, Spencer. I'm simply tired."

"Well, then, I shall let you retire." He gave her a perfunctory kiss on the cheek. "Sleep well, my dear."

"Thank you. Good night."

As soon as the door closed behind Spencer, Olivia picked up the lamp that stood on a table in the entry and started up the stairs. But she paused before she'd gone far.

"I sent your father a telegram saying I'd failed, that you couldn't be found. . . ."

She looked down the hallway toward her father's study.

"Olivia, Mr. Walker didn't lie to you about the telegram. I saw it. . . ."

If only she could be sure . . .

Once again she descended the stairs, then made her way to the room at the back of the house.

The study was her father's sanctuary, his most private domain. Neither Olivia nor her mother was ever to enter unless summoned there by Northrop. It was with an unsteady hand that Olivia turned the knob and pushed open the door before her.

A flood of bad memories washed over her as she stared into the darkened room. She saw herself as she'd once been, a lonely child, seeking her father's approval and affection. She saw the wounded girl who had wondered what was so terribly wrong with her that her father couldn't love her.

It's not my fault.

Her heart quickened.

It's not my fault he can't love me.

She stepped into the room, moving slowly toward the massive desk.

Father can't love anyone. It's not my fault.

A sigh whispered through her lips, and with the corresponding intake of air, she felt a sudden release. She supposed intellectually she'd understood about her father's inability to love, to give of himself, for many years. But feeling and believing it in her heart was something different, something new. Fear for the future seemed to flee from her. No matter what she found here tonight, she didn't have to be afraid anymore.

She sat in the large chair behind the desk, placed the lamp on the desktop, and pulled open the top drawer. She drew in another deep breath, then began her search.

It was nearly four in the morning before she found the two telegrams, both of them folded and wrinkled.

She read the first through a blur of tears:

"Have been unable to find Olivia. If your daughter was ever in Idaho Territory, she isn't any longer. I've found no clues to her whereabouts and believe it is pointless to continue the search. I suggest you save your time and money and accept that she has vanished for good. R. J. Walker."

She skimmed the second telegram, her heart racing with joy as she read the only words that mattered:

"I have located not only Mr. Walker but your daughter. . . . Signed, Gil O'Reilly."

He hadn't lied. Remington hadn't lied about this. He hadn't betrayed her to her father.

She covered her face with shaking hands, only then admitting to herself how afraid she had been.

He hadn't lied about loving her. He'd been prepared to give up a fortune, to give up hope of redeeming Sunnyvale, to let revenge go, all for his love of her.

Tomorrow morning she would go to him. Tomorrow she would tell Remington she loved him.

Tomorrow.

31

Olivia awoke with a start. She sat up and glanced quickly toward the windows. Anemic morning light peeked around the curtains, announcing the coming of dawn.

Remington!

Tossing aside the blankets, she slid her legs over to the side of the high poster bed. Her hair tumbled into her face, and she pushed it back with an impatient hand. She didn't bother to ring for Sophie. She didn't want anyone to know she was awake. She would dress herself this morning. There had to be something in her wardrobe she could manage without the help of her maid.

She hurried across the room and stirred up the fire on the hearth, adding more fuel. Then she performed hasty morning ablutions in the connecting bathing chamber. From her vast wardrobe she chose a dark blue gown with buttons up the front of the bodice. Without thought to wrinkling the fabric, she gathered the full skirts and dropped the gown over her head. She wanted only to hurry.

A short while later she hooked the last button on her
walking shoes, then straightened and picked up her hair-
brush, knowing she would never be able to dress her hair
as Sophie would.

Remington likes it down, she thought.

She smiled. Remington did like it down. He also liked
her hair in a braid, and so did she.

With brisk strokes of the brush, she swept the tangles
from her hair, then wove it into one thick plait, tying the
end with a ribbon.

When she looked in the mirror, she didn't see Olivia
Vanderhoff staring back at her. She saw Libby, and her
heart sang with joy because Remington loved Libby Blue.

Remington had been unable to sleep. Still wearing his
evening attire, he watched from the window of his bedchamber as dawn spilled shades of pink and lavender
across the clouds on the horizon. He watched it and wondered when he might hear from Libby again.

*"I need some time to think, Remington. It's all so con-
fusing. I'm engaged to Spencer. . . . "*

What would she decide? When might he hear from her
again?

Those were only two of the questions that had plagued
him throughout the night. He kept seeing her tentative
smile, kept hearing her whisper that she needed to talk to
him, kept feeling her uncertainty.

He wouldn't let her marry the viscount. No matter
what he had to do or say, he wouldn't let her marry a man
she didn't love, a man who wanted only the fortune her
father had agreed to settle on her. Not that Spencer
Lambert was necessarily a bad sort. But good or bad
didn't matter. What mattered was Spencer wouldn't make
Libby happy . . . and Libby deserved to be happy.

He swore as he turned away from the window, raking the fingers of both hands through his hair. He shouldn't have let her leave the Camerons' home last night. He should have dragged her back here to his place, if he'd had to. He should have held her and kissed her and caressed her until she couldn't think of anything but him.

At the very least, he should have made plans to see her again. He should have made her agree to meet with him today, this afternoon. He would go crazy before he could learn what social function she would be attending next.

What about church? he thought with sudden inspiration.

Of course! He glanced at the clock on the mantel. Why hadn't he thought of that before? The Vanderhoff women had always attended the Presbyterian church no more than a dozen blocks from his brownstone. He'd learned that bit of information when he'd first taken the case. And it was equally well known that Northrop never darkened a church door, having no use for religion.

Remington couldn't be certain if Libby had been back to church with her mother since her return, but he suspected her father would insist she keep up appearances. And since Northrop wouldn't be there himself, Remington didn't have that complication to worry about. He could at least have a chance to see her, even if they couldn't speak.

After glancing at the clock one more time, he decided he had plenty of time to bathe and put on fresh clothes and still be at church before services began.

Libby placed the dark blue bonnet on her head, then turned toward the door. She kept imagining Remington's face as she told him what she'd found, as she told him she was sorry for not trusting him, for not believing him. She could almost feel his arms as they encircled her and brought her close against him.

She reached for the knob, turned it, and pulled. The door didn't open. She felt a sudden heaviness in her chest as she tried it again. Still it didn't open.

The door was locked from the outside.

Her heart skipped. This couldn't be happening.

Once again she twisted the knob and yanked. Again and again and again.

"No," she whispered. "No. No. No."

From the other side of the door, she heard a deep, soft chuckle.

"Father, what are you doing?"

"Your wedding day has been moved forward, and I'm making sure you're here to enjoy it."

"Father!" She pounded on the door with her fist. "Father, open the door!"

"I can't, Olivia."

She dragged in a deep breath, forcing herself to be calm. She wouldn't let him hear her panic. Carefully moderating her voice, she said, "I never said I wouldn't marry Lord Lambert. Please, open the door. Mother will be expecting me to join her for church."

"Your mother won't be going to church, either. She has too many things to do in preparation for your wedding next week." His voice grew deeper, closer. "Olivia, if you think you can simply refuse to marry the viscount when the time comes, do consider what might happen to Mr. Walker. There are so many calamities that could befall him in this city."

Her heart nearly stopped beating altogether. She closed her eyes and wilted against the door.

"Just consider it, daughter."

She heard him walk away. "No," she whispered again as she slowly slid down the door until she sat in a puddle of blue skirts on the floor. "You can't do this. You can't."

*   *   *

Remington's gaze searched every pew, but neither Libby nor her mother was in church this morning. It was probably because she'd been out so late last night, he told himself. Or maybe they didn't attend this church any longer. There could be a dozen reasons why she wasn't here.

Uneasiness nagged at him as he slipped out of the church and headed down the sidewalk toward home.

He remembered the way Libby had looked last night, the way she'd watched him as he'd told her everything. He'd seen a spark of hope in her eyes, a willingness to believe, as she'd listened. He'd known she still cared, whether or not she was willing to admit it.

She would contact him after she'd had time to sort things through, he reassured himself. He had no reason to feel apprehensive. She would send word when she was ready to see him. All he had to do was wait.

Unfortunately, his disquiet wouldn't leave him. It grew with every step he took.

Something's wrong. . . . Something's wrong. . . . The words kept playing through his head, unrelenting, insistent. Logic wasn't able to dislodge the words of warning.

By the time he reached his brownstone, he'd given up arguing with himself. He was going to have to see Libby today. And the only way he knew to do that was to pay a visit to Rosegate.

Libby heard the key turn in the lock and rose quickly from the chair near the fireplace. A moment later Sophie entered, carrying a breakfast tray.

"Your father sent something for you to eat, Miss Olivia."

Ignoring the maid, Libby hurried toward the door. If she were especially careful, she just might be able to—

"It's no use, Miss Olivia. Your father has someone watching the door," Sophie called after her. "A mean-looking sort, he is, from Mr. Vanderhoff's warehouse, I think."

Libby's heart sank, but she refused to give in to despair. She was determined to find a way out. She had to get to Remington. She had lingered too long in apathy, slipping back into an old familiar pattern of letting her father run her life. She wasn't going to do it any longer.

"Sophie, you must help me," she said in a low voice, whirling about to face the maid.

The girl shook her head, eyes wide. "I can't. Your father warned me what would happen if I did. I'm a poor girl. I can't afford to be turned out onto the street without references."

"What about England? Don't you want to go to England with me after my wedding?"

"Your father has promised to send me himself, as long as I do as I'm told, miss. And there'd be no England for me if you have your way. The master told me so."

With a sound of frustration, Libby walked to the window overlooking the street. She looked down, wondering briefly if she could manage to climb down the side of the house. If only there were a ledge or a balcony or even a covered porch! But there was nothing but a sheer, three-story drop to the ground.

There had to be some way to escape. Her father couldn't lock her up this way. He couldn't really force her to marry someone she didn't want to marry.

The black carriage with its bright green trim pulled up to the curb in front of the Vanderhoff mansion. Even before the carriage door opened, she knew it was Remington. He'd come for her!

She tried to twist the window latch, but it was stuck. "Open," she demanded as she saw Remington descend from the carriage. As if in obedience, the latch turned.

Hands on her upper arms gripped her flesh and yanked

her back from the window before she could shout a word of protest. "You're to stay away from the window," a gruff voice ordered.

She twisted, trying to see the watchdog her father had sent to keep her. Before she caught a glimpse of him, he shoved her toward her bed. She tripped and fell facedown into the unmade bedding. She heard his chortle as he left the room, closing the door behind him.

"Sophie—" she began as she struggled back to her feet but stopped when she discovered the maid was gone, too. She hurried over to the door and tried to open it, even though she'd known she would find it locked.

She raced back to the window, but it was too late. Remington was nowhere in sight.

The butler led Remington along a dark-paneled hallway toward the back of the house. Libby's father was waiting for him in a cavernous room, the walls lined with bookshelves, the floor covered with ornate carpeting, and a massive desk, meant to make visitors feel insignificant, set near the far wall.

Northrop rose from the chair behind that desk as Remington entered the study. "Mr. Walker, I didn't know you'd returned to Manhattan."

Like hell you didn't, he thought, crossing the room with confident strides. "I've been back more than a month now."

Northrop feigned surprise. "You have? Then why haven't you sent round your bill for the rest of your fee? I've been expecting it."

"I haven't sent it because I don't want your money, Vanderhoff."

Remington watched Northrop frown, certain the older man took exception to his tone of voice. Fine, he thought. That suits me just fine.

"I've come to see Libby."

"My daughter's name is Olivia." He sat down and motioned to a chair opposite him. "And she isn't receiving visitors."

Remington didn't sit down. "She'll see me."

"And why is that, Mr. Walker?" Northrop asked, raising an eyebrow.

"Because Libby knows you lied to her. You can't force her to marry the viscount. She's a grown woman, and she can make her own choice."

"She *has* made her choice. She and the viscount are to be married next week."

"Next week? But the newspaper said—"

"The newspaper was wrong."

Remington pressed his knuckles against the desktop. "Then let Libby tell me that for herself."

Northrop leaned back in his chair and eyed Remington with a look of disdain, as if he were no more than a cockroach on the carpet.

"Unless you're afraid, of course," Remington added softly.

The seconds were ticked off by the pendulum in the grandfather clock.

At long last, Northrop rose from his chair again. "Very well, Mr. Walker. I'll bring my daughter down to see you. And when she has told you of her plans, I shall expect you to leave this house without further trouble. Is that understood?"

"If that's her decision, I'll go."

Libby didn't turn around this time when she heard the key in the lock. She remained at the window, staring down at Remington's carriage, hardly daring to breathe as she waited to see him leave the house.

"Olivia."

She felt an eerie alarm slide up her spine.

"Olivia, Mr. Walker has come to see you."

She turned slowly, fixing her father with a suspicious gaze. "You'll let me see him?"

"Yes. He wants you to tell him that you've made your decision to marry Lord Lambert. He wants you to tell him I'm not forcing the marriage and that it's of your own choice." He moved across the room to stand before her. He placed his index finger beneath her chin. "Before I take you down, I think I should remind you what might happen to Mr. Walker if you should fail to send him away."

You don't frighten me, she wanted to say. But it wasn't true. He terrified her. He was more dangerous than Timothy Bevins ever thought of being. Bevins had been mad, insane. But her father wasn't crazy. He knew exactly what he was doing. He wasn't mad; he was evil. And he was more dangerous than Bevins because he had the power to do what he wanted and get away with it.

"I ruined Jefferson Walker financially, but I won't stop there with his son. If he crosses me, they'll find him floating facedown in the Hudson River."

"You knew?" she whispered, surprise momentarily eclipsing her fear. "You knew who he was?"

He barked a laugh. "Of course I knew. Do you think me a fool?"

No, she didn't think him a fool. She thought him heartless. Evil. "Have you no feelings at all?" She took a step backward, pressing her thighs against the windowsill. "Don't you care for anyone but yourself?"

"Very little, my dear. Now, shall I tell you what to say to your devoted young man?"

"I won't marry Spencer. You cannot make me."

"Ah, but you *will* marry Spencer, and I *can* make you do it. You'll marry the viscount for Mr. Walker's sake . . . and for your mother's. If you don't want either of them to come to harm, you'll do as I say."

"Mama?" She shook her head. "Not Mama."

"You'll go downstairs and tell Mr. Walker that you have made your decision. You are going to marry the viscount. If you don't, Olivia, your beloved Mr. Walker will find himself in deep water before nightfall. And your mother . . ." He left the threat unfinished.

What choice did she have? Remington . . . her mother . . . How else could she protect them from the man who stood before her?

She met her father's eyes with an unwavering gaze, hoping he could see the hatred that had blazed to life in her heart. "When I was little, I wanted so much to win your love. I wondered what was so terribly wrong with me. Why you couldn't care for me." She lifted her chin. "But now I see there would have been something wrong with me if you *had* cared." She stepped around him and headed for the door. "Someday your transgressions will catch up with you, Father, and you'll find the price you must pay for them is more than you possess."

Libby walked swiftly, with her head held high. She didn't bother to look back to see if her father followed; she knew he did.

On the second-floor landing, she paused and glanced down the hall toward her mother's room. Was Anna locked in, too? Was she all right? She longed to know the answers, but there was no time to discover them now. She moved on, descending the stairway to the ground floor. Her mind searched for an idea, some sort of plan, some way to warn Remington of the danger he was in.

God help me, she prayed as she walked down the hall. Keep him safe.

Remington heard her footsteps just before Libby entered the study. Her father was right behind her.

She hesitated a moment in the doorway. There was

something different about her, he thought as he watched her move with purpose across the room.

She stopped just out of his reach. "Father says you wanted to see me."

He glanced over her shoulder. Northrop stood just inside the room, his arms folded in front of his chest. Glancing back at Libby, Remington said, "I've come to take you away from here."

"I can't go with you, Remington. I'm going to marry Spencer."

He stepped forward, took hold of her arms, and drew her toward him. He stared down into wide green eyes. "Is that what you want?"

Her voice grew softer. "It's what I must do, Remington. And you should take the money Father paid you and return to the Blue Springs. Go away from Manhattan. You don't belong here." She drew a breath, then said in a stronger voice, "Tell Sawyer I love him. Tell him not to forget Libby Blue."

Libby Blue. That was it. That's what was different about her. She wore her hair in a braid, like Libby, and her gaze wasn't cool and remote as it had been. There was feeling in her apple green eyes. He could read love in their depths—and fear, too.

His instincts hadn't been wrong. Something was very much amiss here, and she was trying to warn him.

"Libby?" he asked softly, testing the name.

"Yes."

In that one word, he heard her confession of love.

"Leave with me," he urged.

"I can't."

His fingers squeezed gently. "I understand, Libby. I'll go, since that's what you want me to do." *But I'll be back for you*, his eyes told her. *Don't be afraid. I'll return.*

He could only hope that she understood as he released her arms and walked out of the study, leaving her behind.

32

The Vanderhoff mansion loomed dark and large above Seventy-second Street. Thin clouds blew across the three-quarter moon, and shadows and moonlight played a ghostly dance over the stone facing of the house.

Standing across the street, Remington stared at the third-story window, fourth from the left. Sawyer had said that was where he'd seen her. Remington hoped it was her bedchamber. He'd probably only have one chance to find out.

Moving stealthily, he crossed the street and entered through the front gate, then slipped around the side of the house, heading for the servants' entry. At two in the morning, no one was likely to be awake. With a little luck he could get up to the third floor, wake Libby, and then lead her out. Her absence wouldn't be discovered until she was called to breakfast.

With just a little luck . . .

The servants' entrance was locked, but it took Remington only a couple of minutes to open it. He was grateful the door was kept well oiled. It opened and closed without a squeak.

Once inside, he waited a moment for his eyes to adjust to the darkness. Then he moved forward cautiously, into the kitchen, beyond the pantry and the laundry room, searching for the back staircase. He found it just beyond a large, swinging door. A gas lamp, turned low, cast a dim yellow light on the narrow, steeply pitched stairs.

Glancing up, he took a deep breath, then began the ascent, stepping softly and praying the boards wouldn't creak beneath his weight. His luck continued to hold.

When he reached the third floor, he paused again, finding his bearings, then followed the hallway that would lead him to the chambers facing the street. He nearly stumbled over a chair left in the hall but caught it before it could topple over and send up an alarm.

He breathed a sigh of relief as he righted the chair, then reached for the door to what he hoped and prayed was Libby's room. The key had been conveniently left in the lock.

He glanced to his right, then to his left. All was silent. With a faint click, he turned the key and opened the door, slipping inside and closing it behind him.

The large four-poster bed was off to his left, a giant spiderlike shadow in a room filled with shadows. With heart pounding in his ears, Remington moved toward it, his steps silenced by a thick carpet.

Libby was brought abruptly awake by a hand over her mouth. Terror shot through her, and she tried to pull away, thrashing with her arms, kicking with her legs.

"Libby, it's me."

She quieted instantly. His hand slid away.

"Come on. We need to get out of here."

She sat up. "Remington." His name slipped from her lips, a verbal caress, filled with hope.

Then he was holding her, kissing her, pushing her hair back from her face. She clung to him, savoring the moment, glad for it, no matter how brief. She breathed in his warm, masculine scent and felt comforted by how familiar it seemed to her.

He lifted his mouth to whisper, "We'd better do this back at my place. We aren't safe yet."

"Remington, I can't go." Although she couldn't see him, she could sense his surprise. "Father's threatened to hurt Mother if I don't do what he says. And he's threatened to kill you."

"Don't worry about me. I can take care of myself." He drew her up from the bed. "We'll take your mother with us. You'll have to show me where her room is."

"But—"

"Don't argue with me, Libby."

She couldn't help smiling, despite the seriousness of their situation. "I won't. I'll never argue with you again."

His chuckle was barely audible. "I doubt that." He kissed her again, then said, "Now hurry."

She grabbed her dressing gown from the stool at the foot of her bed, slipped her arms into the sleeves, and then tied the belt securely around her waist. In the dark she found a pair of house shoes and put them on. "I'm ready," she told Remington softly.

He took hold of her hand and led her toward the door. "Where will we find your mother?"

"Second floor, down the hall to the right."

"And where's your father's room?"

"Beyond it one door."

He turned the knob. "Once we're out in the hall, not a word. Understood?"

She nodded, forgetting he couldn't see her in the dark.

He opened the door, and Libby's heart began to pound a riotous beat. If anyone was near, they would surely hear it.

She tightened her grip on Remington's hand as he led her along the hall to the servants' staircase. They descended one floor, and she was thankful for the dim light of the gas lamp, left burning in case one of the Vanderhoffs should ring for something in the night. She was thankful for it because it afforded her a glimpse of Remington, and she took courage from the sight of him.

When they reached the second-floor landing, he turned to her. "Wait here," he said, his mouth beside her ear.

She shook her head.

He ignored her. "If anything goes wrong, run for it. Get to my place, then send for David Pierce. He's a judge here in the city and an old family friend. Mrs. Blake will know how to get in touch with him. David will be able to help you. You can trust him."

She shook her head again, gripping his hand, refusing to let go.

He kissed her cheek. "It'll be all right, Libby," he whispered. "I won't be long."

Libby felt a sudden *whoosh* of air, then heard a sickening sound, flesh against flesh, bone against bone. Remington jerked free of her hold and went crashing to the floor. That's when she saw his assailant. The brute moved with terrible swiftness, driving his boot into Remington's kidney—once, then again and again.

"Remington! Stop!" She tried to intercede but was stayed by fingers closing around her arm.

"I'm afraid your young man is wrong, Olivia," her father said as he turned her to face him. "He will be a long time in returning." He glanced beyond her. "Caswell, dispose of Mr. Walker."

"No, Father! Don't!" She twisted around to see Remington. He lay unconscious at Caswell's feet. Tears clouded her vision as she turned again. "Please, I beg you, Father. Don't hurt him anymore. I'll do anything you want. Just please don't harm him."

"Very touching. Very touching indeed." He motioned with his head. "You know what to do, Caswell."

"Aye, that I do, sir."

A cry tore from her lips as she watched Caswell throw Remington over his shoulder and disappear down the staircase. "Please, Father, don't!"

His grip on her arm tightened ruthlessly. "You should have thought of protecting him before you tried to escape, Olivia. It's too late to help him now."

Remington regained consciousness in the dank, stinking hold of a ship.

He staggered to his feet, feeling his way in the darkness. Although the floor rocked beneath him, he knew the ship was still tied to the pier. He could hear it knocking against the dock as it tugged on its moorings.

He wondered how long he had been unconscious, then touched the back of his head, wincing as he felt the lump and dried blood. Next he felt the bruised places on his side and stomach.

If he ever got his hands on the fellow who'd kicked him . . .

But he hadn't time for that now. He had to get off this ship. He didn't doubt for a moment that he was meant to be fish bait as soon as they set to sea.

And he wasn't about to let that happen. Not when he knew Libby needed him.

33

Remington was dead.

Every day the dressmaker came to Rosegate, to Libby's room, for the fittings of her wedding gown. Mrs. Davenport never let on if she thought the bride's behavior was odd. She simply chattered about the Parisian model gown made of ivory satin, draped with Brussels lace, and trimmed with orange blossoms and said how wonderful it was that Libby was marrying an English lord and how she hoped Libby would still be able to wear her gowns occasionally.

"Never has Manhattan seen such a beautiful bride as you will be, Miss Vanderhoff," she would say each day. "You'll take England by storm. Mark my words."

But Libby cared nothing about England, nothing about her wedding, nothing about anything. Emptiness filled her, stretched before her into her future, a constant reminder of the only thing that mattered: Remington was dead.

He was dead, and nothing else mattered without him.

She tried once to tell herself to fight her father, to refuse to do his bidding, to escape and tell the authorities what Northrop Vanderhoff had done. Remington would want her to fight. He wouldn't want her to retreat inside herself as she had done when she'd thought he'd betrayed her.

But she realized the futility of going to the police, even if she could escape. She had no proof of any wrongdoing. No one other than Caswell and her father had seen Remington inside Rosegate that night. She didn't even have any proof that she'd known Remington, beyond a casual acquaintance. She had nothing, nothing but a life without him.

She longed to be able to see her mother, but Anna was kept from her, too. If only she could lay her head in her mother's lap and weep, perhaps the pain in her chest would become bearable. Perhaps then she could find some spark of life left in her.

At night, in the darkness of her room, she stared up at the ceiling and thought of the Blue Springs, Aunt Amanda, Sawyer, McGregor, Misty, and old Lightning. And Remington. She remembered what life had been like for her in Idaho, and for brief moments of fancy she imagined she could find that happiness, that life, again.

But she couldn't. Not now that Remington was dead.

Spencer Lambert called daily at the Vanderhoff mansion, bringing gifts for his bride. And every day Northrop came to Libby's room and escorted her downstairs to see her betrothed. She endured the viscount's visits as she endured everything else—in silence. He never seemed to mind her remote behavior. Perhaps he was getting all he wanted in a wife—her silence and her money.

Libby supposed she would be glad to leave this house, to leave America. After her wedding she would never have to see her father again. She might have continued to hate him, but it took energy to hate, and she had no strength left, not even for that.

Appropriately enough, Olivia Vanderhoff's wedding day arrived with gray skies and cold October winds.

At dawn Libby watched from her bedchamber window as the sky turned from onyx to pewter. Leaves tumbled from tree limbs, rolling along the street, slipping beneath the wheels of delivery wagons where they were crushed into dust. Extra servants, hired for the wedding festivities, leaned into the wind and held on to their hats as they made their way toward the rear entrance of the Vanderhoff house.

The door opened behind Libby, but she didn't bother to turn around. It didn't matter who it was. Nothing mattered anymore.

"Oh, you're already up, Miss Olivia," Sophie said with surprise. "And here I thought I'd have to wake you."

"No, I'm up." She pressed her forehead against the cool glass, wishing she could open the window and let the wind blow her away like the autumn leaves.

"I'll have your bath ready in no time. You've a big day ahead of you."

"Remington wanted me to marry him."

"What's that, miss?"

She turned toward the maid. "Remington asked me to marry him. I never should have left Idaho. I should have stayed there and married him."

"But Miss Olivia, you're going to be a countess. You should be happy you didn't marry some farmer."

Libby closed her eyes. "He wasn't a farmer," she whispered. "He was everything."

A few moments passed before the maid spoke again. "Miss Olivia, I'm sorry if I've caused you hurt. I was only doing what the master wanted. And what else could I do? There's not many jobs that pay as good, and with your father's promise to send me back to England . . . "

Libby shook her head. "It doesn't matter now." She turned back to the window.

Another long silence gripped the room.

Finally Sophie whispered, "I'll get your bath, miss."

Remington kept his cap pulled low and his head bent forward as he carted chairs into the Vanderhoff ballroom, ever watchful for a chance to slip away from the other temporary help and make his way up the stairs. And just in case he needed any help, Gil O'Reilly had managed to get himself a position working in the kitchen.

Surprisingly enough, Remington owed his life to the Irishman who had first brought Northrop to the Blue Springs. O'Reilly had been responsible for getting Remington off the ship before Caswell could send him to a watery grave, although his rescue had been unplanned.

O'Reilly had been on board the *Vanderhoff Queen* to investigate the disappearance of a sailor from another ship docked nearby. Whether chance or fate, O'Reilly had opened the door to Remington's hold and set him free. Now Caswell was languishing in a jail cell of his own, unable to inform Northrop of Remington's escape, thanks to a friend of O'Reilly's on the police force.

The Irishman also got the credit for stopping Remington from charging back to Rosegate as soon as he was free. "Have yourself a plan," he'd urged Remington. "Vanderhoff's a powerful man who'll stop at nothing to get what he wants. You've seen proof of that already. Sure, and we've got little to fight him with but our wits."

"Why make this your fight?" Remington had asked O'Reilly.

"'Tis sorry I am for the part I played in Miss Vanderhoff's troubles. I saw the way it was when we come back from Idaho, and my heart nearly broke for her. Count this as my way of askin' your forgiveness."

Remington hadn't been about to reject O'Reilly's offer of help. They would probably need both it and plenty of luck to get them out of here today.

Anna walked boldly into Northrop's study and closed the door behind her. Her husband looked up from the papers on his desk, and she saw a flicker of surprise cross his face.

"I must speak with you," she said, hoping he wouldn't notice the slight quaver in her voice.

He set aside the papers he'd been reading. "What is it, Anna?"

"You must stop this farce."

"Stop what?" He leaned back in his chair, a look of mild amusement replacing surprise.

She set her shoulders and moved toward him. "You must not force Olivia to go through with this wedding."

"I'm not forcing her, my dear. Olivia is quite willing to go through with it."

"I don't believe you."

Northrop bolted up from his chair, a dark scowl drawing his brows together, all trace of amusement gone. "You don't what?"

"I don't believe you," she said again, somehow managing not to flinch from him. "Why else are you keeping me from her?"

He was silent a moment, then he shrugged. "Very well, Anna. You may see her." He sat down and picked up his papers, dismissing her without a word.

Anna hesitated, suspecting some sort of trick. Northrop had set a guard at Olivia's door last week, and he had forbidden Anna to go near her room. She knew the reason neither for his edict then nor for his permission now. She waited, thinking he would look up and suddenly laugh at his cruel joke. But he didn't. He continued to ignore her.

Finally she turned and hurried from the room. Quickly she climbed the stairs to the third floor. No one tried to stop her as she hastened down the hall.

She rapped on the door, then opened it without waiting for permission to enter. "Olivia," she called as she stepped inside.

Her daughter stood near the window, gazing down at the avenue below.

"Olivia?" She closed the door.

Olivia made no indication that she'd heard.

Anna moved across the bedchamber, stopping beside her daughter. She laid her hand on Olivia's shoulder.

Olivia turned her head and met Anna's gaze. "Mama," she said softly. "You've come."

"Yes, dear."

Olivia turned once more to the window. "It's my wedding day." She spoke in a monotone, her voice completely without feeling.

"Yes, I know. Olivia, dearest . . . your father says you want to marry the viscount. Is it true? Is this what you want?"

"It doesn't matter."

Anna's fingers tightened on Olivia's shoulder. "What about Mr. Walker? You love him, don't you?"

"He's dead."

Anna gasped and pressed her free hand against her heart.

Olivia looked at her again. "I think I shall be glad to go to England, Mama."

"Oh, my darling daughter," Anna whispered, tears gathering in her eyes. She hugged Olivia, pressing her face into the curve of her neck, stroking her hair. She wanted to comfort her, but she didn't know what to say. She wanted to tell her this was not the right reason to marry the viscount, but she couldn't do that, either. She understood Olivia's desire to go away. She felt it, too.

Wedding guests had already started to arrive at Rosegate before Remington found the opportunity he'd been awaiting. In a brief moment when no one else was around, he slipped away, climbing the back staircase with alacrity, ever watchful.

Just as he reached the third floor, the door to Libby's room opened and a maid stepped into the hall. Remington watched as she hurried away. He waited until she'd disappeared into another room, then strode toward his destination.

The door wasn't locked. He opened it and stepped inside quickly.

His gaze found Libby at once. She was standing before the cheval glass, clad in a wedding gown. Two women fussed about her, an older woman fastening the pearl buttons up the back of the gown, the other, a young woman about Libby's age, kneeling on the floor, doing something to the hem.

The older woman turned her head when she heard the door click shut. She let out a tiny gasp of surprise when she saw Remington. "What are you doing here, sir?"

He ignored her as he started forward.

The woman stepped into his path. "Get out of here at once, or I shall be forced to—"

"Libby."

He saw her stiffen, then she turned around. Color drained from her face. Her lips moved, but no sound came out.

"Jeanette, send for Mr. Vanderhoff," the older woman ordered. "Quickly. Tell him—"

"No." Libby stopped Jeanette with a hand on her arm. "No, please. It's all right, Mrs. Davenport." She came toward him, stepping around Mrs. Davenport, who hadn't budged an inch. "I thought you were dead," she whispered when she'd stopped before him.

"No. I'm very much alive. And you're very beautiful."

She reached up, touching his face with her fingertips. Her eyes were wide, unblinking, as if afraid he might disappear any second. "You're alive."

He grabbed one of her hands, turned it, and brought it to his lips, kissing her palm. "Very."

"How did you escape? Father said—"

"I'll tell you later. Are you ready to go back to the Blue Springs and marry me?"

"I'm ready." She almost smiled, as if just realizing he was real and not an illusion. "I've been ready for quite some time."

Unable to help himself, he drew her against him and lowered his mouth to meet hers. She tasted sweeter than he'd remembered. He longed for the kiss to go on for hours. He longed to be able to stand there and hold her and kiss her and reassure her, but now was not the time. They risked discovery with every passing moment.

Stepping back, he reached into his pocket and withdrew the bank draft he'd brought with him. "This is for your father," he said as he handed it to her.

Libby stared down at the draft. It was made out to Northrop Vanderhoff.

"That's every penny he's paid me," Remington said softly. "I thought we should leave it for him."

Her vision blurred with unshed tears. "You don't have to give this back. You earned it."

"I don't want his money. I only want his daughter. Let's go home, Libby."

Home. We're going home. . . .

But the joy that sang in her heart was stopped by the ominous sound of an opening door. Grabbing hold of Remington's arm, she waited to see who was entering.

Looking lovely in a bright yellow gown, tiny yellow roses in her hair, Anna stopped in her tracks. Her eyes darted between Remington and Libby. Then she glanced into the hall, stepped back in the room, and closed the door, leaning against it. "Mr. Walker, I thought you were dead."

"That was the rumor, Mrs. Vanderhoff. As you can see, it was false."

Libby moved toward her mother. Lowering her voice to a whisper, she said, "I'm leaving with Remington now, Mama. I want you to come with us."

"Come with you?"

She nodded. "You must leave Father. For your own sake, Mama, you must leave this house. Please. Come with us."

Anna shook her head. "It's nearly time for the wedding. Your father will be looking for you soon. We must get the both of you out of here. I'll worry about what I should do later." She touched Libby's cheek. "Don't worry about me. I'll be fine."

Libby glanced over her shoulder at Remington. As if he understood what she was thinking, he came forward and joined his voice to hers.

"Don't put it off, Mrs. Vanderhoff. Come with us to the Blue Springs. Libby is right. You shouldn't stay here. And you'll like it in Idaho. You'd be happy there."

Anna smiled softly. "Libby." She looked at her daughter. "I haven't heard anyone call you that since you were a girl, still in the nursery." She leaned forward and kissed Libby's cheek. "I'm so glad for you both."

"Mama, please."

Anna shook her head again, then looked at Remington. "What is your plan, Mr. Walker?"

"I was hoping we could disguise Libby as one of the servants and slip out the way I came in."

"I can send for Sophie," her mother offered.

"No." The single word was emphatic, determined.

Both Remington and Anna turned toward her with looks of surprise.

"I'm not sneaking out of here. I'm not running away anymore." She faced Remington, gazing up into his beloved blue eyes, beseeching him to understand. "I've run away too often in the past. I'm not running again."

He touched her cheek. "You're right. If we run, he'll have won, won't he?"

She nodded.

"I think it's time to go downstairs." He took hold of her arm. "Ready?"

"Yes."

"Then let's go face your father."

34

Northrop became aware of a hush rippling across the crowd of guests. He looked up to find his daughter standing in the doorway to the ballroom. She looked spectacular in her wedding gown, every inch a countess. But with her, dressed like one of the servants, stood Remington Walker, holding her arm with fierce possessiveness, and Northrop knew in that instant his daughter would never be a countess.

"Who is that with Olivia?" he heard someone whisper.

Someone else answered, "That's Remington Walker. What's he doing dressed like that?"

"And why's he with Olivia?"

Then Northrop saw Anna. She was wearing a yellow silk gown, appearing scarcely old enough to be the mother of a bride. Yellow, her favorite color. Yellow, the color he'd forbidden her to wear all these years.

He tasted the bitterness of defeat on his tongue.

*　　　*　　　*

For the first time in her life, Libby was completely without fear. She felt free, like an eagle soaring high above the rugged Idaho mountains.

With her gaze locked on her father, she and Remington moved through the throng of guests. They parted like water before a ship's bow. She heard their whispers but ignored them. She didn't care what was said or by whom. She had come only to say good-bye. To her father, but even more so to Olivia Vanderhoff.

Northrop glared at them as they approached. She saw his frustration in the set of his mouth, knew he was controlling a blinding rage that would erupt later. Pity the poor person who was nearby when it happened.

Stopping a few feet away, she held out the bank draft Remington had given her upstairs. "We've come to give you this, Father."

His frown deepened as he reached to take the draft.

"And to say good-bye. I'm not going to marry the viscount." As a collective gasp arose behind her, she shifted her gaze to her erstwhile fiancé. "I'm sorry, Spencer. I cannot marry you when I love someone else." Once more she looked at her father. "I won't be sold like some product in your warehouse, Father, and I won't be held prisoner in my room. I'm going to walk out that door, free to do as I please. I'm going to marry Remington, and then I'm returning to our ranch in Idaho."

The buzz of voices increased.

"Everything you paid for me is there. You can't keep us apart, no matter what lies you tell, no matter what else you do."

Remington's hand tightened on her arm, and she glanced up at him.

"Our love means more than any amount of money."

Remington bent down and kissed her. She heard more gasps of surprise, perhaps even indignation, but she didn't care. She didn't need anyone's approval to be who she was or to love the man she loved.

Left breathless by Remington's kiss, Libby remained encircled by his arms as she turned to find her mother. "Mama, come with us," she encouraged softly. "You'll be happy there. Come with us."

Indecision warred in Anna's eyes.

"You deserve to be happy, Mama."

"Yes," her mother whispered. "Yes, I do." She glanced at Northrop, saying more loudly, "I do deserve to be happy for a change."

Northrop's face blazed red with fury. "Anna, I'll not tolerate—"

"You have nothing to say about it, Northrop." Anna turned toward the shocked guests. "I'm sorry, everyone, but the wedding you came to witness will not be taking place. Now, you must excuse me. I must pack a few things. You see, I'm leaving New York." She smiled at her daughter. "I'm going to Idaho with Libby and her new husband. Believe it or not, I'm going to raise sheep instead of roses."

The wedding ceremony was held that same afternoon in Judge David Pierce's parlor. It was a simple affair, with only Anna, Sawyer, and Remington's new friend, Gil O'Reilly, in attendance.

After the vows had been spoken and Remington had kissed his bride, the newlyweds slipped away to the Plaza Hotel at the corner of Fifth Avenue and Fifty-ninth Street. Remington ordered a sumptuous meal delivered to their suite, but Libby could scarcely eat a bite. And it seemed her husband had little appetite, either.

At least, not an appetite for food.

Remington rose from his chair and came slowly around

the table. Libby's heart raced with eagerness as he drew near. She had been waiting for this moment for hours, days, months.

He leaned down and kissed the curve of her neck. Gooseflesh rose along her arm. She closed her eyes and let her head drop back, savoring the sensations coursing through her.

"You make a beautiful bride, Mrs. Walker," he whispered in her ear, causing another shiver of delight.

She met his gaze. "Mrs. Walker," she repeated with wonder. "Mrs. Remington Walker."

He switched to the other side of her neck. "Beautiful," he murmured against her skin.

She wasn't quite sure how it happened, but somehow she found herself standing. His fingers moved deftly down her back, slipping the buttons free, opening the bodice, allowing cool air to caress her skin. Again she shivered, this time with anticipation.

He turned her toward him and cradled her face between his hands. He stared down at her, his gaze a caress, full of promise and love. She felt her insides turning soft and liquid.

"Thank you, Libby."

"Thank you?" she echoed.

He kissed her lips, her nose, her eyelids. "Yes."

Her heart quickened. "For what?"

"For giving me something worthwhile to live for. I'd forgotten what was good and beautiful in the world. All I had was anger and bitterness and a desire for revenge. You showed me there was something better. There was you." He kissed her again, long, slow, lingering.

She wrapped her arms around his torso, her legs weak with wanting. There was so much in her heart. So much she wanted to tell him, but the words wouldn't come. Not now when he was kissing her that way. Not now as his hands began to roam over her body, removing her gown and her petticoats and her corset and her stockings.

Later. Later she would tell him how much she loved him. Later she would tell him what he'd taught her: that freedom wasn't something she could find if she ran away from her troubles. It was something she could find only if she stood and fought. Liberty wasn't being alone. It was giving herself, her heart, to others.

Later. She would tell him all that and more later. After he'd carried her to bed and lain with her there. After he'd laved her breasts with warm lips and joined his body with hers. After they'd touched the heavens and stars and tumbled back to earth.

Later. There would be time for that and so much more. They were free to love each other for the rest of their lives.

Epilogue

May 1894
Blue Springs Ranch, Idaho

From the living room window of the ranch house, Libby Walker watched the pink fingers of dawn caress the western mountain range. Slowly the deep colors of night gave way to vibrant shades of morning, and the valley that was home came to life with familiar sounds. A crow of a rooster. The bark of a dog. A bleating of a lamb. Even Melly's impatient moo.

This was Libby's favorite time of day, when the house was still quiet and she could reflect on the pleasures of life. And the pleasures of her life were many.

She lowered her gaze to the infant suckling on her breast. Her son let go of the nipple and grinned up at her, gurgling a milky laugh, as if he understood what she was thinking.

"Hello, angel," she whispered as she closed her bodice.

Then she raised the baby to her shoulder and patted his back.

Jefferson Walker, twelve weeks old today, had been a sweet-natured baby from the day he was born, quite unlike his sister. Amanda Ann, almost three years old, was an impatient soul, headstrong and willful. Remington said she was like her mother, but Libby thought Amanda Ann would be ever so much more than Libby had ever dreamed of being.

"If I ever commission a portrait of you," Remington said from the hallway, "I want you posed just like that."

She turned and watched as he walked into the room.

"With your hair down," he continued, "the morning sun coming in the window at your back, and holding our baby in your arms." He gave her a kiss, long and sweet, the way she liked them best. Then he kissed the fuzzy dark hair on his son's head. "Morning, Jeff."

Libby's heart swelled to overflowing. Even after nearly four years, she could sometimes scarcely believe this was real, that Remington was her husband, that she spent every night wrapped in the safety of his arms, that he had given her two children to love and cherish.

"Are you going over to your mother's today?" he asked as he lifted the baby from her arms.

"Mmm. I promised I'd help her with her new rose cuttings."

"What's McGregor think of all those flowers surrounding their house?"

Libby laughed softly, thinking of her stepfather's expression when the last shipment of cuttings had arrived. "Och, woman," she mimicked, "will ye have us buried in roses before ye're done?"

Remington's laughter joined hers.

She smiled up at him. "McGregor makes Mama so happy. He may grumble, but he'd plant rosebushes 'til doomsday if it pleased her, and she knows it."

Libby never got tired of seeing her mother's contentment or the way McGregor cared for her. The old sheepherder had already fallen in love with Anna before her divorce from Northrop had miraculously been granted two years before. McGregor had proposed the very next day after word arrived, and to Libby's surprise, her mother had said yes just as quickly. After their wedding, they'd purchased the old Bevins place and made it their home.

A tiny frown creased Libby's brow as thoughts of her mother's divorce reminded her of her father. Northrop Vanderhoff's railroads had been bankrupted by the financial panic of 1893. The falling stock market in June of that year had cost him Vanderhoff Shipping, Rosegate, and his fortune. Shortly afterward, Ellen Prine had married a man from San Francisco and had taken her sons to California, well out of Northrop's reach.

In a gesture of reconciliation that had surprised even Libby, she had written to her father, inviting him to come to the Blue Springs to live with them. His reply had been hateful and bitter. She'd lost all track of him after that, as if he'd disappeared from the face of the earth.

She seldom thought of her father these days, but sometimes she wished he could still learn to love. Sometimes she wished he could have seen his grandchildren and discovered there was so much more to life than wealth and control and power.

The back door slammed shut, and Libby was pulled from her sober thoughts as she recognized the sound of Sawyer's footsteps coming through the kitchen and down the hall. A moment later he appeared in the living room entry.

At fourteen, their adopted son was no longer a boy. Sawyer had shot up this past winter and was now taller than Libby. His voice had already changed to the deeper voice of a man. He'd even started to shave, although

Libby suspected he didn't need to do it more than once every couple of weeks.

"Mornin'," he greeted his parents. "I've got the milking done, Dad. You still going to help me with the colt this morning?"

"Right after we eat," Remington answered.

Sawyer grinned, his eagerness to begin training his young horse making him resemble the boy of Libby's memories. "I'll bring in the eggs, Ma." He turned and disappeared down the hall.

She felt a familiar warm glow, thinking again how blessed she was. "I guess I'd better get busy with breakfast if I'm going to get you men out of my hair."

Remington leaned down and whispered in her ear, "I'd rather be in your hair, Mrs. Walker. I'd like to run my fingers through it and spread it across the pillow like a fan."

She shivered, remembering their lovemaking last night. She would have suggested they put off breakfast for a little while, but then she heard Amanda Ann call, "Mama," and she knew her day had begun in earnest—a day more wonderful, more full, than she had ever dreamed was possible, thanks to the man beside her.

She remembered the words of the poem she'd read last night.

> *If I have freedom in my love,*
> *And in my soul am free,*
> *Angels alone that soar above*
> *Enjoy such liberty.*

She smiled at the simple truth, feeling as if the poet had written those words just for her. Only when she'd given herself in love had she become truly free. Only when she'd risked her heart had she found the ability to soar like the angels.

"Mama!"

"I'm coming, Amanda Ann," she called, then looked up into Remington's eyes of blue, saying softly, "I love you, Remington Walker."

And she knew she always would.

AVAILABLE NOW

Liberty Blue by Robin Lee Hatcher

When Libby headed west, running from her ruthless father and her privileged life, she never looked back. Remington Walker will take any risk to find her, as long as her father keeps paying him. But when he finally catches up with the beautiful, spirited woman, he realizes she's worth more than money can buy.

Shadows in the Mirror by Roslynn Griffith

Headstrong society beauty Iphigenia Wentworth is determined to go to West Texas to find the illegitimate daughter who was taken from her at birth. As an excuse to get there, she answers Monte Ryerson's ad for a mail-order bride, never expecting to love this distant rancher with a troubled past.

Yesterday's Tomorrows by Margaret Lane

In this time-travel romance, Montana rancher Abby De Coux finds herself magically transported back to the year 1875 in order to save her family's ranch. There she meets ruggedly handsome Elan, who is powerless to defend himself from Abby's passionate fire—or from recklessly gambling his future to make her his forever.

The Covenant by Modean Moon

From the author of the acclaimed *Evermore*, a moving present-day romance expertly interwoven with a nineteenth-century love story. "Ms. Moon writes with a spellbinding intensity that will keep you up till the wee hours of the morning until the last page is turned."

—*Romantic Times*

Brimstone by Sonia Simone

After being cheated at the gaming tables by seasoned sharper Katie Starr, the Earl of Brynston decides to teach the silly American girl a lesson. But soon the two are caught in a high stakes game in which they both risk losing their hearts.

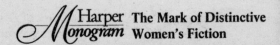 **Harper Monogram** The Mark of Distinctive Women's Fiction

COMING SOON

Touched by Angels by Debbie Maconber

From the bestselling author of *A Season of Angels* and *The Trouble with Angels*. The much-loved angelic trio—Shirley, Goodness, and Mercy—are spending this Christmas in New York City. And three deserving souls are about to have their wishes granted by this dizzy, though divinely inspired, crew.

Till the End of Time by Suzanne Elizabeth

The latest sizzling time-travel romance from the award-winning author of *Destiny's Embrace*. Scott Ramsey has a taste for adventure and a way with the ladies. When his time-travel experiment transports him back to Civil War Georgia, he meets his match in Rachel Ann Warren, a beautiful Union spy posing as a Southern belle.

A Taste of Honey by Stephanie Mittman

After raising her five siblings, marrying the local minister is a chance for Annie Morrow to get away from the farm. When she loses her heart to widower Noah Eastman, however, Annie must choose between a life of ease and a love no money can buy.

A Delicate Condition by Angie Ray

Golden Heart Winner. A marriage of convenience weds innocent Miranda Rembert to the icy Lord Huntsley. But beneath his lordship's stern exterior, fires of passion linger—along with a burning desire for the marital pleasures only Miranda can provide.

Reckless Destiny by Teresa Southwick

Believing that Arizona Territory is no place for a lady, Captain Kane Carrington sent proper easterner Cady Tanner packing. Now the winsome schoolteacher is back, and ready to teach Captain Carrington a lesson in love.

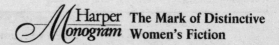

Harper Monogram The Mark of Distinctive Women's Fiction

ATTENTION: ORGANIZATIONS AND CORPORATIONS

Most HarperPaperbacks are available at special quantity discounts for bulk purchases for sales promotions, premiums, or fund-raising. For information, please call or write:
**Special Markets Department, HarperCollins Publishers,
10 East 53rd Street, New York, N.Y. 10022.
Telephone: (212) 207-7528. Fax: (212) 207-7222.**